MW01236276

TREASURE COAST

Revival

EMERALD BAY
BOOK 4

LEIGH DUNCAN

Treasure Coast Revival
Emerald Bay, Book #4

Copyright ©2024 by Leigh D. Duncan

This book is a work of fiction. The characters, events, and places portrayed in this book are products of the author's imagination and are either fictitious or are used fictitiously. Any similarity to real person, living or dead, is purely coincidental and not intended by the author.

Digital ISBN: 978-1-944258-40-5
Print ISBN: 978-1-944258-41-2
Gardenia Street Publishing

Published in the United States of America

Welcome to Emerald Bay!

After a lifetime of running the finest inn in Emerald Bay, Margaret Clayton has to make a decision...sell the Dane Crown Inn to a stranger or put her hopes for the future in her family's hands. For most people, the choice would be simple. But nothing about her family is simple...especially not with her daughter and four nieces whose help Margaret needs now more than ever.

The five cousins know the inn as well as Margaret does. As young girls and teenagers, they spent every summer keeping the cottages and suites spotless, and enjoying the gorgeous beach as a tight knit family. Thirty years later, though, these five women have complicated, important, distant, and utterly packed lives. The last thing any of them can do is drop everything and save the inn. But, when it comes to family, the last thing is sometimes the *only* thing.

As the once-close cousins come together on the glorious shores of Florida's Treasure Coast, they learn that some things never change, but others can never be the same. And the only thing that matters is family which, like the Dane Crown Inn, is forever.

One

Kim

The breeze off the ocean stiffened as the sun dipped below the dunes that stood between the beach and the Dane Crown Inn. In the twilight, a salty haze filled the air. The waves of an incoming tide crept ever closer. The latest rush of water left a ring of foam on the dampened sand a scant three yards from where Kim and Natalie sat on a tree trunk that had washed ashore months earlier.

"So what's up with you and this guy Craig?" Natalie broke off a piece of driftwood and drew stick figures in the sand at their feet.

Kim stifled a sigh. The sky had darkened while her daughter had rambled from one topic to another. So far she'd mentioned her brother, Josh, and his new girlfriend, asked about the remodeling of the inn that had been in the Dane family for more than three generations, and nailed down a few details about the Memorial Day reunion. The one subject she hadn't broached was the one that had driven them to the beach in the first place. Namely, Natalie's announcement that her life was over.

"He seems nice," her daughter prodded when Kim didn't respond. "Did I hear someone call him *Mayor* Mitchell?"

Kim smiled despite herself. "Yes, Craig's the mayor. But before you start thinking that makes him a bigwig, just remember, Emerald Bay is a very small town. It's nothing like New York." She held her breath, hoping the mere mention of the city Natalie had fled would finally lead to the discussion her daughter had been avoiding.

"Still, mayor." Natalie whistled softly as she deftly sidestepped the trap. "That's something, isn't it? You two look good together. Do you like him?"

"Would that be a problem?" Caution straightened Kim's smile. Her daughter didn't hold out hope that she and Frank would get back together, did she? That wasn't going to happen. Not now. Not ever.

"You and Craig?" Natalie shook her head hard enough to flutter the blue streak in her naturally blond hair. "Not at all. You deserve to be happy, Mom."

That was a relief.

"I am. Happy, that is," Kim admitted. "Not just about Craig, though. I love Emerald Bay. I didn't realize how much I'd missed being around my family until I got here. Plus, where else would I have the chance to start my own business?" With her aunt's permission, she was using the inn's kitchen to launch her catering business. Already, six clients had signed up to receive weekly deliveries from Royal Meals. At this rate, she'd be operating in the black long before her customers received their first orders.

"Let me know if you need any help building your online presence, Mom."

"For something so small?" Kim couldn't mask her surprise. She'd planned to rely on word of mouth to spread the news. After all, gossip spread faster than wildfire in a town the size of Emerald Bay.

"Mom, every business needs a website. You should probably have a Facebook page, too. Instagram wouldn't hurt." Dragging her bare foot over the sand, Natalie erased the stick figures she'd drawn and started over. "I can help you with all that."

Kim nodded. If anyone knew the ins and outs

of social media, Natalie did. A year ago, she'd walked away from a prestigious job with a top advertising agency in order to embark on a career as an influencer, a move Kim admittedly didn't understand. "I'd be happy to take you up on the offer, but...does that mean you're sticking around?"

Natalie lifted one shoulder in a defeated shrug. "For a while, I guess. I can't go back to New York. My life there is over. I really messed things up."

Determined not to overreact to her daughter's insistence that she'd ruined her life beyond repair, Kim focused on a sparkle of lights coming from a passing ship that sailed north toward the port at Cape Canaveral. Watching it, she told herself she should be thankful. At least Natalie had chosen to spend Christmas with her in Emerald Bay instead of seeking to escape her problems on a holiday cruise. Not that the girl could afford a cruise. Hadn't she maxed out her credit cards buying a First Class ticket to Florida at the very last minute? Natalie, or Nat as she'd recently insisted on being called, had arrived on the doorstep of the Dane Crown Inn without enough money to even pay her cab fare from the airport. Though why she'd hired a cab to take the fifty-mile trip when there was a perfectly good shuttle available at a fraction of the cost, Kim had no idea.

Whatever her reasoning, one fact remained clear—Nat had worn out her welcome in New York City. Waiting to hear all the details in her daughter's tale of woe, Kim fought a motherly urge to wrap her arms around her youngest child and assure her that everything would be all right, that Mama would fix things, as she'd done a thousand times before.

But would she? Should she?

She shook her head. At twenty-four, Natalie—Nat—was a grown woman. It was high time she took responsibility for her own life. Her failures, as well as her successes.

Not that Kim intended for one second to go all tough love on her daughter. Not without learning what had spurred Nat's impromptu trip to Florida on Christmas Eve and whether her career and her life, as she claimed, were over. Like the tide, worry rushed in to fill all the blank spaces in Kim's mind. Trying to push it back, she brushed a windblown strand of hair firmly behind one ear.

"So what happened? The last time you called, you were on your way to New York for the 'party of the year.'" Kim made air quotes around the phrase Nat had used when she'd called in a panic, insisting her entire career depended on making an entrance at an event where she'd rub elbows with America's latest celebrity sweethearts. "Didn't you make it in time?"

The answer can't be that simple, can it?

"Oh, I got there. And it was everything I thought it would be. If I'd known what would happen next, though, I would have skipped it." The night breeze ruffled the wisps of hair around her face when Nat hung her head.

"What happened?" Kim asked. She hated to pry, but sometimes getting answers from her daughter could be more difficult than wresting the pit from an unripe avocado.

"Mom, you've never seen anything like it. It was Dayglo's birthday, and his studio went all out." The young actor starred in a family-friendly sitcom called *The Fieldmans*, Nat explained, though she needn't have bothered. Kim watched the show when it aired each week.

"I don't even want to think how much money the party cost. The flowers alone must have run twenty, thirty grand. Champagne fountains in every corner. An open bar. Red-carpet treatment all the way. Of course, it had to be with that guest list. All of Dayglo's costars were there. And Sasha's closest friends. You know who she is, don't you?"

Kim stifled a laugh. She wasn't so old that she was completely out of touch. She knew, for instance, that the actress had starred in her own TV show at age ten. Now approaching thirty, she'd earned a solid spot at the top of Hollywood's A-list. "Didn't she just land a leading role in David Heyman's next movie?"

"Yeah," Nat said dreamily. "With her star power and his backing, it's sure to be a hit. Which is why everybody who's anybody wanted to be at that party. Taylor and her entourage dropped by. Brittany, Jharel, Jenna." Her eyes sparkled as she recited a list of entertainers whose photos regularly graced the cover of *People* magazine.

"Sounds like quite the event," Kim acknowledged. She'd been to a few of those back in the day. She and Frank had even thrown a couple. Of course, that was before she'd learned that the money to pay for the bottomless glasses of champagne and the valet parking and all the rest had come straight out of the pockets of the investors in her husband's latest get-rich-quick scheme. Once she'd learned the truth, that Frank's business ventures were little more than Ponzi schemes, she'd turned her back on him and his lavish lifestyle. Her life hadn't exactly been a bed of roses since then, but she'd chosen a clean conscience over her ex's ill-gotten gains.

Her only regret had been the rift the divorce had caused between her and her children. When the court made them choose, Josh and Nat had both elected to live with their fun-loving dad. As soon as he'd turned eighteen, though, Josh had distanced himself from both parents. Nat, on the other hand, had grown closer to her father, which made the girl's presence in Emerald Bay all the more out of character.

"Not only was it a total blast," Nat continued breathlessly, "Sasha and I really hit it off." She tilted her head toward her mother. "I have you to thank for that. Remember when I was in college and I got red wine on my dress? You told me to blot the stain with alcohol?"

Kim nodded. As she recalled, Nat had borrowed the satin gown from one of her sorority sisters and had been positively distraught when her date drenched the bodice while making an enthusiastic toast.

"Well, at the party, Dayglo popped the cork on a bottle of sparkling pinot imported from France especially for his birthday. Wine sprayed everywhere. Some of it landed on the cuff of Sasha's dress. Really, it was only a drop, but she was in tears. I asked one of the waiters to find me a bottle of rubbing alcohol, and I followed her. I did just what you said. I dabbed the spot with alcohol, and that's all it took." She snapped her fingers. "We were instant besties. The next few weeks were heavenly. We lunched at Buvette. Shopped at Barney's. She mentioned my Insta page to a couple of friends, and the next thing I knew, I had more sponsors than I could handle." She gave a humorless laugh. "I even signed a lease for an apartment."

"Sounds like things were working out exactly like you'd hoped they would." When Kim had questioned why a business would pay for the candid shots Nat posted on her social media accounts, her daughter had informed her that traditional ads were passe. Influencers were the wave of the future, she'd said, and it was just a matter of time before her career as one took off.

"Yeah, it was a blast...until it wasn't." Nat ran her fingers through her hair.

"What changed?"

Nat's breath escaped in a long, slow sigh. Her head dropped nearly to her chest, taking her voice with it. Kim leaned forward to catch her daughter's next words.

"We were at a club." Nat's voice was barely audible above the sound of the waves. "I ducked into the ladies' room for a minute. Next thing I knew, Sasha was there, too. She'd caught Dayglo with some other girl, and she was having a major meltdown."

"Ouch!" Kim exclaimed.

"I did my best to console her, but she…Whoa! She lost it—mascara and tears running down her cheeks. She told me to get out my phone and make a video. Then she just went on a rant. One of those, Am-I-The-Bad-Guy things. You've seen them on YouTube, haven't you? Like when a bridezilla plans a destination bachelorette party and wants to know if she's the bad guy for sticking her bridesmaids with the bill."

"I've seen a couple of them," Kim admitted. They usually struck a false chord with her. She thought they were long on drama and short on substance, like most of the reality shows on TV.

"She really let Dayglo have it. Said he had been the one true love of her life and talked about all she'd given up to be with him, only to have him betray her. When she finished, she insisted I post it right then and there."

"Tell me you didn't!" Kim held her breath. She could list a dozen reasons why uploading a video of a hysterical movie star to social media was a bad idea.

"I tried to talk her out of it, Mom." Nat shifted uneasily. "I told her she should wait. That she might feel differently in the morning. But she was adamant. And, well, she is Sasha. She didn't leave me much choice."

"So you did it? You put her video out there?" Kim shook her head. This had all the ingredients of a disaster in the making. Much as she didn't want to, she could see one looming.

"Yeah. After it was done, she fixed her face—she refused to walk through the club looking like a sad clown—and we piled into the limo. We went straight back to her hotel. By the time we got to her suite, that video had thousands of views. By the next day, it had gone viral. That's when things really started to get weird. Sasha's fans went wild. They boycotted *The Fieldmans. Its* ratings plummeted overnight. A couple of other women claimed they'd had affairs with Dayglo. Advertisers pulled their ads. There was talk of canceling the show or kicking him off it."

"Intense," Kim said softly.

"Yeah. That's when the studio stepped in. They staged the most romantic make-up scene ever. Dayglo—in full tux and tails, no less—hit the flower market, where he bought practically every long-stemmed red rose in the place. He loaded most of them into a little red wagon. Another vendor handed him such a huge bouquet, he couldn't see over the top of it. Then he walked—*he walked*—across town pulling that wagon and trailing roses all along the way. I've seen the pictures. It was amazing. The studio must have tipped off the media, 'cause by the time he got to Sasha's hotel, a crowd had gathered. There were newscasters and police escorts, the whole nine yards. Like a scene out of a movie, he stood below Sasha's balcony and begged her to take him back. Of course, she did."

Kim nodded. She'd heard about the breakup and the consequent reunion. Hadn't everyone? But something Nat had said bothered her. "You say you saw the pictures. You weren't there?"

"No." Nat's shoulders folded in on themselves. "Sasha, she...she'd sent me to the airport to meet her sister's plane. At least, that's what she said. But Devon—that's Sasha's sister—she never showed up. I found out later it had all been a ploy to get me out of the way."

Kim's stomach tightened. She might not have been privy to Frank's schemes, but she'd spent enough time with the man to recognize a setup when she saw one. This had all the markings of a well-thought-out plan. Sasha couldn't forgive a cheater and still maintain the respect of her fans. No, she had to shift the blame onto someone else's shoulders. And who better to take the fall than Natalie?

In the fading light, she saw tears glistening

on her daughter's cheeks. Her heart clenched. She'd give anything, everything, to undo what had happened. She swallowed, hard, imagining the scene.

"I was duped," Sasha would claim. "Dayglo never cheated on me. It was all a publicity stunt pulled by someone I mistakenly trusted."

And, as Nat relayed the rest of the story in a shaky voice, that's more or less what happened. Although, Kim had to admit, even she hadn't expected Sasha to accuse Nat of creating the video out of thin air. Or of faking dozens of other photos that showed Nat as one of her inner circle. But that was exactly what the movie star did.

"I'm so sorry, honey." Kim slipped one arm around her daughter's waist and squeezed her tight.

"I should have let it go. I should have walked away. But I had to try and fix things," Nat continued. "Sasha wouldn't return any of my calls. She'd blocked all my texts. I thought if I could just talk to her, we could straighten things out. I mean, it all had to be a huge, horrible mistake, right?"

The tide had crept another two feet up the beach. While Kim watched, ripples washed away Nat's latest set of drawings.

"I knew she'd be at Avenue last Friday. She always goes there when she's in New York. But I couldn't..." Nat sniffed. "I didn't even make it past the entrance. The bouncer had my name on a list and not the good kind. He told me to get lost. That's when I knew for sure it was over.

"And that's the whole, sordid story," Nat said at last. She wiped her eyes. "I lost all my sponsors, my apartment, everything. My podcast is dead. Haters kept flagging my Insta and TikTok pages, so I had to take them down. What am I going to do, Mom? I can't go back to New York. I'll never be able to show my face there again."

"Not right away, maybe," Kim soothed. "Forever is a long time." Elephants didn't forget, but people did. That much she knew for a fact. The stage and screen and even politics were filled with people who'd reinvented themselves after getting caught shoplifting at Saks or flunking out of rehab for the umpteenth time or stealing from the public cookie jar. Nat, too, could come back from this. She just needed to step away from the public eye for a while.

"But what am I going to do in the meantime?" Nat asked. "I have no money, no place to live. I even owe you and Aunt Belle for my taxi fare." She'd always referred to her mother's cousins as her aunts. The habit was so ingrained now that she was unlikely to change it.

The pain in her daughter's voice cut deep, but Kim forced herself to stay strong. "I don't have all the answers, but I have a pretty good idea who we can ask."

Over the past few months, the Dane Crown Inn had become a haven for people who were starting their lives over. The matriarch of the family, Aunt Margaret was leading the charge by getting the only home she'd ever known ready to put on the market. Behind her was Margaret's daughter, Belle. After years of sitting at the top of the pop charts, she'd returned home to lick her wounds and reinvent herself. Then there was Kim's cousin, Diane, whose whole world had imploded when her husband left her. Diane hadn't let it destroy her, though. She and her daughter were creating new futures for themselves here in Emerald Bay. When rumors that she was selling out threatened her bakery's bottom line, Diane's sister, Amy, had countered by announcing she'd soon open a second location for the bakery she'd started from scratch only a few years earlier. Kim's own sister, Jen, had held more jobs and lived in more places than anyone else in the family—she knew all about making a fresh start. As for herself, Kim had faced her own challenges and learned to meet them head on. Between them all, the women of the Dane family could surely offer Nat some well-founded advice.

"Thank you for telling me everything you're going through. It means more than I can say that you'd come to me. That you'd trust me with all this." Nat had rarely sought her advice in the years following the divorce. "I wish I could say I had all the answers, but I don't. I do think it might help you to know that you're not alone — your aunts and I, we've all been through our own challenges. What do you think about talking it over with them?"

Nat pitched her drawing stick into the waves. "It can't hurt, I guess."

Kim took a breath. "Tomorrow's going to be busy, what with everyone moving into the cottages and all." The move was necessary, since workers were slated to start refinishing the hardwood floors throughout the inn this week. "But why don't you join us at the firepit tomorrow night?" Now that the weather had turned cooler, she and her cousins had moved their nightly gab fests there from the deck. "In the meantime, don't worry. I'm here for you. We all are."

Kim lifted her feet high above a new wave

that rushed ashore. When the water receded, she gave her daughter's shoulders another squeeze. "For now, though, I think we'd better head inside before we get soaked."

Beyond the French doors that opened onto the deck, rain drummed against the windows. Water trickled out of the downspouts in a steady stream. Standing in the kitchen, Kim cast a final glance in the direction of the firepit. At least the unexpected storm had held off until they'd finished moving into the cottages, she thought. Besides, it gave them one last chance to enjoy the fireplace in the front room.

Tomorrow, workers would descend on the inn. The buzz of electric sanders, combined with the fumes from the stain and poly, would render the main house uninhabitable until the floors were finished. Though the supervisor had promised to complete the work in two weeks, Kim had managed enough large-scale projects in her former life to know they were invariably fraught with delays. Who knew when the family would have a chance to sit in the comfy living room again? Returning to her task, she finished loading the glasses of wine and cups of hot chocolate onto a heavy wooden tray.

"That's it in a nutshell. Nat's really hurt and doesn't know what to do next. I thought maybe we could try and cheer her up tonight." Kim had filled the others in while they'd toted their personal belongings down the stairs and into the cottages earlier, but this had been her first chance to speak with Amy, who'd spent a long day at Sweet Cakes.

"I'll tell you one thing: Sasha is dead to me. I'll never watch her in another movie. And you can take that to the bank." Amy lifted a platter of heart-shaped cookies off the counter. The recipe was a new one, and if it passed tonight's taste test, she planned to add the item to the bakery's Valentine's Day lineup.

"You and me both," Kim agreed. "I've watched my last episode of *The Fieldmans*, too." After the needless harm they'd caused her daughter, she'd never be able to look at either Sasha or Dayglo the same.

"I'm not sure what I'll have to add to the conversation, but if she's looking for work, I could always use an extra pair of hands at the bakery."

"She might just take you up on that. Poor kid, she's flat broke. At least she has a place to stay.

She's going to bunk in with me for the time being." Carefully balancing the drink tray, Kim headed for the parlor where her sister and her cousins lounged on overstuffed couches and chairs.

"Well, aren't you a comfortable group." Amy peered over Kim's shoulder.

Taking in Belle's flannel pajamas and Jen in a pair of nearly threadbare sweats, Kim chuckled. She waited to lower her tray until Diane removed her feet from the coffee table.

"What if a guest came in and saw this motley crew? What would they think?" Amy huffed.

"You're just jealous 'cause you came here straight from work and didn't have a chance to change." Diane hiked the cuffs of a fuzzy pair of socks higher on her calves while she eyed her sister's jeans and the T-shirt that bore a Sweet Cakes logo. "Relax. We don't have any guests."

"Are you sure?"

"Yep," Belle chimed in. "The Carsons checked out this morning. That was the last of them." She and her mom had canceled a pitifully small handful of reservations once the work on the floors had been scheduled.

"So that's it, just us?" Amy set the cookies on the coffee table beside the drinks Kim had placed in the center.

"Caitlyn went back to Tampa with Tim and Nick." Diane squeezed closer to Jen and patted the empty spot she'd cleared on the couch. She didn't seem to mind when Amy plopped down on one of the occasional chairs instead. "I have to pick up her transcripts before school starts. I'll bring her back then." After a semester of home school, the teenager had begged to start the new year at Emerald Bay High.

"And Aunt Margaret?" Jen checked the time on her phone. "It's a little early for her to turn in, isn't it?"

Belle nodded. "I didn't let her help much, but moving out of the family quarters and into our cabin still took a lot out of her. She crashed right after dinner."

"I, for one, enjoy having the place to ourselves for a change." Jen tucked her feet beneath her on the couch. "We were never allowed to sit in here when we were kids."

"We had a lot more guests back then," Kim reminded her younger sister. There'd been a time when each of the inn's fifteen suites and six cabins were fully booked on a regular basis. Reservations had all but dried up after the accident that had taken their Aunt Liz's life and left Aunt Margaret reliant on a cane to get around. As the years slipped by, the inn had fallen into disrepair. In the six months since Kim's arrival, though, she and her cousins had made significant strides in restoring the property to its former glory. So far, they'd put a new roof on one of the cabins and refurbished the rest, painted and hung new wallpaper in the guest suites upstairs, and replaced the carpet throughout. The gardeners had been hard at work trimming overgrown plants and clearing the paths that meandered through the twenty-acre property. Having the decades-old wood floors refinished was the last of the major items on their list before they gave the exterior a fresh coat of paint.

"Do you think business will pick up once word gets around about all the improvements we've made?" Belle brushed a piece of lint from the arm of the Queen Anne chair she occupied.

"That's the hope," Diane answered, her voice firm. "Once the inn is profitable again, it'll make it much easier to find a buyer."

"One willing to keep the doors open." Kim reminded everyone of the condition their aunt had placed on selling the place.

"Whew." Jen blew across the top of the mug of hot cocoa she'd taken from the coffee table. She took a sip and delicately licked her upper lip. Setting the cocoa aside to cool, she asked, "Is there any chance Aunt Margaret will change her mind and decide to keep the inn? After working so hard to fix it up, it's a shame to have to let it go."

Belle slowly shook her head. "Mama's getting too old to run this place on her own anymore. The next time she gets hurt trying to make a simple repair, it could be something far worse than a broken arm." Margaret had reluctantly confessed that she'd taken several spills before the one that resulted in surgery and months in a heavy cast.

"Anyone here have a burning desire to dedicate the rest of their life to running the inn?" Kim asked. She surveyed the faces of her cousins, her sister and her daughter. One by one, each woman either averted her eyes or gave an outright *no*. No surprise there. Except for Nat, they all had careers or businesses of their own to run. And as much as she'd love to see her daughter make a permanent home in Emerald Bay, she recognized that Nat had her sights set on bigger and better things.

"I guess the next step is to finish the repairs and do our best to pack this place full of happy, satisfied customers, then. I think Nat might be able to help us with that." She turned to her daughter. "Didn't you say something about a website?"

Slowly, Nat blinked. "Does the inn even have one?"

Belle nodded. "It does. Dad set it up." She frowned. "I don't think it's been updated since he died." Eric Clayton had suffered a fatal heart attack nearly ten years earlier.

"Whoa. That's ancient. Think of the website as the first impression a potential guest gets of the inn. If it's old and dated, then guests will think the inn is, too," Nat offered. "A good website with an impressive amount of traffic is critical in today's business world."

"Would you be willing to work on that...as long as you're here?" Kim asked.

Nat nodded. "Yeah, sure."

"Speaking of which, do you have any idea how long you'll be staying?" Diane asked. "Not that we want you to go," she hurried to add. "We want you to stick around for as long as you can."

"About that. My career has hit..." Nat's voice faltered, and she shot her mom an imploring look.

"A stumbling block?" Amy suggested. "Been there. Done that."

"The skids?" Jen put in. "I can relate."

"Hit the proverbial brick wall?" Belle chimed. "It's no fun when you're stuck exploring new options. Believe me."

Nat's jaw unhinged. "I don't believe that.

You're Belle Dane. You can do anything."

Belle chose a glass of wine from the tray and hoisted it. "You think it's easy for me to start over at fifty? Think again, kiddo. The older you get, the harder it becomes to recreate yourself. People—managers, fans, the media—they all see you a certain way. They have expectations that have turned rock solid over the years."

Holding her wine in one hand, Belle stretched a languid arm over her head. Sweeping her fingers through the air, she bent, ending with a flourish at her toes. When she straightened, it was if she'd parted a magical curtain. Gone was the mystique of the great Belle Dane. In its place sat a middle-aged woman dressed in silky PJ's, her hair in a turban. Without makeup to hide them, the faint lines around her eyes and mouth showed. "Re-inventing myself won't be as easy for me as it will be for you. You're just starting out. You have all the choices in the world ahead of you."

"But...but becoming an influencer was my dream," Nat protested.

"So you'll get another dream." Amy slipped off her shoes and wriggled her toes. "Remember Colonel Archer?"

"He was in the Army, wasn't he? Vietnam?" Kim had spotted the man at church last week.

"That's the one. He's nearly eighty now and still carries himself like a soldier. Anyway, his son Mark was one of the most popular boys in my class at Emerald Bay High. President of the student council, captain of the basketball team, voted Most Likely to Succeed. He was headed to West Point after graduation. Wanted to follow in his dad's footsteps. Two weeks before he was supposed to leave, Mark was playing beach volleyball with a bunch from school and hurt his back. Turned out he'd herniated a disc. West Point disqualified him when he couldn't pass the physical."

"He must have been devastated," Kim murmured.

"His dad, too," Diane said.

"The thing is, his life wasn't over. He took a gap year and, by the time he was ready to go back to school, he'd found a new calling—environmental science. He went to Stanford, earned a Master's and then his PhD. He holds patents that have made him a millionaire several times over. With some of the money, he founded a charity that provides water purifiers to areas hit by natural disasters."

An appreciative murmur swept through the group. All except Nat, who didn't seem to see the point.

Diane nibbled on one of the cookies Amy had left on the coffee table. "You don't have to be a superstar like Belle or the inventor of the next cutting-edge device to save the planet in order to start over. Look at me and Caitlyn. We got the rug pulled out from under us when Tim left us. It wouldn't be a lie to say Caitlyn lost her way for a bit there. Got cut from the soccer team. Suspended from school. Lost all her friends. But coming here has been good for her. She's making new friends, doing well in her studies. She feels ready to transfer to Emerald Bay High and go out for the soccer team here."

Diane grabbed a napkin and spat what was left of her cookie into it. "Amy, these aren't your best work," she declared. Her face scrunched. "All I can taste is red dye." She balled the napkin and dropped it into the round metal trash can at the end of the couch.

Amy shrugged. "Back to the drawing board, I guess."

"Guess you'll have to...*start over*." Jen laughed. Giving Nat a pointed look, she sobered. "At some point in our lives, we all have to re-invent ourselves. You get blackballed in Biloxi and Vegas isn't much better. Your husband walks out on you." She reached for Diane's hand and gave it a squeeze. "The stellar career you've built suddenly falls apart." She lifted her chin to Belle before turning to Kim. "Your company reorganizes. Just pick up the paper or scroll through the news feed on your phone. There's always a story about an athlete who's suffered a career-ending injury. Or a star who gets some debilitating disease and is forced to retire. The thing is, you can't let any of that stop you. You have to punt or pivot or spin or whatever you want to call it."

"'Cause if you don't, you stagnate. That's the road to bitterness and misery," Belle said with a knowing look.

"Everyone in this room recognizes that what happened to you was a bad thing." Amy leaned forward, her elbows propped on her knees, her expression fierce. "If it was up to us, we'd teach Sasha and Dayglo a lesson about loyalty and friendship." Her shoulders relaxed. "But they aren't our concern. You are. You have to decide whether you're going to sit around all day wailing about your misfortune."

"Or dust yourself off and set yourself on a new path. One that will be different from the one you thought you should take." Diane met Nat's gaze and held it with a look that said she had firsthand knowledge of the subject at hand.

"But one that interests you and offers at least

the hope for happiness," Belle added as if reciting part of a well-rehearsed speech.

Confusion filled Nat's face. Her expression announced that the advice she'd received hadn't been at all what she'd expected. Tears welled in her eyes. "But what if I can't? What if I have no idea what comes next?"

The log burning in the fireplace broke in two. The ends collapsed, sending a shower of sparks up the chimney. In a rare show of speed and agility, Belle sprang from her seat. Grabbing the poker, she scooted a tiny glowing ember to the rear of the hearth. The problem dealt with, she turned to Nat. "That's for you to decide. Just know this failure is a turning point, a deciding moment in your life. And you're the only one who can decide how you'll react and what your future will look like."

Diane cleared her throat. "That doesn't mean you can sit on your hands all day and contemplate your navel. There's plenty to do around here, and we could use your help while you figure out your next step."

"I've already said I'd help with the website. And I promised Mom I'd help build a social media presence for her catering business." Nat expelled a thready breath. But if she was looking for sympathy, she'd come to the wrong crowd.

"That's a start," Belle pointed out. "You'll need to get a job, too. Amy said she'll hire you part-time at the bakery. And I had to let my assistant go when I moved here. Believe it or not, I do get the occasional piece of fan mail. How's your cursive?"

Nat shrugged. "Pretty good."

"If you're interested, you can help me answer those letters. Just until you figure out what's next."

"I think I'd like that a lot. All of it." Nat thought for a moment. "But it might take me a while to, you know, think everything through."

Kim, who'd remained quiet throughout the discussion, cupped one hand over her daughter's. "Honey, the inn is your home until you decide it's time to move on."

"Or until Aunt Margaret sells it. Then we'll all be looking for a new place to live," Diane mused aloud.

"Even then, you'll always have a home with me," Kim said firmly. And for the first time since Nat had arrived in Emerald Bay, she saw an honest-to-goodness smile on her daughter's face.

Two

Diane

"Are you sure it's okay for us to go inside? Shouldn't we wear respirators? Or masks?" Diane studied the inn's side entrance. Beyond the heavy door stood the laundry room, a pantry the size of her daughter's bedroom back in Tampa and a spacious kitchen. For the past five days, hammers had pounded, sanders had buzzed and vacuums had whirred while Jonas, the crew supervisor, and the rest of the workers prepared to stain and seal the hardwood floors throughout the inn. The noise had been so loud, so constant, her head had started throbbing to a beat not unlike that of the kettle drums the boys in the back row of the high school orchestra used to play.

"Relax." Kim inserted the key into the door. "Jonas said it was all right for us to pick up a few things before they actually apply the stain and sealer. After that, we won't be allowed inside until the house has been properly aired out."

Kim turned the handle. The door creaked open, revealing a wintery scene. Instead of snow, though, grainy sawdust covered the washers and dryers, the counters and shelves. It even clung to the walls. This despite the heavy curtain of plastic that separated the laundry room with its tiled floors from the rest of the house.

"Oh, my," Diane whispered.

"It is worse than I imagined," Kim admitted with a frown. "I sure wouldn't recommend spending the night in here." Dust danced in the air when she coughed.

The pungent smell of freshly sanded wood filled Diane's nose. She sneezed. "I'm perfectly content staying in our little cottage," she said when she stopped sniffling. "You think they'll clean all this up before they leave?"

Kim laughed. "I think it's a good thing we allowed a couple of extra days in the schedule. We're going to need it." So far, Jonas was proving to be a man of his word. Everything was moving along without delay in a precisely choreographed dance.

Diane traced one index finger through the fine layer of dust that coated the washing machine. "I think we should put everyone on notice. We're going to need all hands on deck if we're going to get rid of all this mess before we reopen."

"Probably ought to alert Irene and Eunice, too." The housekeepers were enjoying an extended holiday while work on the floors proceeded. From the looks of things, their time off would come at a price. "Let's not linger. I want to grab a ham hock and some black-eyed peas out of the freezer for New Year's Day."

"And I need to get Caitlyn's extra shin guards from our room." Nick had complained that his legs were black-and-blue from helping his sister prepare for the upcoming soccer team tryouts at Emerald Bay High.

"You're going to Tampa in the morning?" Kim brushed aside the curtain and they traipsed down the hallway to the family room and the kitchen.

"I don't think I could stand the noise another day." Even now that the workers had all left for the day, her temples still throbbed.

"Jonas told Belle they're finished with all the sanding and repairs. The guys will vacuum and run tack cloths over the floors tomorrow and again the next day. Things will quiet down when they start applying the stain."

"Good, but I still have to get on the road. I promised Caitlyn and Nick we'd spend New Year's Eve together." She didn't bother to explain that it might be her children's last chance to enjoy a holiday in the house where they'd spent their childhood. She and Tim would probably sell the two-story Colonial if she carried through with her plan to make the move to Emerald Bay a permanent one.

"You'll miss our spa day," Kim complained with good-natured grace. "Belle and Jen are going to help Amy and me get ready to go out that night. Nails, hair, facials—the works."

"Sorry." Diane's foot skidded on the dust-covered tile. "Careful," she warned. "That stuff's slippery."

"You can say that again." Kim slid to a stop just beyond the kitchen, where she pointed to the multiple layers of plastic that sheathed the granite counters, appliances and cabinets. "I hope that means we won't have to wash all the dishes, pots and pans."

"Probably not. It looks like they did a better job of sealing things off in here than in the laundry room," Diane agreed. She brushed a sprinkling of sawdust from her sweatshirt.

As she stepped beyond the kitchen, air sifted through Diane's lips. She'd known, of course, that the rooms had been emptied. Bookcases and floor lamps, dining chairs and tables crowded the deck and the front porch, where heavy tarps protected the sturdy furniture from the weather. Upholstered items had been shoved into every available carpeted space, the doors to those rooms sealed tight with wide blue tape. Whatever was left had been toted out to the parking area and stashed in two temporary storage units. Still, the sight of all that empty space nearly took her breath away. She peered down the hall, unable to remember if or when she'd ever seen it completely empty.

"Whoa!" She nearly jumped out of her skin when her voice echoed across freshly sanded floors and bounced off the plastic sheeting that covered the windows.

Beside her, Kim grinned. "Halllooow!" she called.

Another echo resounded.

"Hey. I could get into this." Kim loosed a mournful howl.

"Don't." Diane stilled her cousin by placing a hand on her forearm. "Gives me the creeps."

"Really?" An evil twinkle lit Kim's eyes.

"Yeah. Makes me think some ghostly wraith

will shimmer into existence right in front of us." Not that she believed in ghosts.

"If they do, it'll be a race to see which one of us is the first one out the door. Woo-hoo," Kim said so softly the sound barely echoed.

Diane aimed a sharp look in Kim's direction. "Come on. Let's get what we need and get out of here."

"Fine by me." Kim backtracked toward the pantry, where the freezer had been swathed in several large protective sheets. "This will take a minute. I'll need to wipe everything down before I open the door. Unless you'd like a little extra fiber in your diet? Me, neither," she agreed when Diane shook her head. "Are you okay to go upstairs yourself?"

"Yeah. But if I'm not back in ten minutes, send out a search team."

Though she tried to sound lighthearted, Diane couldn't hide the whisper of unease that shot through her. She swallowed. It wasn't just echoes that gave her the creeps. The empty rooms gave off a ghostly vibe. Which was weird, because no one had ever actually died in the house. In the sixty-plus years the inn had been in existence, no guest had ever passed away in their sleep. If they had, she'd have known about it. The closest their family had come to that misfortune had been when her Uncle Eric collapsed on the front lawn. According to the paramedics, he'd been dead before he hit the ground, the victim of a massive heart attack.

Of course, there were all those stories about the fleet of Spanish treasure ships bound for King Philip's court that had wrecked off the coast in 1715. A handful of survivors, some carting gold doubloons and gems salvaged from the heavily laden ships, had made it ashore. The largest group of them had camped several miles north of the inn, but remnants of smaller camps had been discovered as far south as Fort Pierce. Lacking supplies or shelter, threatened by animals and disease—to say nothing of marauding pirates—few made it through that first winter. It wasn't too far-fetched to think that one or more of those unfortunate souls had died in the very spot where her grandparents had elected to build the inn.

"Hmmm." She pressed her lips together. If ghosts did inhabit the house, could one of them point her in the direction of their hidden loot? Millions of dollars' worth of gold, silver and jewels had been aboard the eleven ships when most of them broke apart in a hurricane. Though a great deal of it had eventually been recovered, a fair amount had never been accounted for, and the coins sometimes washed ashore. Unfortunately, she and her cousins had never unearthed so much as a single piece of eight. Not in all the many treasure hunts they'd embarked on when they were kids.

Which was a shame, she mused. What with her aunt's insurance carrier canceling their policy on the inn and the need to pay substantially higher premiums for new coverage, they could use a fresh influx of cash. An emerald or two, say, or even a gold doubloon would come in handy right about now.

She laughed at herself. She didn't hold out any real hope of stumbling across a chest filled with long-lost treasure on the grounds of the Dane Crown Inn, did she? It had been one thing to believe such things could really happen when she was a youngster and following a map some long-forgotten relative had probably drawn to entertain his own children. It was quite another to count on the remote possibility of making a once-in-a-lifetime discovery in the hopes of solving a real-life problem. No. Paying the bills and balancing the accounts required a measured, practical approach. Rather than hoping for a three-hundred-year-old windfall, she needed to be thinking more along the lines of selling a two-story Colonial in a much-coveted part of the state and investing some of the profits in her family's inn.

Leaving a trail of dusty footprints behind her, Diane crossed to the staircase. In another part of the house, a board creaked. She paused, grabbing the banister to steady herself. "Don't be absurd," she said out loud. "There are no such things as ghosts."

Her shoes made hollow scuffing noises as she mounted the treads. On the second floor, doors opened onto empty suites, and she hurried toward the two smaller rooms tucked into a corner at the end of the corridor. Thankful her daughter had stored her extra gear in the Beryl suite's closet rather than in a dresser that was now who-knew-where on the property, she studied the top shelf. Sure enough, a bulky sports bag sat exactly where Caitlyn had said it would be.

A waterfall of sawdust poured down on her when Diane grasped the handles. She tugged the bag off the ledge and let it fall to the floor. It landed with a thud, sending more dust swirling. She sneezed once and then again.

"You okay up there?" Sounding as if it were rising from the bottom of a deep well, Kim's voice floated up the stairs.

"Yeah!" Diane called out. "I dropped the bag. It was heavier than I expected. I'll be right down."

She made quick work of unzipping the duffle. Shoving aside a pair of worn-out soccer cleats and a brand new Plant High sweatshirt that she couldn't blame her daughter for leaving behind, she grabbed the shin guards and stuck them under one arm.

She had just returned the bag to its shelf when the protective plastic that had been taped over the windows billowed. A loud bang rang out from downstairs. At the same time, a whoosh of air and a low moan swept in from the hallway. Blinking, Diane swung her head, certain she'd heard someone call her name. When the plastic rattled again, the hairs on the back of her neck stood on end and chill bumps raced down her arms.

"Hey! Where is everyone?"

Ready to bolt, Diane froze when Belle's voice reverberated through the house.

"In here." Kim's voice echoed from the kitchen.

One hand pressed over her thudding heart, Diane took a second to regain her composure. "There are no ghosts," she whispered before she stepped into the corridor and retraced her steps to the top of the stairs. "I'm on my way down," she announced after making sure she had a firm grip on the banister.

"Oh, wow! The acoustics in this place are amazing." Belle ran through the scales. "Do-re-mi-fa-so-la-ti-do."

Diane had no doubt whatsoever that if anyone else had launched into "The Old Rugged Cross," she would have bowled both of her cousins over on her way out the door. But as Belle's version of the haunting melody filled the house, an unexpected peace soothed all her fears.

"Did anyone ever mention that you have a gift?" she asked, joining Belle and Kim in the kitchen.

Though Belle's cheeks pinked, the serene expression on her face didn't waiver. "Once or twice," she admitted.

"A voice like that is a terrible thing to waste." Kim waved her finger in a circle around the redhead's face. "You really ought to do something with it."

Belle's head drooped. "I'm working on it." She sighed heavily. Less than a minute later, her shoulders squared. "Now where are we with the floors? Jonas says everything is right on schedule."

From what Diane could tell, not a single floorboard had been left in its original condition. "They're doing a great job," she offered. "But…"

"But?" Questions formed in Belle's green eyes.

"But we'll have to clean the house from top to bottom before we can move back in, much less open the inn to guests. Everything—the walls, the railings, the counters—they're all covered in sawdust." Kim brushed her hand over the closest wall. When she opened her palm, a grayish-brown residue coated her fingers.

"Yuck!" Belle immediately pulled the neck of her sweatshirt over her mouth to create a makeshift mask. Her voice muffled, she asked, "Do you have everything you need?"

Kim hefted a shopping bag that Diane assumed held the makings for a traditional New Year's dinner—several packages of black-eyed peas for good luck along with the meaty ham bone she'd pulled from the freezer. "I'm good."

Diane waved the shin guards she'd retrieved while she was upstairs.

"On that note, then, I think it's time we make tracks."

Which was exactly what they did. With Belle leading the way, they proceeded down the hall, through the laundry room and out the side entrance. Stepping into the sunlight of a winter day, Diane reached behind her to close the door. A tiny dust devil swirled at her feet, and she once more had the sensation of someone calling her name.

"Ridiculous," she whispered. Ghosts don't exist, she reminded herself, although she couldn't entirely banish the idea that one might be trying to deliver a message.

Her foot on the brake, Diane swigged the last of the coffee from her travel mug and resettled the steel cup in the center console. Though she'd slipped behind the wheel of her car shortly after the first rays of sunshine had brightened the eastern horizon beyond Emerald Bay, an accident on Route 60 had forced her to detour north to the Beachline and landed her in Orlando just in time for the morning rush-hour. At the rate she was traveling—or rather, not traveling—it would take at least another hour before she neared the Gulf Coast and Tampa, the third largest city in the state. Eyeing the heavy traffic that clogged all five of I-4's westbound and exit lanes as she neared the final turnoff to a popular theme park, she took a steadying breath.

In front of her, chalk curlicues and drawings of cartoon characters adorned the rear window of a van with out-of-state plates. Diane applied more pressure to her brake pedal when the van's driver signaled his intention to take the next exit. The lane he wanted was, unfortunately, filled with vehicles carrying families who were just as eager, if not more so, to spend the day in the area known as "the happiest place on earth." The other drivers ignored the van's blinking turn signal and edged past him, trapping him in place. Meanwhile, cars in Diane's lane came to a complete standstill. Around her, horns blasted. Diane tsked. The added noise wouldn't convince anyone to give an inch. Finally, in a move that reminded her of the bumper cars Nick and Caitlyn had loved when they were younger, the driver of the van nosed forward, the fender of his vehicle practically scraping the paint off an SUV when its driver hesitated just a hair too long.

With the lane ahead now clear, Diane hit the gas but not before she glimpsed a tiny princess strapped into one of the van's car seats. She smiled and waved to the youngster, recalling all too well her own children's excitement when they used to visit the theme parks as a family.

How long ago had that been?

Six or seven years, at least.

She gave her head a slight shake. After she'd started to climb the corporate ladder, she'd taken precious little time away from the office. Besides, once Nick and his friends got their driver's licenses, they preferred to hit the parks without parents hovering over their shoulders. That left Caitlyn, who'd shown more interest in a bouncy, black-and-white ball than the characters who stepped out of the pages of children's books.

But the girl did love her roller coasters, Diane admitted. The taller and the faster, the better. Maybe she and Caitlyn should start back to Emerald Bay early, just the two of them. She'd splurge on tickets and they could spend a day riding the rides and gorging on fried foods.

Reluctantly, she put thoughts of the adventure on hold. This time of year, thanks to schools that were on break across the country, crowds formed hours-long lines that wrapped around every attraction. But that was one of the many advantages of living in Florida. Besides ready access to beautiful beaches and pleasant weather even in the middle of winter, she and Caitlyn could visit the many theme parks whenever they wanted. And they would, she promised, more to herself than to her daughter. Once the new year was underway and schools started up again, the crowds would thin. Then the two of them would pick a day and play hooky.

That was, they would if everything went well with Caitlyn's transfer to Emerald Bay High. Diane worried an earring with the fingers of one hand. Had she made the right decision by letting her daughter return to public school? Was it too soon? For that matter, how sure was she that staying in Emerald Bay was the right choice at all?

Very sure.

Of that, she had no doubt. She might not know where she and Tim were headed or whether they'd be able to fix their broken marriage, but she did know that moving to Emerald Bay had been the best choice for her daughter. Surrounded by the aunts and cousins who loved and supported her, Caitlyn had blossomed. She was no longer the angry, sullen child who'd gotten kicked out of school for fighting. She'd formed new friendships, gotten involved in community projects like Habitat for Humanity, and grown close to her Aunt Margaret. Plus, tryouts for the soccer team would begin in two weeks, and Caitlyn was working hard to be ready for them. From daily phone calls with her daughter, she knew Cait had insisted on twice-daily practice sessions with her brother. Nick swore she didn't go easy on him, and he had the bruises to prove it.

Diane shifted her weight on the comfortable leather seat. Though Caitlyn was and had to be her first priority, the teen wasn't the only one who'd benefited from their time in Emerald Bay. She had, too. It had taken her a long minute to realize it and even longer to admit it, but she'd gotten so wrapped up in earning the next promotion that she'd lost sight of the important things in life. Her daughter's problems had broken the cycle and forced her off that treadmill. Once she'd had both feet on the ground, she'd seen how damaging her headlong rush to get to the top had been. For her. For her family. For her marriage.

These last few months in Emerald Bay with her sister and her cousins and Aunt Margaret had helped her refocus. On her children. On her health. Now that she had her bearings, she wanted to put down new roots, start a new life. She could think of no better way to do that than by dusting off her dream of owning her very own boutique accounting firm. And now that ill health had forced Emerald Bay's lone accountant into a sudden retirement, the town had a very real and immediate need for someone with her skill set.

So why hadn't she already hung out her shingle and gotten to work? The answer came swiftly and cleanly.

Tim.

What would he think of her business plan, of making her move to Emerald Bay a permanent one? Would he support her decision? Or would it deliver another body blow to a relationship that was already in trouble?

Yes, she'd made the mistake of not making her marriage a priority. Of striving so hard to get ahead, she'd lost sight of the reasons success was important in the first place—her husband, her children, her home. Those were her mistakes, and she owned them.

But Tim had dealt his own cruel blow to their marriage when he'd taken off on a two-week cruise without her. Now he said he'd come to his senses, that he'd been wrong to walk out on her, that he wanted to mend things between them.

And, oh, how she wanted that, too. She missed listening to him whistle show tunes as he made the coffee or fixed breakfast for Caitlyn in the mornings. How many times over the last few months had she wished she could ask his advice, feel the comforting weight of his hand on her shoulder or have him nag her about getting enough exercise. She wanted him in her life, at her table, in her bed.

But could they ever heal what was wrong with their marriage? Could they start over together?

Only time would tell.

She reached for her coffee cup, remembered that it was empty, and swallowed. Her speed just above the limit, she whizzed past a T-Rex and a line of brontosauri outside the entrance to Dinosaur World. She'd made good time, despite the detour and the usual slowdown around Orlando. Minutes later, her stomach tightened as Tampa's skyline came into view. For over twenty years, seeing the towering Regions Building had meant she was nearly home. But no longer. Now her home was on the opposite side of the state, in a sleepy little beachside town so different from Tampa's hustle and bustle that it might as well be in a different country.

She had a lengthy list of things to do before she could head back there. Some were pleasant, but she'd need to keep all her wits about her for the first two items on her agenda. As she approached the bridge over the Hillsborough River, she shoved all her other concerns aside for the moment and focused on what she wanted to say once she got to Plant High.

At the far end of the hall, a teenager in jeans and a yellow T-shirt disappeared into an open doorway seconds before chimes sounded through overhead speakers to announce the beginning of the next class. Diane tugged on the handle of the door beneath a gold and black banner promoting school spirit and stepped inside the main office. A whiff of sweat mingled with perfume floated in the stale air. The smell stirred a thirty-year-old memory of the day she'd been called to the principal's office. Though she hadn't been in trouble, she'd been so nervous she'd nearly thrown up. As if it, too, remembered that day, her stomach rumbled. She shushed it and strode across the room to the Formica counter that separated the staff from students and visitors to Plant High.

"Mrs. Keenan." Wearing a smile better suited to a used-car salesman than a school secretary, Bonnie Barrett hurried across her side of the room to greet Diane. The younger woman straightened the lapels of the gold polo shirt she wore under a black cardigan. "So nice to see you again," she gushed. She scoured the space on either side of Diane with an expectant gaze. "Isn't Caitlyn with you?"

"No." Wanting to pick up her daughter's records and leave, Diane kept her answer short.

Quick. Simple. To the point.

"Oh!" Bonnie's smile lost some of its glow. "I was hoping you'd bring her. I thought once she saw her friends and teachers, maybe she'd change her mind and want to stay at Plant High."

Was she delusional, Diane wondered. Or had the school secretary simply forgotten all that had transpired last fall?

"Uh, that's not going to happen." Diane gave herself points for staying cool and collected, if not exactly calm.

"Well," Bonnie said, sounding peeved. "When you do see Caitlyn, please wish her well for me. How's she doing?"

Diane arched one eyebrow. Given their conversation the last time she'd visited the school—the day her daughter's former best friend had struck Caitlyn so hard she'd ended up in the school clinic nursing a black eye—Diane had expected a cooler reception. If not a downright adversarial one. At the very least, she'd anticipated being directed to one of the chairs reserved for troublesome students and told to cool her heels for a lengthy period. But not only had the school secretary immediately greeted her, the extra dose of friendliness she'd crammed into her tone was completely out of character for the woman who dealt with teens and their parents day in and day out.

"Caitlyn is fine," Diane answered, all the while wondering at the secretary's odd behavior. "She has excelled in her homeschool program, is involved in community service projects and is excited about starting classes at Emerald Bay High next week. Which is why I'm here—to pick up her records." A fact Bonnie already knew, thanks to the phone conversation they'd had shortly after Caitlyn had begged to return to public school.

Rather than produce the requested file, the secretary continued to prattle as though she and Diane were old friends catching up after a lengthy time apart. "And Nick? We were all so surprised when he chose Virginia Tech over Gainesville."

"He's home for the holidays." Diane chose not to address the woman's unspoken question. Not that it was any of Bonnie Barrett's business, but Nick and his high-school sweetheart had planned to attend the University of Florida together, a plan that had fallen apart when the two broke up shortly after graduation. Unable to face the prospect of spending four years on the same campus as the woman who'd betrayed him, Nick had opted for a school nine hundred miles from home.

Diane gave her watch a pointed glance.

"Do give Nick my best," Bonnie continued brightly. "He was one of our best students."

An understatement, to be sure. Captain of the golf and chess teams, Nick had been the valedictorian of his class at Plant High. An honor Diane and Tim had hoped Caitlyn would hold, as well. But that dream had gone up in smoke when their daughter had been suspended, a move that practically guaranteed she'd fail all her classes. At the reminder of how badly the school had treated her daughter, Diane clenched her jaw and repeated her request through gritted teeth. "I'm here to pick up a copy of Caitlyn's records. You do have them ready, don't you?"

"Yes, but..." Some of Bonnie's enthusiasm drained from her face. "I wish you'd reconsider. Won't you speak with Principal Goshen about re-enrolling Caitlyn at Plant High?"

"Why on earth would I do that?" Diane blurted, her anger and frustration with the entire situation getting the best of her. She would not, could not force her daughter to finish out the year at a school where she'd been attacked and then punished for defending herself. It was ludicrous to even suggest such a thing.

"It's important these students face the consequences of their actions. Don't you think?"

Obviously expecting Diane to agree, Bonnie widened her smile.

In disbelief, Diane slowly shook her head. She wasn't one of those parents who clung to the mistaken belief that her child could do no wrong. She'd never denied that Caitlyn and her friends had hosted a party where underage teens had been drinking. The moment she'd found out about it, she'd grounded her daughter and had been pleased when the parents of the other girls had followed suit. That should have been the end of it, but things had escalated when Caitlyn's best friends—former best friends, she corrected—had blamed her child and cornered her on school grounds.

Diane let her voice drop to a frigid temperature. "I think we both know that ship has sailed. The file, please." She extended her hand, her palm open and expectant.

With little choice in the matter—Diane was well within her rights to enroll her daughter in a different school—Bonnie withdrew a thick manila envelope from beneath the counter. Though she placed one end in Diane's outstretched hand, she held on to the other. "We can...we can still count on Dr. Keenan's sponsorship for our golf and soccer programs, can't we?"

Ah! There it was—the real reason the school

secretary had been so ingratiatingly sweet. She and Tim had always supported the youth sport organizations near their home. Even though neither of her children had played baseball, for over a decade at least one Little League team had marched in the opening ceremonies wearing brand-new uniforms donated by Keenan Dental. The same had held true for basketball and field hockey leagues. Their donations to Nick's golf teams and Caitlyn's soccer teams had been even more generous and, this year alone, had included new gym bags, cleats and sweatshirts for the entire soccer program. It made sense that the school would hate to lose such important donors.

Diane swallowed hard against an urge to parrot Bonnie's own words about consequences back at the woman. Instead, she mustered a thin smile and said, "I'm sorry, but whatever contributions we make in the future will go to Caitlyn's new school, Emerald Bay High. I'll take those records, if you don't mind, and be on my way." With a firm grip, she wrenched the folder from Bonnie's grasp and stuck it in her purse.

Her head high, she left the school secretary to stare after her as she exited without saying another word. Her footsteps sure and steady, she marched to her car. Only when she was seated behind the wheel did she pause to take a long, shuddery breath.

One down and one to go, she told herself when she'd calmed sufficiently. But, knowing her next stop would be fraught with just as much tension as this one, she didn't relax. There'd be time enough for that when she was done. Putting her car in gear, she pulled out of the parking lot.

Noise bounced off the cement walls of the parking garage beneath the headquarters of Ybor City Accountants when Diane braked to an abrupt stop near her assigned parking space. Or what was supposed to be her space. She peered over her steering wheel in disbelief. Someone had parked a shiny black SUV in her spot. Grabbing a pen and tearing a sheet of paper from the notebook she always carried, she scribbled a note to the interloper. Seconds later, she climbed out of her car.

But a glance at the signage bolted to the wall in front of the vehicle stopped her before she could tuck the slip of paper beneath the SUV's windshield wiper. Shaking her head, she quashed the irritation that churned in her stomach. The spot, her old spot, had been reassigned to Blake Larson, her chief rival at the accounting firm and the man who'd taken over the WEXX account in her absence. The stiffness in her shoulders eased, and she crumpled the paper into a ball.

Change was inevitable, she reminded herself as she hurried back to her car. Three months had passed since she'd visited the home office; she couldn't expect things to be exactly as she'd left them. That included her coveted parking spot.

Behind the wheel again, she shifted her foot from the brake to the gas. Slowly moving forward, she drove up and down the rows, searching for an empty space. The task took longer than one would expect, considering the timing. Many companies all but shut down during the week between Christmas and New Year's so their employees could spend time with family and friends. But not Ybor City Accountants. Here it was business as usual, with just as many vehicles in the garage as on any other day in the year.

She was nearly to the exit before she found an empty spot, pulled in and shut off her engine. Slipping her keys into her pocket, she stashed her purse under a jacket she kept in the back seat. Seconds later, the sound of her heels broke the silence of the otherwise quiet garage as she hiked to the employee access, which was only a few steps from her old parking space.

As part of the fitness routine she'd begun shortly after moving to Emerald Bay, she chose the stairs over the elevator. She emerged into a lobby where bright sunlight streamed through floor-to-ceiling windows and glinted off marble floors. Pleased to find she was less winded than she would have been three months ago, she straightened the badge she wore on a lanyard around her neck. The receptionist behind the tall marble counter that stood beneath a gleaming company logo nodded, and Diane turned toward the bank of elevators against the back wall.

"Hey, Joe," she said as she approached the familiar security guard. Her footsteps slowed when the guard didn't return her greeting with his usual smile but grabbed a clipboard instead.

"Haven't seen you around lately, Ms. Keenan." Muscles bulging under his gray uniform shirt, Joe ran a finger down a list.

Diane gulped. Was this another unexpected change? Had she been barred from the facility? She held her breath until Joe returned the list to its place atop a podium that served as the guard station.

"Welcome back." A familiar smile replaced the serious expression on Joe's face. "We've missed having you around lately."

"It was nice to have some time away from the office," she answered as tension seeped from her shoulders. She didn't bother to explain that, in all likelihood, today's visit would be her last. Once she finished signing papers in the HR office and turning in her badge, she'd have no reason to visit the building again.

"How's Linda? Did Freddie and Carla have a good Christmas?" she asked, inquiring about Joe's family while she waited for the arrival of one of the four elevator cars.

"The best." Joe's grin widened. "Linda said I should be sure and thank you. The money helped us make the twins' Christmas a special one."

Though Ybor City Accountants provided every employee with a certificate good for a turkey or a ham from a local meat market each year, Diane made a point of tucking a little something extra into the cards she signed for members of the support staff. It warmed her heart to know her gift had made Christmas better for Joe and his family.

A bell dinged, and the doors of the elevator opened with a nearly silent swish. Diane stepped aboard. She reached toward the operating panel. Before she selected a floor, she asked, "Have you seen Mr. Thomlinson today?"

"Yes, ma'am. He's upstairs. Seemed like he was in a hurry when he came in about an hour ago." Joe squinted. "Not sure how long he plans to be in the office, either. His car and driver are waiting for him out front." With a slight frown, he inclined his head toward the main entrance. Beyond it, a long town car idled at the curb.

"Probably on his way to the golf course." Diane grinned. The company founder played eighteen holes several times a week, a habit that was well known among all the staff. "I'm glad I'm not the one keeping him from his tee time."

She sobered. Jeff had once been her staunchest advocate at the accounting firm. Lately, though, things had grown increasingly strained between them, and their most recent interactions hadn't been pleasant—to say the least. The last thing she wanted was to get into another argument with the man on this, her final day with his company. But considering all he'd done for her over the years, she owed him the simple courtesy of saying goodbye in person, didn't she?

With a nod to the security guard, she pressed the button that would take her to Executive Row. The soft music that played while the elevator glided upward did nothing to dampen the nervous energy that surged through her. Before she could rethink her choice, however, two soft chimes announced her arrival. The doors opened onto the tenth floor's hushed atmosphere.

Diane straightened the lapels of her suit jacket and stepped into the carpeted hallway. Focused on one office in particular, she strode past the open doors of the VIPs who, with very few exceptions, worked sixty- and seventy-hour weeks year in and year out. She tsked silently.

Once she'd longed to trade her corner office on this floor for an even bigger, better one on Executive Row. But that had been before. Before she'd learned firsthand how much it cost to reach the top. The price had been much higher than she'd wanted to pay, leaving her no choice but to walk away from the career she'd built. Not that there'd been anything easy about leaving. Now, though, her future held new possibilities, and she felt ready to embrace them.

Outside the suite of offices reserved for the company founder, his personal assistant, a diminutive woman named Barbara, raised one finger while she spoke quietly into a headset. "I miss you, too, sweetie. I'm coming straight home after work. In the meantime, you have fun with Daddy."

Diane felt a bittersweet pang as she listened to the half of the conversation she could hear.

How many times had she promised her own children that she'd see them soon? And how many times had she broken those promises in order to deal with one crisis or another at work? Far too many, she admitted. She'd missed out on so much of Nick and Caitlyn's childhoods while her focus had been elsewhere. Now they were practically adults—Nick in college and Caitlyn already a sophomore in high school. Could she ever make up for the time she'd lost with them? Her knees went weak, and she sank onto one of the side chairs in the anteroom while Barbara tried to reassure her own child, one who apparently wasn't happy with *soon* and wanted her mother to come home *now*.

After issuing one last promise that she'd be home as quick as she could, Barbara ended the call. Removing her headset, she sat for a long moment, her eyes closed.

Though it really wasn't her place to offer advice, Diane quietly asked, "Why aren't you home, enjoying the week off with your family?"

Barbara's eyes sprang open. She blinked slowly before answering in a shaky voice. "I asked for the time off, but you know Jeff."

Diane nodded. "I can practically hear him." Their boss often used children's fables to motivate his employees. In her gruffest imitation of the founder's voice, she said, "Remember what happens when you fiddle your time away."

"You gotta make hay while the sun shines," Barbara finished.

Giggling like a schoolgirl, Diane glanced at her friend's desk. As Jeff's personal assistant, Barbara had moved as high as she'd ever go with the company. With her boss out of the office for the rest of the day, what was she going to do all afternoon—file her nails? "You know, your daughter's only going to be four once."

"Don't I know it," Barbara answered wistfully. She paused for a moment, then pressed her hands to her head. "Oooooh, I feel a headache coming on," she moaned, though her smile betrayed her. "As soon as Jeff heads for the golf course, I'm going to punch out for the day."

"That's the ticket." Diane smiled her encouragement.

Barbara stood. Coming around the desk, she opened her arms wide. "Diane!" she exclaimed. "I've missed you! I didn't know you were coming back today!"

Drawn into Barbara's hug, Diane blinked away a rush of tears. The hardest part of moving on with her life was leaving her friends behind, and Barbara had been a good friend. Though their careers had followed different paths, the two of them had started working for Ybor City Accountants at the same time. Through the years, they'd compared recipes at company potlucks, swapped stories about their children and husbands during the occasional girls' night out and complained about their bosses whenever they had the chance. They'd grown so close that five years ago, she'd even hosted a shower at a local restaurant when her friend was expecting baby number three.

"I can't stay long, Barb." Diane smiled through her tears. "Today is my last day with the firm. I just popped in to say goodbye before I process out."

"No!" Barbara protested. "You're leaving?" The woman's eyebrows lifted.

"I'm afraid so." Diane had always known Jeff played his cards close to his vest, but learning he hadn't shared the news of her resignation with his assistant surprised her.

Barbara's hand fluttered as she slid a tiny gold star along the chain she wore around her neck. Curiosity and compassion filled her gaze. "Do you have any idea what you're going to do next?"

Diane lifted one shoulder in a gentle shrug. "Nothing is set in stone yet, but thought I'd try being my own boss for a while."

"You're going to start your own accounting firm? Here? In Tampa?" Barbara's voice climbed until it squeaked. She cleared her throat.

Diane muffled a laugh. No doubt her friend was imagining how her boss would react. And no wonder. Jeff would have serious qualms if she opened a competing firm within a hundred miles of Tampa.

"In Emerald Bay," she corrected, putting the woman's—and Jeff's—concerns to rest. "Everything's in the planning stages, but I'm looking into opening a small office that will cater to the needs of the local business community." She needed to hash out all the details with Tim, but she grew more certain about the idea every day.

"Well, then. Best of luck to you."

"Thanks, Barb. You, too. I had hoped to see Jeff while I was here. I wanted to thank him personally for all he's done for me throughout my career here." Diane eyed the darkened office behind Barbara's desk. Jeff's suite was outfitted with motion-activated sensors that would turn on the lights at the slightest movement. "Apparently, I've missed him."

Barbara's gaze dropped to the calendar on her desk. "He's in a meeting with Blake," she admitted.

"No problem." Diane shrugged. "Next time

you see him, let him know I stopped by. Okay?"

"I will. I'll tell him first thing...tomorrow." Barbara added a cheery grin.

Diane checked her watch. She had an hour before her appointment with HR. That gave her just enough time to box up the awards, plaques and mementos she'd left behind.

"I understand Blake has moved into my old office." She felt a sharp pang at the thought of her longtime rival enjoying the spectacular view from the window that had once been hers. Her regret quickly faded. She'd been so buried under a heavy workload that she'd never been able to take the time to look out the window, much less enjoy the membership in a health club or any of the other perks that had come with her most recent promotion.

"Yes." Barbara nodded slowly.

"Do you know where they moved me to? I'd like to collect my belongings before I process out."

"You're on the sixth floor with the rest of the WEXX team. Hold on a sec." Barbara moved the cursor on her desk. Her monitor sprang to life, and she clicked a few keys.

While she waited, Diane compared her management style to Blake's. When she'd been in charge, she'd insisted on having her team nearby. She'd always kept her door open in case someone had a question or ran into a problem they couldn't solve on their own. Blake, on the other hand, liked to keep his distance. He was fond of saying it fostered independence, and perhaps the added peace and quiet made him more effective. For his sake, she hoped so. The WEXX contract was huge, and transferring it from its current accounting house to theirs was a mammoth undertaking. She should know. If she'd stayed on at Ybor City, she'd have been in charge of the transition.

"6310," Barbara said at last. "Do you need directions?"

"Nope. I'll find it." Diane pictured the standard layout of the lower floors. Looking for her assigned space would give her the chance to poke around a bit. And who knew? It might be nice to run into another co-worker or two before she closed the chapter on this part of her life.

After giving Barbara a goodbye hug, Diane retraced her steps to the bank of elevators at the end of the hall. A minute later, she blinked as the doors parted on the sixth floor. The first thing that hit her was the noise. The cacophony of conversations, ringing telephones and clicking computer keys—so different from the quiet atmosphere of Executive Row—rolled over her like waves on the beach during a storm. Next came the acrid scent of burned coffee mixed with the buttery smell of popcorn and the fish someone had heated in a nearby microwave. Over that rode the fragrant blend of dozens of different perfumes, colognes and body sprays.

Diane coped by taking shallow breaths while she got her bearings. To her left and her right, glass walls opened into small offices reserved for senior accountants. Stepping into a corridor the width of two sidewalks, she checked the numbers on the doors. She gulped. Her new office was not one of them. Instead, she'd been assigned a space in the rabbit warren, an area behind a chest-high gray wall that contained hundreds of tiny modular spaces.

Tears pricked at her eyes. No doubt Blake had intended the assignment as an insult, a reminder of how the tables had turned, making him her boss instead of the other way around. He probably thought she'd be furious, but all she felt was incredibly sad that her former rival had stooped to such petty tactics. She sniffed and blinked away her tears. If it weren't for the photos of Nick and Caitlyn she'd left in her office, she'd head on down to Human Resources now and turn in her badge. But she did want those pictures, and with no other option for getting them, she began looking for her assigned space.

A short while later, she stood at the threshold of a tiny cubicle more suited to a new hire than someone who'd been with the company as long as she had. The standard-issue space had no door, just a gap in the depressingly gray walls. The furniture, such as it was, consisted of a built-in desk, a single overhead storage bin and an office chair that listed to one side. In one corner, a cardboard box that used to hold copier paper sat on a serviceable guest chair. Laughter bubbled up from her midsection, along with a renewed sense that her decision to leave Ybor City Accountants had been the right one.

She crossed the bare floor tiles in two strides and lifted the box lid. Setting it aside, she sorted through the contents. Among the framed photographs, certificates of achievement and awards, she found a calculator and a stapler that weren't hers. She set those on the desk and replaced the lid.

"Diane?"

She whirled at the sound of her name. Recognizing the junior accountant who'd worked for her on a number of recent projects, she smiled warmly. "Marcus," she said. "I was hoping to run into some of the old gang while I was here."

"You look good, Diane."

"You look…" Diane paused while she studied the young man. Fatigue had darkened the circles under his eyes. His hair was several weeks overdue for a cut. His shirt and pants were so wrinkled, she wondered if he'd slept in them. She suspected he'd doused himself with cologne to mask the smell of body odor. "You look like Blake's been running you ragged," she admitted finally.

"Ain't it the truth. I haven't had a day off in two weeks except for Christmas."

"I take it the WEXX account is giving you problems?"

"It's a hot mess. I'm on the tax team. We shoulda been done already, but every time I think we're finished, we get a whole new set of requirements. We've had to start over from scratch three times already." The moment the words escaped his lips, Marcus's face paled. "But—but you didn't hear that from me."

"Hear what?" Forcing a puzzled look on her face, Diane cupped one hand behind her ear. She refused to offer any advice. Though Blake and his team were cutting it awfully close if they were going to meet the deadline for filing the first reports of the year, Ybor City's newest account was not her problem.

Marcus shot her a thankful glance before his gaze shifted to the tiny cubicle. His expression soured. "Wow! Blake really stuck it to you, didn't he? I never dreamed he'd put you down here with the rest of us grunts."

"Yes, well." Diane scuffed one heel against the carpet. A lot of people would rant and rave about the unfairness of being given such a minuscule office, but what would be the point in that? It wasn't like she'd be here long enough to actually use it. "It's okay," she reassured Marcus. "They just stored my stuff here until I could pick it up."

The tall man's eyes widened. "You're leaving?"

"Turned in my notice two weeks ago." Diane nodded. "I'm moving to Emerald Bay."

"Where?" Marcus's face pinched.

"It's a small, beachside community on the opposite coast." When Marcus still looked bewildered, she added, "Between Vero and Sebastian."

He propped his arm on top of the modular wall. "Why move to such an out-of-the-way place?"

"It's where I'm from." Diane shrugged. "My family owns an inn on the beach, and my aunt is getting too old to run it by herself." She fell short of telling the young man the rest of her plans and let him fill in the blanks however he wanted.

Marcus's eyebrows dipped low over his eyes. "I didn't see anything about a going-away party."

"I didn't want one." Though, if she were being perfectly honest, no one had offered to organize one. She gestured toward the beehive of activity around them. "Considering how busy everyone is these days, it just didn't seem right."

"Everyone deserves a proper send-off," Marcus protested. He tugged on his chin. "Um, how about I get the team together for drinks after work? For old times' sake."

Diane shook her head. "Thanks, but I have plans for this evening." She'd promised to be home in time for dinner with Nick and Caitlyn. Besides, if she knew anything about working and Ybor City Accountants—and she did—Marcus and his coworkers would be at their desks long after the supper dishes had been washed, dried and put away.

When Marcus looked as though he might argue, she hefted her box of personal items. "I'd love to stay and chat, but I need to get moving. It's time for my meeting with HR. Will you give my best to everyone?" she asked.

"Sure." He leaned forward, his voice

dropping to a conspiratorial level. "I always enjoyed working with you, Diane. If you ask me, they should have given the WEXX account to you. I'm not sure Blake…"

Juggling the box, Diane held up one hand to stop the man from saying anything more. "Just so you know, Mr. Thomlinson did offer me the WEXX account," she said softly. "I turned it down." She regained her grip on the box that was growing heavier by the second. "As for Blake, he's an excellent manager. I'd appreciate it if you gave him your full support. Like you always did for me."

His face coloring slightly, Marcus nodded. He eyed the box she held. "You want me to carry that for you?"

"Nah, I got it. But thanks, Marcus, for everything."

With that, she headed downstairs to turn in her badge.

An hour later, the last item on her list of things to do completed, Diane carried her personal items out of the HR office. She felt naked without the lanyard she'd worn around her neck since the day she'd first reported to work at Ybor City Accountants, but she'd handed it over in exchange for the usual raft of exit paperwork. Taking the elevator this time in deference to the heavy box, she nudged the button for the garage with her elbow. Shrugging aside a few last-minute doubts, she started toward her car when the doors opened. She made it as far as the curb before the sound of hurried footsteps echoing off the walls of the stairwell stopped her. She glanced over her shoulder just in time to see Jeff Thomlinson speed down the final few steps.

Her brow puckered. What was the company founder doing in the parking garage when his own town car waited for him upstairs? For that matter, why hadn't he left for the golf course ages ago?

"Diane! Hold up a minute," Jeff called before she could resume her long walk to the other side of the garage where her own car waited.

Lowering her burden to the cement, she stayed put while he closed the gap between them. Her confusion deepened when, slightly out of breath, Jeff wheezed to a stop in front of her.

"I heard you were in the building. I'm glad I caught you." He eyed her box of personal effects. "You aren't leaving already, are you?"

Touched that he'd wanted to say goodbye in person, she stuck out her hand. "I stopped by your office earlier. I was sorry I missed you."

"It's good to see you. Good to see you." Jeff clasped her outstretched hand. Rather than giving it his customary shake, he held her in his grasp. "I was hoping we'd have a minute to talk."

A horn sounded from somewhere in the depths of the garage. The noise startled Jeff, who relinquished his grip. Scouring the area as if muggers and thieves might lurk behind every pillar, he asked, "Do you mind if we go to my office?" he asked.

Diane tilted her head to one side. "Don't you have a golf game?"

A chagrined expression passed over Jeff's face. "My earlier meeting didn't, uh, didn't go as well as I'd hoped, but I'm still hoping to play nine holes."

"Oh?" Questions burned in Diane's stomach. Hadn't Barbara mentioned a meeting with Blake this morning? She throttled her curiosity. Whatever problems Jeff faced in the firm, they were no longer her concern.

"Let's go upstairs where we can talk in private." Jeff pointed to her box. "Can I carry that for you?"

Diane shook her head. "I'm sorry. I'm on my way out. And I'm in a bit of a hurry." She'd timed her departure to get ahead of the heavy afternoon traffic. Accompanying Jeff to his office would use up an hour or more, making her late for dinner with the kids. She'd vowed not to let work interfere with her family ever again. On the other hand, she didn't want to appear totally heartless. Hoping she wasn't making a big mistake, she toed the box at her feet. "Was there something I can help you with?"

"You can come back," Jeff blurted.

Come back where? Diane pressed her lips together as she eyed the elevator behind Jeff. "I just told you I'm headed home."

"Come back to work here. For me. I'll give you your old office back. Or a better one. Name your price. A new title? A raise? You'll be in charge of the WEXX account. Just come back, please. We need you here." He took a breath. "*I* need you here."

Diane stared at the man who'd grown Ybor City Accountants from a one-person office into one of the largest accounting firms in the state. She would have sworn she knew all his moods, all his emotions. After all, she'd watched him handle two of his three divorces and at least one hostile takeover attempt with an unwavering confidence. She'd felt his disappointment after a potential client had chosen to go with a different firm. She'd witnessed his chest swell with pride the day his daughter gave birth to his first grandchild. Or when his son passed the bar on his first try. Oh, Jeff could rant and rave with the best of them—especially if one of his managers missed an important deadline. Sometimes, though, she'd wondered how much of his anger was real and how much of it was an act designed to spur his staff to work harder, be better.

But in all the years she'd known him, she'd never once heard Jeff beg. And there was no doubt in her mind that that was exactly what he was doing now—begging.

For a second, a heady sense of vindication threatened to overwhelm her while the ways she could use the situation to her advantage flashed before her. The corner office. The expense account. A host of other perks. Extra vacation days.

At the thought of having more time off, though, she steadied. Only minutes earlier, she'd literally been walking away from a job that had demanded so much of her time, energy and dedication it had destroyed her marriage and damaged her relationship with her children. Why would she even consider going back to it?

She swallowed. Hard. There'd been a time when Jeff's offer would have been music to her ears. When she'd have given him a resounding

Yes without considering the effect her answer would have on her husband, her children, her own health. But no more. "I appreciate the offer, Jeff. You can't know how much it means to me to hear that you want me back at Ybor City Accountants. But—" She inhaled deeply. "But I've made my decision, and it's final."

"I refuse to accept that answer." A hint of the old Jeff, the in-charge Jeff, showed in the way he drew himself to his full height. "There has to be something you want. Some way I can change your mind."

Diane rocked back on her heels. She could think of only one set of circumstances that would allow her to put her family first and still work for the firm, but the last time she'd broached the idea with Jeff, he'd rejected it outright. She didn't think he'd ever change his mind. Not even now.

You'll never know if you don't ask.

She took a breath. "Are you willing to let me handle the job from Emerald Bay? To come into the office once or twice a week, like I suggested?"

It wasn't a perfect solution. They'd both have to compromise in order to make it work. She'd have to delay her dream of starting her own business for another year, at least. He'd...Well, she wasn't sure what he'd give up, so she searched the man's face for an answer as well as for some sign that he was willing to compromise.

Jeff only frowned, his features tightening. "There's too much riding on the WEXX account. It's too big, too important. Now is not the time to introduce a whole new way of doing things. Maybe sometime in the future. Some other project. But not—"

"Well. I guess that's your answer then." She interrupted Jeff before he could continue. She didn't need to hear anything else. She'd seen the steely glint in his eyes. She knew how his mind worked. He had no intention of ever letting her work remotely. Not on this contract or any other. Like he did all the managers who worked for him, he wanted her at his beck and call. And not just during normal working hours, but any hour of the day or night. He wanted, needed to see her burning the midnight oil. Only then would he be assured that she was doing all she could to complete the project on time and under budget.

"Thanks for the offer, but I'm not interested." Picking up her box, she put a couple of steps between her and the company founder.

"You're not serious," Jeff protested. "What's it going to take? Really."

Diane gave her head a firm shake. "There's absolutely nothing," she said, almost afraid to admit how much she enjoyed Jeff's look of shock and disbelief. Taking pity on the man, she paused. "I will offer you one piece of advice, though."

"What?" Jeff asked, sounding like a petulant child.

"Tell Blake to trust his gut and quit trying to reinvent the wheel," she said, thinking of her earlier conversation with Marcus. "Blake needs to pick a plan for how to handle things and stick with it. Even if it's not perfect. Even if someone comes up with a better idea. The way he's going—scrapping the current method in favor of a different approach every five minutes—he's never going to finish on time."

"And that's how you'd handle it? Just lay out a path and go with it?" As though he were begrudging the point, Jeff folded his arms across his chest.

"It's how I've always done things. And it worked, didn't it?" Jeff was fond of pitting his managers against one another. She didn't need to remind him how often her team had beaten Blake's in those not-so-friendly challenges.

"See, that's exactly why you're needed here. Not galivanting off across to the other side of the state."

Diane adjusted her grip on the box. "Like I

said, pick a plan and stick with it. I've chosen mine."

Jeff's shoulders rounded in a sign of defeat. "I can't change your mind."

"No, sir." She'd made her choice.

"Well, then." He cleared his throat. "I guess this is goodbye."

"Yes, sir. I think it is." She nodded briefly. "Thanks again...for everything."

Without another word, her former mentor walked to the elevator.

Watching him go, Diane resisted the urge to scratch her head. Jeff was a millionaire several times over. He owned one of the largest accounting firms in the state and regularly wined and dined with the rich and famous. Yet he'd been divorced three times that she knew of, and other than to ask for money, his children rarely spoke with him. In her mind, she'd always picture him as a sad, lonely man who had nothing to live for other than his company and his golf game.

She breathed a sigh of relief. She'd come close—too close—to becoming exactly like him. She had a chance now to start fresh, to carve out a different future for herself and her children. Maybe, just maybe, she and Tim could work things out between them, too.

And, putting one foot in front of the other, she headed for her car and the start of her new life in Emerald Bay.

Three

Belle

Jen's eyes widened in surprise as she scanned the room Belle had transformed into a day spa. "Whoa! I like what you've done with the place." In a move reminiscent of an actress from the '50s, the brunette waved a hand through the air. "You must give me the name of your decorator, dah-ling."

With some help from a couple of the gardeners, Belle had arranged three overstuffed chairs and matching ottomans in a circle in the middle of the main room of the cozy cottage. Draped in soft linens, the furniture created the best impression of a spa she could manage under the circumstances. Hating the doubts that made her voice unsteady, she asked, "Do you think Amy and Kim will like it?"

"I think they'll love it," Jen declared. She crossed to the island that doubled as a dining table. "Good grief, cuz," she exclaimed. "Did you buy stock in Sephora? I haven't seen this many cleansers and oils since I worked in a spa." Setting down her mug of coffee, she twisted the lid off one of the jars Belle had lined up on the granite surface. She lifted the container to her nose. "Oh, yum. That smells delicious."

Belle glanced at the sparkling yellow bottle her cousin had chosen. "That one's a blend of honey and apple. An excellent moisturizer for mature skin."

"Just exactly what are you implying?" Jen propped one hand on her hip. "Do I need to remind you I'm younger than you are?" She dabbed a tiny bit of the cream on one finger and replaced the lid. The air filled with a sweet scent as she rubbed the lotion into the back of her hands. "Ahhh." She gestured toward the long line of jars, bottles and tubes. "Makes me feel all girly."

Belle's soft laughter filled the room as she eyed the array of beauty products. She wished she could have added pouches of diamond powder exfoliant from Baccarat, but her days of dropping a cool grand to bathe in a refreshing tub of Evian or to have her face and hands slathered in youth-defying caviar were over. For today's facial scrubs, she'd selected masks made of pure Peruvian mud—which were pricey enough, thank you very much.

Thinking back over what Jen had said, Belle felt her eyebrows bunch, something they did too often now that her latest Botox injections were wearing off. "Did you say you worked at a spa? I thought you were a cocktail waitress."

"Mostly I was, but I've done a little bit of everything." Jen slowly examined each of the cosmetics as she talked. "Whatever it took to keep a roof over my head and food in my belly. From slinging burgers at fast-food joints to tending bar, I've done it. Including a stint or two in hoity-toity spas. At first, I just folded towels and cleaned up after the clients. After a while, I started helping with treatments. I liked it well enough to think about getting into one of those cosmetology schools."

"You have your license?" Belle fought to keep her jaw from dropping. Her cousin was full of surprises.

Jen shook her head. "Never got quite that far. I was just looking into it when I went to work at the River Delta. Tips there were good, so I figured I'd save the cosmetology stuff for when I got too old to work the floor of the casino." Her smile wobbled as she ran a hand over her hips and thighs. "That day came a lot sooner than I expected."

"You're not old," Belle protested. To prove her point, she gave the slim woman a once-over. Jen's skin stretched tautly over high cheekbones and a chiseled jaw. With her long legs, waspish waist and well-endowed chest, she looked half her age in skintight leggings and a T-shirt that strained so much across her ample bosom it would earn a disapproving glare from at least one of Emerald Bay's matrons. "You're in great shape," she said firmly.

"Hey, when you got it, flaunt it." Jen struck a Betty Boop pose that made them both laugh. Straightening, she gave her head a shake. "It's not the looks. It's the speed. Those twentysome-things run rings around me," she admitted while her dark curls shimmied.

"I hear you," Belle commiserated. "It's getting harder and harder for me to compete with the Taylors and the Brittanys of the world. Before my last tour was canceled, I spent more time in the gym than I did in the practice studio."

Sympathy clouded Jen's features. Her head canted to one side. "Do you miss it? The record deals and the performances? Having an entourage at your beck and call?"

The usual vague response about taking advantage of new opportunities and looking forward to a change began to roll off Belle's tongue. She stopped it. White lies were good enough for neighbors and acquaintances. But family and loved ones deserved to hear the truth. Jen definitely fell into both categories.

Belle cleared her throat. "I'd be lying if I said I didn't." She wiped the sad smile from her face with a shrug. "But what are you going to do? Sometimes life hands us lemons. We all have to decide what to do with them. I'm determined to make lemonade out of mine."

"Count me in on that, too." A mix of concern and curiosity pooled in Jen's dark eyes. "But what *is* next?"

"That's the question, isn't it?" Cousins or not, Belle wasn't quite ready for that conversation. Fortunately, the muffled sound of her mother moving around in the tiny bedroom gave her an excuse to remain quiet.

"To be continued," Belle said. Whatever the future held in store for her or for Jen, they'd have to discuss it another time, another place. Today was all about Amy and Kim and helping them look their best for New Year's Eve. She motioned toward the array of products. "I'm so glad you offered to help out today. I've been on the receiving end of all this a million times, but I've never given someone else the spa treatment before, and I want to do it right. Amy and Kim deserve to look absolutely fabulous for their dates."

"That they do," Jen agreed. "And Aunt Margaret, too. She's done so much for us. She deserves a day of pampering." When Belle nodded, she asked, "What time are we getting started?"

"Mom should be out in a minute." Belle swung toward the bedroom. It had been a while since she'd heard the shower shut off. "Amy texted to say she was on her way. Kim and Natalie should be here any minute."

"I better finish my coffee while I can." Jen picked up the mug she'd set aside and drank deeply.

"There's plenty more. I made a fresh pot." Belle no sooner got the words out than the front door of the little cottage opened. A burst of cold air and a shaft of bright sunlight spilled through the gap. Kim and Natalie quickly stepped into the room and closed the door behind them.

"Brr," Kim announced. She cinched a thick terrycloth robe tighter around her waist. "I hope it's not going to be this cold tonight. I don't look good in chill bumps, and my dress is sleeveless."

"It's supposed to warm up," Jen said from the kitchen counter where she was refilling her coffee cup. "You won't need more than a light sweater or a shawl."

"You can borrow one of mine. I have plenty to choose from." Belle eyed the wisp of blond hair that peeked out from beneath the turban Kim wore. "How'd you like the shampoo and conditioner?" She'd given Kim some of her own and told her to use it instead of the inexpensive brand she'd been using.

"Oh, my goodness. It's the best," Kim declared. "My hair's never felt so silky. You have to tell me where I can get some."

"It's just something I picked up in New York," Belle hedged. She didn't dare mention the name of her favorite salon in Midtown where the owner had created a custom line of shampoo and conditioners just for her. The one-of-a-kind treatment came with a hefty price tag. One she was pretty sure her cousin couldn't afford. Not that she could, either. Not now that her circumstances had changed.

Belle turned to greet Nat next but stopped when she noticed a striking difference in the girl. Gone was the brilliant blue that had reminded Belle of the plumage of a colorful bird. In its place, strands of dark blond framed the younger woman's face. "You've done something different with your hair, too, haven't you?"

Fluffing her short lengths with her fingers, Nat preened. "What do you think, Aunt Belle?"

The greeting warmed Belle's heart. According to all the genealogy charts, she and Nat were first cousins once removed, but she'd been the girl's Aunt Belle since the day Kim gave birth. "Your natural color is beautiful," Belle answered, eying the golden highlights that sparkled among her niece's darker strands.

"It was her idea." Nat pointed to Jen. "Thanks for suggesting the baking soda. It took out every bit of the blue."

Belle arched an eyebrow at her cousin. "Baking soda?"

"For the dye," Jen explained.

"Oh?" Though she dreaded the day she found a single gray strand among her dark curls, so far Belle had been lucky enough to avoid dying her own hair.

"Nat's wasn't permanent," Jen explained. "It would have faded on its own after a couple of washes, but the baking soda helped the process along."

"Good to know." Belle filed the information away and hoped she'd never need it. "The change suits you, Nat." She rubbed her hands together. "Want to get started? We have a lot to do today."

"What about Amy and Aunt Margaret?" Kim asked.

"Mom's almost ready." A shadow passed by the window. "And if I'm not mistaken, here's Amy now."

After a quick knock, the door inched open. When Nat and Kim stepped aside to let it swing wide, Amy eased into the room carrying a covered tray.

"Oooh, something good?" Nat took the tray and peeked inside. Her lips pursed, and disappointment spread over her features. "Cucumbers? I was hoping for breakfast."

"The cucumbers are for our facials, but don't worry." Amy held up a cloth sack adorned with the Sweet Cakes logo. "I brought bagels."

"None for me, thanks." Kim patted her slim hips. "Not if I'm going to fit into that dress tonight." She'd taken one look at the landscape print she'd borrowed from Belle's closet and immediately gone on a diet.

"I'll have one." Nat took the bag from Amy's outstretched hand. She poked around inside. "You brought cream cheese, too? Thanks! How about you, Aunt Margaret? Want to split one?"

"I could use a little something to eat."

Looking a bit overwhelmed, Margaret stepped from the bedroom.

"You can set those in the kitchen while I help Mama." Belle smiled at the velvet dressing gown that threatened to fall off Margaret's thin shoulders. "Mama, that color brings out the blue in your eyes," she gushed. "Let me just roll the collar for you and tighten the belt." She made quick work of adjusting the fit of the gown.

"It is pretty." Margaret idly stroked the soft fabric. "But I don't know why I couldn't just get dressed for the day. I'm not the one with a hot date."

"You don't have to have a date to feel special, Mama," Belle soothed. Tucking her mother's arm in her own, she slowly guided the older woman to the seating area. "Today is your day to be pampered. Yours and Amy's and Kim's. Now, if you three ladies will take your places, we'll get started."

Once her mom stopped protesting and settled into her chair, Belle turned on an infuser. Soon, the soothing scent of lemongrass filled the air. While classical music played softly in the background, she directed her helpers—Jen and Nat—to prepare the first treatment. A short while later, their feet soaking in small plastic tubs of water, Amy and Kim sipped from tall glasses of fruit-flavored water while Margaret had her usual cup of coffee and nibbled on a half of a bagel.

"Are you ready for this, Aunt Margaret?" Nat brushed a stray crumb from her shirt before she sank cross-legged on the floor in front of the chair.

Margaret eyed the young woman over the rim of her cup. "This isn't going to hurt, is it?"

"Don't worry. I'll be very gentle." As if to prove she meant it, Nat carefully folded the hem of Margaret's dressing gown up to her knees. Grabbing a jar of exfoliant, she let the older woman sniff it while she explained, "Now the first thing we're going to do is slather this buffing cream on your legs and then I'm going to massage them. We'll do the same thing with your arms. You'll be amazed at how wonderful your skin will feel when we're done."

From the spot where she knelt in front of Kim, Belle listened to Nat's patter and smiled. The girl had showered her mother with kindness and love from the moment she'd arrived on the inn's doorstep. Someone that caring deserved the best life could dish out, and she wished nothing less for the girl she considered her niece. Brushing a sudden dampness from her eyes onto her shirt sleeve, Belle scooped a plum-size portion of body scrub from her jar and began working it onto Kim's legs.

As the air filled with a nutty scent, she asked, "Tell me, what are the plans for this evening? Is Craig taking you somewhere spectacular?"

"Mmm, that feels like heaven," Kim practically moaned. "Forget the date. I'm perfectly content to stay right where I am."

Jen looked up from Amy's feet. "Aren't you looking forward to spending New Year's with Craig?" Her sister and the mayor had been seeing each other for several months.

Kim's smile deepened. "Of course I am. He wouldn't tell me where we are going, just to wear a pretty dress, but I'm sure he has something wonderful planned. That's the kind of man he is. He's the most thoughtful and caring man I've ever dated." Concerned about her daughter's feelings, she shot Nat an apologetic look. "No offense to your dad, honey."

"None taken," the girl responded. "Even I'll admit that Dad can be more than a little self-centered."

Sensing they'd ventured onto treacherous ground, Belle tried to make light of the conversation. "I'm glad you've found someone who makes you happy, Kim."

"I'm just trying to live in the moment. And in

this moment, I'm very, very happy." Kim purred contentedly.

In the chair between Margaret and Kim, Amy gave a groaning sigh. "Ooooh, do that some more." She pointed to the foot Jen had been massaging. "Ah, yes," she whispered a moment later. "Much as I'd like to stay here all day and let you do whatever it is you're doing to my feet, I'm not going to let anything stop me from spending the night with Max."

"Oh?" Belle hiked her eyebrows. This was news. Amy hadn't shown a serious interest in anyone since her marriage fell apart, and that had been ages ago. "Are you saying that tonight is *the* night?" Aiming at a spot below her cousin's waist, she circled her finger in the air. "Did you take care of things down there?"

Amy squeaked a protest. "Belle!"

Margaret, who'd been staring so intently at Nat that no one thought she was listening, asked, "Take care of what things?"

Belle's face heated. With her fingers coated in exfoliant, she barely resisted the urge to clamp one hand over her mouth. The very thought of explaining what she'd meant to her mother was too embarrassing for words. Looking for help, she searched the faces of the other women. She needn't have bothered. Nat handled the matter with her usual grace and charm.

From her spot in front of Margaret, Nat tipped her head. "They're talking about shaving around her bikini line. You know, so she's not all bushy."

Margaret blinked several times before she let out a surprised gasp. "Oooh!" Her eyes narrowed into inquisitive slits as she peered at Amy. "Did you?"

The baker's color brightened. She held up both hands, calling for a stop to the conversation. "For everybody's information, 'down there' is nobody's business but my own." She sat up straighter. "And it's certainly none of Max's business."

"Okay, then." Belle's hearty laughter joined with the others'.

Kim waited for the laughter to die down before she said, "I think we were talking about plans for the evening." Giving Amy an evil, cousinly grin, she added, "And I guess now we all know what's *not* on your agenda."

Belle shushed Kim by giving her calf a playful pinch. "Sorry," she mock-apologized. Glancing over her shoulder, she addressed Amy. "So what *are* you and Max going to do tonight? If you're not going to...you know."

"Puh-leeze." Amy flopped back in her chair. "I don't know the man well enough for that. It's way too early to get serious. But to answer your question, I have no idea. He said he wanted to surprise me."

"Sounds intriguing." Cupping water in her hands, Jen began removing the exfoliant from Amy's legs. "That could be just about anything."

Amy bit her lower lip. "He's made it his mission in life to find a restaurant I've never been to. I keep telling him it's a lost cause. Between growing up here in Emerald Bay and constantly checking out the bakery's competition, I've eaten at every place from here to Fort Pierce at least once. If they were any good, I've been back often enough to memorize the menu." She lifted her shoulders in surrender. "But he keeps trying."

Belle dried Kim's legs with a towel. Laying a fresh one across Kim's lap, she plopped another dollop of the rich exfoliant on her cousin's arms and went to work. "What time did the boys say they'd pick you up?"

"At six," Amy answered.

"Craig will be here at six thirty."

Belle glanced at the digital display on the microwave. Nat had already finished with Margaret and was rinsing her soaking tub in the sink while Jen tidied up the area around Amy's chair. Aware of how much they had left to do, she said, "I think we'd better move to the next step if you ladies are going to be ready on time." Leaving Kim to soak up the ambience of their makeshift spa, she carried her own tub into the kitchen.

With Jen's help, she removed the lids from an assortment of moisturizers and arranged the open bottles and jars on a mirrored tray. "Nat, if you'll take these around and let Mama and the girls choose whatever they like, it'll help a lot."

While Jen refreshed drinks and passed around a plate of tiny cookies, Nat helped the others select one of the rich lotions. Soon, the scents of apple, lavender and blue tansy rose from the fragrant honey-based cream Nat worked into Margaret's skin while Jen applied their choices to Kim's and Amy's hands and feet. Meanwhile, Belle scooped ample portions of the imported mud mask onto small silicone bowls. Into yet another one, she poured a rich blend of hibiscus and rosehip seed oil that was all but guaranteed to work wonders at erasing the lines from her mother's face. Once their three "clients" were stretched out comfortably to let the detoxifying masks do their work, Belle handed bowls and small towels to Jen and Nat. She kept a third set for herself.

Nat gave the contents of her bowl an appreciative sniff. She wasted no time before dipping up a smidge and smearing it on her chin. She giggled. "It tingles."

Jen frowned. "Are you sure, Belle? I know how expensive this stuff is."

Jen's concern touched Belle's heart, and she smiled warmly. "Please. We deserve a little treat after working so hard this morning, don't we? Besides, I can't very well put it back in the jar."

Jen's frown smoothed. "Well, if you insist." Following Nat's example, she began applying the rich mud to her chin and cheeks. "Don't forget your neck." She sank onto one of the chairs Belle had shoved against the wall. "They say the décolleté shows your age quicker than crow's feet."

When they were properly covered in the dark paste, Belle set the timer for twenty minutes. She leaned back in a chair, closed her eyes and let the powerful leaching properties in the mask work their magic. She must have drifted off, because when the timer on her phone chimed, it seemed like mere seconds had passed instead of nearly a half hour.

All six women made quick work of rinsing their faces. Lunch, served on bamboo trays, came next. While the others dug into their scoops of chicken salad on beds of artfully arranged spinach leaves, Belle lugged an oversized case out of the bedroom. After clearing a space on the counter, she flipped the latches and popped open the lid. A collective gasp rose from the group when drop lights over the counter shone down on an extensive selection of eyeshadows, blushes and contouring powders.

"Oh, man!" Kim whispered. Setting her lunch aside, she began examining the makeup collection. "I had no idea eyeshadow came in so many shades of green." Turning to Belle, she gave her a puzzled look. "What did you need all this for? Whenever you were going on stage, you had professionals do your hair and makeup, didn't you?"

Belle sighed, remembering. "Makeup girls get stuck in traffic. Or they get the directions wrong and never show up. After I waited for my stylist at Webster Hall one night when she thought the gig was at the Palladium, I started carrying my own makeup bag." She eyed the extensive collection with a wry smile. "It kind of grew over the years."

Amy forked up the last bit of her salad and joined Kim at the counter. "Ooooh," she breathed. "This reminds me of those big boxes of crayons we used to get for Christmas each year."

"Sixty-four colors." Kim grinned at the memory. "With a sharpener built into the side of the box."

"I loved those." Amy ran one finger over no less than six different silver shadows. "This is even more fun." Her eyes glinted at Belle. "You can get me one of these next Christmas."

"I'll get right on that," Belle said, her tone dry.

Jen crumpled her napkin. "Okay, ladies. We still have nails, hair and makeup to do, and time's a'wasting. How are we going to do this?" She looked to Belle for the answer.

"Nat volunteered to be our nail technician for the day." The younger woman had assured everyone she was up to the challenge, and from the looks of her beautiful nails, Belle didn't doubt it.

Nat curled her fingers inward and examined her polish. "I've been on the road so much it seemed better to learn how to do them myself than to have to search for a good salon wherever I was."

"And Jen, you're going to do Amy's and Kim's hair. I think I have everything you need. That leaves the makeup for me." She pointed to the kit. "I'm pretty good at that."

"Sounds good," Jen said. "I guess we'd better

get started then. Who wants to have their hair done first?"

Kim raised her hand.

"Good." Belle nodded. "Amy, let's have Nat do your nails, and Mama, I'll do your makeup. Don't worry. I won't go overboard." She paused when Margaret didn't answer. "You'll let me do your makeup, won't you, Mama?"

"Oh, posh." Margaret looked up from the last few bites of her salad long enough to give her fingers a dismissive flick. "A little powder, a little blush—that's all I ever wear." She took a sip of coffee and swallowed. "No, you focus on Amy and Kim. I don't need anyone fussing over me. I'll probably fall asleep before the ball drops on TV anyway."

Jen reached over and squeezed her aunt's hand. "I'm not going out tonight. I thought we could play some Hand and Foot this evening." The card game was Margaret's favorite. "I hope you're up for it."

Interest sparked in the older woman's eyes. "You'll keep score?"

"Of course," Jen assured her.

Margaret sat up a little straighter. "I wouldn't mind beating the pants off you." Margaret's eyes sought Nat's. "You and Belle are welcome to join us. We'll play teams."

Nat hedged. "I've never heard of Hand and Foot," she said. "Is it easy to learn?"

Belle chuckled. "It's like Rummy but a lot more complicated. I'm afraid, though, Mama will have to teach you another time. I volunteered to help with the youth group at church tonight. And as much as today wore me out, I gave my word that I'd be there. I was hoping you'd come with me."

"Oh?" Nat's eyebrows rose.

"Unless you'd rather stay home," Belle quickly amended. Though she wanted Nat to join her, the choice was really up to her niece.

"Sure thing. Whatever you need." She turned to face Margaret and grinned. "I guess that means you'll have to teach me another time. This week sometime?"

"Nothing would make me happier," Margaret assured the girl.

Belle felt her mother's eyes search her face.

"If you don't mind, I think I'd like to take my nap now. All this pampering has plumb tuckered me out. I need to get some rest if Jen and I are going to play cards tonight."

Belle and Jen exchanged satisfied looks. "That's fine, Mama. Nat can do your nails when you wake up."

"I have a soft peach I think you'll absolutely love," Nat offered.

"Pink is fine," Margaret said, though she looked about as happy as someone who'd sucked on a lemon. Holding her tray at an awkward angle, Margaret attempted to stand. "Fire engine red is better."

"Oh, ho!" Nat said while everyone else chuckled. "Red it is!"

Belle hurried to her mother's side. "Here. I'll take care of your tray while you get ready for your nap. I'll come in and check on you in a few minutes." Ever since the fall that had broken her arm, her mom had been fighting to regain her stamina. Her afternoon lie-downs, which had been little more than catnaps before the accident, now regularly stretched out for an hour or more.

When Margaret disappeared into the bedroom, Belle and Jen took care of the lunch dishes and Nat straightened things in the spa area before they all went to their stations in the "spa." For the next several hours, the bright smell of polish and hair care products filled the air while Belle, Jen and Nat worked their magic, first on Kim and Amy and, once she woke, on Margaret. Shortly before Max was due to arrive, the three pampered women adjourned to the bedroom to slip into the clothes Belle had steamed and hung in the closet.

Belle, Jen and Nat applauded when Margaret,

wearing a silky pantsuit that had been a Christmas present, stepped out of the bedroom. Though she leaned heavily on her cane, the eighty-year-old managed a decent spin before she sank onto the couch beside her daughter. She placed a hand on Belle's forearm and whispered, "Thanks for all this. You really outdid yourself."

Belle patted her mother's thin hand. "I couldn't have pulled it off without Nat and Jen." She eyed her mother's face. "I'm going to get you some of that blush. It's a great color on you."

"Oh, honey," Margaret protested. "You've given all of us such a perfect day. You don't need to give me anything else."

Belle opened her mouth to argue but snapped it shut when the door to the bedroom re-opened. This time, Amy emerged in a little black dress covered in sparkling crystals. When Belle caught sight of the baker all gussied up like a fairy princess, she nearly wept for joy. "Oh, Amy. You look beautiful," she gushed.

"You're going to knock Max's socks off when he sees you in that dress," Nat declared.

And that wasn't all. Jen had worked wonders with Amy's hair, sweeping the dark curls into an utterly feminine updo, the very opposite of the tight bun she wore to work each day. The spa treatments had banished every trace of the fatigue and worry that came from managing a growing business. From the makeup that highlighted her rosy cheeks and deep-set eyes, down past glittery, silver nails to matching silver heels, Amy looked simply stunning.

"Turn around. Let me see the back," Jen ordered.

After complying with the request, Amy cupped her hands under her breasts. "You were right," she declared, her eyes on Belle. "No extra padding required."

Belle nearly laughed out loud as she recalled their conversation the day she'd suggested the LBD in her closet would make the perfect dress for Amy to wear to ring in the new year. Her cousin had argued that she'd need help to fill out the top. But Belle had been certain the scoop-necked dress would fit Amy to a *T*, and she'd been right. "That dress looks perfect on you."

"I'm not sure how long I'll last in these shoes." Letting the four-inch heel dangle from it, Amy struck out a foot.

"You're preaching to the choir," said Jen, who regularly worked an eight-hour shift in heels.

Belle shrugged. "Men would never believe all we go through to look good. Be sure to give your feet a break by kicking your shoes off under the table during dinner."

"You don't have to tell me twice." Amy slipped onto a nearby chair to wait for Kim.

Seconds later, the door to the bedroom flung open and Kim strutted out like a model on a runway. Her gown, a multicolored Oscar de la Renta, whispered around her calves with each step. Just as Jen had predicted, a warm front had rolled in during the day, bringing the temperature outside to a nearly balmy seventy-eight and making the light green wrap Kim had borrowed along with the dress the perfect accessory.

"Do you think I should have worn my hair up?" Kim asked.

Belle eyed the glossy tresses that fell around her cousin's shoulders. "Your hair looks great. You look fantastic."

Kim smoothed her hand over one of the skirt's wide pleats. Her week had paid off. Not even the tiniest bulge showed at the snug waist. "I've never worn anything so elegant before. My wedding gown wasn't even this nice." A stricken look crossed her face. "Maybe I shouldn't wear it. What if something happens—I get a stain on it or something?"

"Relax. It's just a dress," Belle assured her cousin. One that cost several thousand dollars, to be sure, but a dress all the same. No matter what it cost, the price wasn't worth nearly as much as seeing the happy glow on Kim's face when the skirt flared out as she spun on one heel.

A knock on the door a few minutes before six sent everyone scurrying.

"It's Max," Nat announced, after peering through the curtains at the front window.

While Belle went to let him in, Amy scooted into the bedroom in order to make an entrance.

"Max! Happy New Year's Eve," Belle called. She swung the door wide. Used to seeing the handyman in jeans and a T-shirt, she nodded her approval at the dark blue suit and crisp white shirt he'd donned for the occasion.

"Happy New Year's Eve to you, too." Max's deep voice boomed through the small cottage as he exchanged greetings with everyone.

"So, Max." Jen folded her arms neatly across her chest. "Where are you taking Amy tonight?"

"It's a secret," Max said with a smile, his expression mysterious.

"But—" Jen began. She stopped speaking when Amy stepped out of the bedroom.

Max's head swung, and he gave a low, strangled whistle. "Wow! You look..." He scanned the rest of the faces in the room as if looking for help.

"Incredible?" prompted Kim.

"Amazing?" suggested Nat.

"Beautiful?" Belle asked.

"Yeah, all that. And more." He hurried to his date's side. "You're even more gorgeous than usual. Do you still want to go out with me?"

Belle felt her own heart hitch when Amy tilted her head and smiled sweetly at Max.

"I can't think of anyone I'd rather spend New Year's Eve with," she whispered. Letting her eyes roam up and down the handyman's tall figure, she added, "You sure cleaned up nice."

"I aim to please." He glanced at the cap sleeves of the dress Amy wore. "Our car and driver are waiting in the parking area. I'm sorry we couldn't get any closer. Do you need a sweater?"

In response, Amy slipped her arm in his. "I don't think I'll need one as long as I have you to keep me warm."

Belle positively loved the way Max's smile deepened while color crept up his neck to stain his cheeks. The big man tucked Amy's hand in his larger one.

"Just so you know, I take my duties very seriously," he assured her.

Amid a flurry of goodbyes and at least one, "Have a good time," Max led a beaming Amy out into the night. Twenty minutes later, a similar departure scene played out when Craig arrived to collect Kim. Craig didn't hesitate to answer Jen's questions, announcing that he'd made dinner reservations at the Gaylord Palms in Orlando, followed by dancing and drinks at one of the area's premier hot spots. They'd finish up the evening closer to home, he insisted, without divulging where they'd be at the stroke of midnight.

"Hey." Craig stared, unable to take his eyes off Kim. "A guy's got to have some secrets, doesn't he?" he asked before he whisked his date out the door.

"Two bucks says he kisses her before they reach the car," Nat piped with a grin.

"I never bet on a sure thing," Jen declared. "Did you see the way those two were looking at each other? They've got it bad."

Belle pressed one hand to her heart. Seeing her cousins and their dates leave for the evening made all the effort she'd put into the day worthwhile. Still, she couldn't deny that it also stirred a longing to have her own special someone.

Had she already found him? Thinking of her former boss's upcoming visit, she sighed dreamily.

"What's the matter, Nat?" Belle asked. She'd been watching the younger woman idly push bites of the excellent fillet around her plate for the last five minutes. So far, the girl hadn't actually consumed a single morsel.

"It's nothing," Nat protested.

"It's not nothing if you can't eat. You're going to need your strength for church tonight."

Nat looked out the window as if she wanted to be anywhere but where she was at that particular moment. She heaved a sigh. "It's just that, if I was in New York, I'd be ready to hit the town with my friends. A group of us would make the rounds of all the best parties. We'd probably start at the Electric Room, and when things grew stale there, we'd move on to the Fish Bowl. We'd finish up on at a rooftop bar overlooking Times Square, where we'd drink champagne and celebrate when the ball dropped."

Jen, who'd carried her dishes from the card table they'd used as a dining table to the sink, languidly bent and touched her toes. "Ugh. I, for one, am looking forward to a quiet evening with

Aunt Margaret." She sent a warm smile winging toward her aunt. "I've worked every New Year's Eve for as far back as I can remember, and it's always a madhouse."

"If you hated it so much, why'd you work it?"

"The tips." Dollar signs practically sparkled in Jen's eyes. "I'd rake 'em in every New Year's. I usually made enough to pay my expenses for an entire month on that one night."

"Didn't you ever, like, just go out and enjoy yourself?" Nat's incredulous expression said what she thought of that idea.

Jen shrugged. "I had rent to pay and mouths to feed. Mostly mine."

Nat shook her head in disbelief. "How about you, Aunt Belle? You must have been to some phenomenal parties."

"A few. Some better than others." Belle glanced at her mom. Margaret had devoured her steak and baked potato like she hadn't eaten all week. She lifted the woman's empty plate and carried it along with her own to the sink.

"The most outrageous was in a villa in Tuscany," she said over her shoulder. "The host was some dot-com billionaire. He turned the massive ballroom into a three-ring circus. Trapeze artists literally swung from the rafters in one.

A lion tamer worked with big cats in another. In an iron cage, of course."

"Of course." Jen said with a touch of sarcasm. "'Cause who wants to start off the new year by getting mauled."

"Exactly." Belle nodded. "All the guests dressed up like clowns. And the food was typical midway fare—cotton candy and corn dogs, pretzels and funnel cakes. When the clock struck twelve, a band played "Entry of the Gladiators.""

"That sounds a little over-the-top," Nat commented.

"Oh, I see what you did there. *The Big Top*." Belle made air quotes. "Yeah, it was. After about five minutes, I'd had my fill, but I couldn't leave. The host had invested heavily in my record label." Belle paused. "The thing is, Jen and me, we've done the whole party circuit. When it comes right down to it, there's nothing better than spending the holidays with family and friends." She glanced at the clock. "Speaking of which, we'd better get moving. We're supposed to be at the church by eight."

Nat's eyes scrunched. "A little late for a church service, isn't it?"

Belle blinked. "It's not a service. We're helping out with the lock-in."

"The what?" Nat's eyes narrowed.

112

"The lock-in. It's for the youth group. They spend the night at the church," Jen explained.

"You girls used to go every year." Margaret's gaze fell on Jen. "Your Aunt Liz would send two huge pans of baked ziti, and it would disappear in a flash."

"Yummy." Jen licked her lips.

"All the kids in the church show up. It's fun," Belle assured her niece.

"Yeah. Fun," Jen said dryly. "If you call sleeping on hard pews and trying to keep fifty hormonal teenagers from doing something they'll regret *fun*."

"Don't let her mislead you. It's so much more than that. We'll sing and play games all night. There'll be testimonies and a band. And food— every kind of junk food imaginable." Belle's eyes filled as she recalled how much she'd looked forward to the lockdowns when she was younger. Now she had the chance to create those special memories for a new crop of teenagers, and she wasn't about to miss the opportunity. "Get your pillow and your toothbrush. I already put our sleeping bags in the trunk of Mama's car."

"Um, okay." Doubt flickered across Nat's face as she carried her plate to the sink and scraped her leftovers into the trash. She ran a hand over the slim-fitting leggings she'd worn all day. Tiny flecks of mud from their masks dotted her shirt. "I'd better change, too."

"Don't dawdle," Belle told her. "We need to leave in fifteen minutes."

While Nat headed for the cottage she and her mother shared with Jen, Belle turned to her mom. "You don't mind that I won't be here to celebrate the New Year with you?"

Margaret's gaze was pure disbelief. "I suggested you help out at the church because you're needed there." She lifted a flowered cloth bag onto the dinner table and began removing stacks of cards from a plastic container. "Just like Jen needs me to teach her a thing or two about Hand and Foot."

"Oh, ho!" Jen chortled. "You're on!" She grabbed a stack of cards, which made riffling noises as she shuffled them. Barely looking up from her hands, she canted her head toward the door. "Go ahead and go," she said. "We'll be fine."

Three hours later, Belle stood on one side of the open doorway and the youth pastor stood on the other. They both counted as teenagers and young adults filed into the rec hall.

"Thirty-nine. Forty. Forty-one. Forty-two," Belle whispered. A clump of girls streamed past.

"Forty-six. Forty-seven. Eight." When the last straggler had entered the room, she met the pastor's eyes. "I had forty-eight. Is that right?"

Samuel Colter checked the total against the numbers on his ever-present clipboard and gave a satisfied grunt. "All present and accounted for. Time to bar the doors before any of them escape." The smile he sent winging toward Belle acknowledged the futility of trying to stop anyone bent on leaving, especially a teenager. "How you doing? These kids can run you ragged if you let them."

"I'm good." Belle smiled. So far, she'd call the evening a success. Of the nearly fifty kids who'd shown tonight, she'd only had to chastise one older girl for poking fun at the younger teens while they sang songs around the campfire. Everyone else had been on their best behavior while they cooked hot dogs and roasted marshmallows.

"Glad to hear it. We're really blessed that you and Nat could help out tonight."

Samuel clapped his hands, a move that immediately drew the attention of the four dozen members of the youth group and their chaperones. "Everybody! Before we move on to the next event, it's time to lock the doors."

After making a show of pulling the wide

double doors shut, the young man, who barely looked old enough to have graduated from seminary, took a roll of crepe paper and wrapped the streamers around the handles. "There," he said when the job was finished. "No one goes in or out until morning."

"He knows that won't keep a two-year-old inside, doesn't he?" Nat whispered at Belle's elbow.

"Right." Belle's smile deepened into a grin. "But the fire department frowns on using real chains and padlocks." She held up grimy hands and sniffed. The smell of the hot dogs she'd spent the last hour threading onto sticks for a campfire weenie roast filled her nose. "I need to wash up."

"Me, too." Nat scanned the roomful of teens. Most had migrated toward the far end of the room where guitars, mics and a drum set crowded a slightly raised platform. Under the direction of the chaperones, several of the teens were pulling chairs into a rough semicircle in front of the stage. Others had plopped down on the tiled floor or milled about in groups, talking. A few had apparently shared the same thought as Belle and headed toward the bathrooms. "Can they spare both of us at the same time?"

"I don't see why not. There are half as many

chaperones as there are kids. We won't be missed for a few minutes."

But as they walked into the restroom a few seconds later, the cluster of girls gathered at the sink made Belle regret the timing of her trip. In the center of the group, the girl she'd chastised earlier held court.

"What's she even doing here?" the leggy blonde asked no one in particular. "She doesn't have kids."

"My mom says she used to go to church here," one of the others said. "She was pretty amazing at the candlelight service."

"Sorry I missed it." Sarcasm weighted her words as the ringleader fluffed her hair in the mirror. "Just 'cause she used to be a big star or something, everybody's all gaga over her. Those days are over. She's basic now. She doesn't have any right to boss people around."

Tell me what you really think.

An urge to deliver a tongue-lashing that would cut the girl to ribbons surged through Belle's chest. It took every ounce of the poise she'd developed in her thirty-plus years at the top of the heap for her to keep her cool, but she managed. Barely. Instead, she threw her shoulders back and marched straight past the girls to a stall.

Only when she was safely hidden from the teenagers' prying eyes did she let her guard down. Her shoulders slumped, and she rested her head against the back of the door while she listened to the sound of rapidly shuffling footsteps and the silence that followed. Belle remained where she was until someone rapped softly on the stall.

"You all right in there, Aunt Belle?" Nat's voice carried an unusual note of concern.

"I'm fine." She stepped out and joined Nat at the sink.

"Someone needs to teach that girl some manners." Nat's fingers fisted.

"I'll admit, there's a part of me that wants to throttle that child, but that wouldn't be very Christian of me, would it?" She stared after the girls.

Nat scuffed her feet on the tiled floor. She muttered a grudging, "I guess not."

"Besides, it's not anything I haven't heard before," Belle said with a sigh.

"You won't let her get away with that kind of talk, though, will you?" Nat asked.

"I can't control what anyone else thinks or says, Nat. That's between her and the Lord."

She studied the door that had swung closed behind the retreating group. "And she did have a point—I *don't* have any children. Maybe I *shouldn't* be here."

"No, Aunt Belle," Nat protested. "Don't even think like that. Didn't the youth pastor ask you to help out tonight?"

"He did, but…" Had she agreed to come out of a desire to be of service? Or simply to relive a good memory from her own childhood.

"There's a reason you're supposed to be here, Aunt Belle." Water poured from the tap when Nat twisted the spigot. "And I don't think it was just to hear some…" Obviously searching for the right words, she fell silent. When she'd apparently decided what she wanted to say, she made air quotes. "You aren't here just to hear some *mean girl* vent."

"Good advice," Belle murmured. Her niece had a point—much as she'd enjoyed the New Year's Eve lock-in as a kid, she'd never have shown up tonight if the pastor hadn't asked her to come. That wasn't all, though, was it? She'd felt compelled to be here. But why? Whatever the reason, she was pretty sure it didn't include an angry response to the conversation she'd overheard.

Closing her eyes, Belle sought the still, small voice that had never failed her. Seconds later, she nodded, certain she had something to say. While she pumped soap from the dispenser and thoroughly scrubbed her hands, she let the idea percolate. By the time she turned off the tap, she knew what she was supposed to do.

"The schedule says the next hour is for testimony." Belle grabbed several paper towels and dried her hands. "I need some clay."

"Some what?" Question marks filled Nat's blue eyes.

"Clay. You know, modeling clay. Or Play-Doh. Something along those lines."

"O-kay." Nat said slowly. Her gaze roamed the bathroom walls as if she expected it to materialize out of thin air.

"There's probably some in the nursery or kindergarten classroom," Belle said, amused. "Why don't you ask that nice Pastor Samuel to let you go get it? Tell him I need it, and he won't give you any grief." Though certain people might argue about it, she was fairly certain her name carried at least that much clout.

"What about you, Aunt Belle? What are you going to do?"

"I'm going to stand right here and pray for a bit. Once you find the clay, bring it to me out in the main room."

They split up, Nat going in search of the needed materials while Belle searched her heart for the right words. A short time later, she joined the rest of the group of teens and chaperones who'd gathered around the stage. Bearing a decent-size hunk of clay, Nat slipped in beside her.

Certain she'd know when the time was right for her to speak, Belle listened intently while, one by one, a handful of the teens and chaperones shared what was in their hearts. She wept along with the others when a young girl of twelve or thirteen recounted the year she and her family had lived in their car and how thankful she was to everyone at the church who'd helped them get off the streets and into an apartment of their own. Craig's nephew, Toby, rose from his place beside the daughter of the senior pastor, Tom Collier. In an emotional speech, the young man shared the story of losing his father several years earlier. He'd been angry after that, he said, and would have wandered into dark places if the Lord hadn't surrounded him with people who'd kept him on the right path. The experience had filled him with a desire to do the same thing for others. After he finished, a few others came forward, offering simple testimonies of faith and love, before the room quieted.

"Anyone else have a story to share?" Pastor Samuel asked.

Around the room, the teens shifted nervously and darted looks at one another, but no one raised their hand.

"All right, then…" the youth pastor began.

"If there's time for one more, I'd like to speak." Belle raised her hand. At the minister's nod, she carried the clay to the stage, where, ignoring the mics, she folded her legs beneath her at the edge of the raised platform.

"You all know I grew up here in Emerald Bay, and this has always been my church home. When I was the same age as many of you, I spent New Year's Eve at the church lockdowns, same as you're doing right now. And, like many of you, I didn't know what I was going to do when I grew up," she said, making eye contact with one person and then another while she kneaded and shaped the clay with her hands. "The Bible tells us that a potter makes many vessels. Some have honorable tasks—they become baskets that hold gold or silver or myrrh." Without so much as a glance down, she held up a basket she'd woven out of the pliant clay. "I hoped the Lord would help me become one of those, but I knew he also made vessels for trash and the like." She shook her head and, with a few deft moves, transformed the basket into a trash can. "I didn't want to be one of those."

Laughter rippled through the group, though from the sound of it, no one knew exactly where Belle was headed. She reformed the can into a blob. "As I grew, my purpose in life became clearer. I recognized that the Lord had given me a gift, one I was supposed to use. And I did. For a long while—for years, in fact—I sang and danced my way across stages throughout the world."

As she'd suspected it might, the next creation she held aloft sent a surprised murmur through the group. Instead of a basket or a trash can, this time the shape came out as a curly-haired doll that held a mic in one hand.

"That's phat," one of the kids called.

"How'd you do that?" another asked while an appreciative murmur sped through the room.

"You like it?" Belle asked. She studied the doll. Even she had to admit that she and the figurine shared an amazing resemblance. "I did, too. Until last year, when everything fell apart. The fame and fortune I once held, they all disappeared." With firm but determined hands, she reworked the clay into a smooth, round ball.

"Now, I could sit in my fireplace and throw ashes on myself and cry, 'Oh, woe is me!' But I'd rather let the potter remake his creation. I don't know what shape it will take this time. All I know is that if I trust Him, if I believe, the result will be even better than anything He's made before."

She held out her hands. Cupped in her palms, leaves and flowers sprouted from a vine that circled the ball of clay.

Her talk finished, she rose and dusted off the back of her jeans. Her eyes swept the assembly. She took a path that led her past the girl from the bathroom. As she moved past her, Belle dropped the clay, which was smooth and round once again, into the girl's lap. Without saying another word, Belle returned to her seat.

Four

Amy

Amy's arm shot toward the bleating alarm on her nightstand. Before she silenced the device, she heard four paws strike the hardwood floor when Socks, who'd spent the night curled up on the pillow beside hers, leapt from the bed. Mewing all the way, the big cat strode into the kitchen in search of breakfast.

"I'll be right there," Amy called when the cat's complaints grew more insistent. Through sleep-bleary eyes, she grabbed the robe she'd left at the foot of her bed before she turned in last night.

This morning, she corrected. A smile crept unbidden across her face. Everything about the previous day and night had been sheer perfection, from the spa day that left her feeling

125

utterly feminine and beautiful, to the restaurant Max had chosen and the spot where they'd welcomed the New Year. Thinking of their date, she stretched as languidly as her cat did when he was lying in a pool of sunlight. Max had delivered her to her front door a little before two. As difficult as he'd been to resist, she had not invited him in for a nightcap that would have, undoubtedly, led to her waking up with more than Socks for company in the big four-poster.

Her lips twisted into a half-smile, half-grimace. Her cousins would probably tease her over that decision, and a part of her did regret it. But another part held firm. She couldn't get around the fact that sex changed things in a relationship. Before she took that step, she wanted to know more about Max, wanted to be sure they had a future together.

Thinking of her cousins, though, she knew she'd have to get a move on if she was going to join them for breakfast. They'd no doubt demand to know every detail about her date. Not that she could blame them. She was equally curious about Kim's night on the town and would have her own questions to ask. She rolled out of bed, took care of business and headed to the kitchen, where Socks was waiting for her, mewing over his empty bowl as if he hadn't devoured an entire can of his favorite cat food the night before. Or feasted on an abundance of the fish flakes he loved while she and Max were ringing in the New Year.

"How's my boy?" she asked, squatting down to rub the big cat's head and belly.

Socks replied by butting her hand in a not-so-gentle reminder that the dry food in his bowl didn't count as real food.

"Okay. Okay. What'll it be?" Taking two cans from the pantry, she held them out to the cat. "White meat chicken?"

Socks sat on his haunches and stared up at her.

"Or trout and tuna?"

Purring loudly, the cat twined between her legs.

"The master has made his wishes known." She pulled the tab off the can and spooned the seafood into a clean cat dish. "How 'bout it, buddy? Did you have a good time last night? You didn't let the fireworks scare you, did you?" Such a thing was highly unlikely. Her cat, unlike others who retreated under the bed at the first sound of a firecracker, had most likely spent the night enjoying the bright flashes of light and the pop and sizzle of fireworks from his perch on the windowsill overlooking the street.

While Socks scarfed down his breakfast, Amy

ground the beans for coffee. By the time the last drop of life-sustaining liquid dripped into her cup from the machine in one corner of the large, airy kitchen, the rich scent of coffee had overpowered the lingering scent of Socks's favorite breakfast food. After carrying her cup to the kitchen table and the window that provided a view of her small garden, she alternated taking sips with treating her cat to a thorough petting.

"Do you have big plans for the day, Socks?" she asked. "Going to sleep for a few hours?"

A loud purring was her only answer. When she'd first brought him home, Socks had been a ball of energy. It had taken a year or two before he'd calmed down enough to play with paper bags without destroying them in five minutes flat or to simply enjoy getting his belly rubbed while Amy watched TV at night. But at the mature age of ten, Socks spent most of his time napping in a sunny spot or curled up in one of the cat beds scattered about the house.

Amy scratched under the cat's chin. She missed the rambunctious kitten he'd been. Should she adopt another kitty? She lifted Socks's front paws and stared into his face. "Would you like that? Would you like some company? Another friend to play with?" In answer, Socks only wiggled out of her grip.

Okay, so she wouldn't bring a kitten home anytime soon, she decided. Now was not the right time to try and introduce a new member of the family anyway. Not with the reunion coming up in a matter of months. Not while she was getting used to having a business partner and juggling the expansion plans for the bakery. And certainly not until she found out if Max had any allergies she should know about.

Thinking about Max reminded her that she had places to go and people to see. But first, there was a little matter of a picnic lunch to assemble since, due to the holiday, few restaurants would be open. Those that were open for business were apt to be woefully short-staffed.

She drained the rest of the coffee from her cup. Setting it down with a slight thunk, she stirred just enough to let Socks know his petting time was over. The big cat recognized his cue and leapt to the floor as if that had been his plan all along. His tail held high, he walked to his drinking fountain, where he lapped politely at the flowing water.

After rinsing her cup and washing her hands, Amy cut thick slices of bread from a loaf of sourdough, added a selection of cheeses and meats and packed the sandwiches into insulated containers. Into another container, she stacked tomato slices on top of crisp lettuce leaves. She layered cookies into a plain plastic tub before, as a final touch, she filled a bag with tiny packets of mayonnaise and mustard, salt and pepper, napkins and plasticware. She placed it all in a wicker basket and latched the top closed.

"Stay out," she told Socks, who, thanks to a cat-proof lid, would leave the food alone.

After showering and pulling on a warm sweater and stepping into a pair of jeans, she breezed through the kitchen one last time. She made sure Socks had plenty of fresh dry food and doled out a hearty serving of his beloved fish flakes. Then she was out the door, juggling the picnic basket and a box of assorted cookies and brownies her cousins and her aunt were sure to enjoy.

Twenty minutes later, Amy left the basket on the front seat of her van, hefted the container of sweet treats and struck out for Regala, the cottage Aunt Margaret and Belle were sharing. Sunlight filtered through the leaves of the tall hedge that ran along the walkway and dappled the pavered path with shadows. In the stillness of the morning, the chirps and coos of a flock of monk parakeets brought a smile to her lips. The birds had taken up residence in a stand of tall palm trees several months ago. So far, they appeared satisfied there. She crossed her fingers and hoped she'd see fledglings trying out their new wings by spring.

Reaching the largest of the six cabins on the property, she knocked lightly, twisted the unlocked knob and let herself inside. Though each of the six cottages had its own kitchen, Regala had become the gathering place while the family waited for the workers to finish working on the floors in the main house.

She stepped inside, not at all surprised to find her Aunt Margaret seated on the couch, a cup of coffee on the end table beside her. In the small but efficient kitchen, Jen scurried about. Trying not to lose her grip on the box of sweet treats, Amy brushed a kiss through her aunt's hair.

"Happy New Year, Aunt Margaret. How are you this morning? Did you sleep well?"

"I slept straight through the night." Margaret's blue eyes twinkled. "I was dreaming about all the money I won off Jen."

In the kitchen, Jen propped both hands on the center island that doubled as a counter and breakfast bar. "Be careful when you're playing with this one. She's crafty," she warned. "She won't have a single seven on the board and then—bam! She lays down seven sevens all at once and goes out on you." She nodded toward Margaret. "I lost twenty bucks at a penny a point."

"Oh, boy!" Amy whistled. Directing the comment to her cousin, she said, "You got trounced."

"Twenty-one dollars and seventeen cents," Margaret corrected. She patted the pocket of the robe she wore over flannel pajamas. "Treat me right, and I'll take you out to lunch this week," she teased.

"It's a date," Amy and Jen said in unison.

"You're right on time." Turning away from the counter, Jen opened the door to the oven and peered inside. Steam rose through the gap, instantly filling the room with a mouthwatering smell. Nodding to herself, Jen closed the oven and shut off the heat.

"Hmm." Amy sniffed the air, which carried a spicy note she didn't quite recognize. "What's that you're cooking? It smells wonderful."

"A recipe I picked up while I was in Vegas. Eggs, chorizo, cheese, green chilis. I added jalapenos for a bit more kick but just on one half.

I wasn't sure everyone would appreciate the heat." Jen placed a trivet in the center of the counter. Beside it, she added a bowl of mixed fruit she took from the fridge.

"I'll try anything once," Amy said. "But you're right—peppers would give Aunt Margaret heartburn. I'm not sure about the others."

Jen studied the box Amy held. "What do you have there?"

"Nothing special—just cookies and brownies. In case anyone needs a sugar rush later."

Jen waved a hand toward an empty spot on the counter. "You can put them there. They won't last long, though. For a little bit of a thing, Nat can put away some sweets."

Amy laughed. "That she can." She'd seen her niece scarf down cookies by the fistful.

Jen glanced over her shoulder at the closed oven. "That can sit for a bit till the others get here. You want coffee?"

"I'll get it." Amy took a mug down from the cabinet by the fridge and poured herself a cup. "I only had one at the house. I knew I'd have more with breakfast."

Light spilled into the room when the front door opened to admit a bedraggled Belle.

"Good grief!" Amy took in her cousin's rumpled clothes. Belle's hair, normally her pride and joy, stuck out in all directions. "You look like they put you through the wringer last night. Are you okay?"

"Exhausted." Belle dumped a sleeping bag into the corner and yawned. "Riding herd over a bunch of teenagers is hard work. Remind me of that when next year's lock-in rolls around."

"I'll do better than that. I'll show you." Amy whipped her cellphone out of her back pocket and snapped a picture. She held it out for Belle to see.

The redhead groaned. "Please delete it." She reached for the phone.

Amy swirled around, tucking the device under her arms to keep Belle from getting her hands on it. She took another look at the photo. Despite her disheveled appearance, her cousin's face bore a calm expression that some might call serene. "Uh-uh," she said. "I'm keeping it."

Belle's hands dropped to her sides in surrender. "At least promise me you'll never post that on social media."

Amy nodded. Though the tabloids would pay handsomely for the snapshot, she'd never betray her cousin. "I promise. It just stays between us."

"Pinkie swear?"

Amy giggled. From the time they'd barely been able to talk until they all scattered in different directions, the most solemn of oaths had required the joining of fingers. "Okay. Pinkie swear." She crooked her little finger and hooked it with Belle's. "I'll never, ever show this picture to anyone outside the family."

Belle cast a baleful eye at the image of her frazzled hair and bare face. "Let me go freshen up. I won't be long."

"You'd better not be," Jen warned. "I cooked. And the eggs will be ruined if they get cold."

"I'll be right back," Belle said before disappearing into the bedroom.

She'd no sooner closed the door than Nat wandered in. The younger woman held her hands out before her and shuffled, zombie-style, toward the kitchen. "Coffee," she said in a guttural monotone. "Must. Have. Coffee."

Before she reached the counter, Jen had filled a cup, which she pressed into Nat's outstretched hands.

"Oh, you're a godsend," Nat gushed. She doctored her cup with sugar and cream from the dispensers on the counter. After taking a long sip, she looked around as if seeing the room for the first time that morning.

"Aunt Margaret. Amy. Jen. Happy New Year!"

"Happy New Year!" Amy's voice joined Jen's and their Aunt Margaret's.

"Did you have fun last night, honey?" Margaret patted the empty cushion beside her in an invitation for the younger woman to sit. Nat joined her.

"Fun?" Nat blinked. "Yeah, surprisingly. It was nice. The kids mostly behaved themselves. I think it helped that Sam kept them busy—"

"Sam? Who's Sam?" Jen interrupted.

"Samuel Colter. He's the youth pastor." Margaret answered without skipping a beat. "This is his first post since seminary."

"He might be new to all this, but he knew what he was doing," Nat said on his behalf. "He had activities planned down to the second from the time we got there until the last parent picked up their kid this morning."

"I noticed the two of you spent quite a bit of time together," Belle said, walking out of the bedroom. Her hair was piled into a messy but stylish topknot. Her freshly washed face glowed, and a light gloss shone on her lips.

"Sheesh. Don't go making anything out of it. He asked for my help organizing some of the games and stuff." Nat leaned toward Margaret, and her voice dropped. "He's a couple of years older than me. We're both new to the area."

"Did he get your phone number?" Margaret asked.

"No." Nat's face scrunched. "Why would he? He's a minister."

"He's also single," Amy pointed out.

"And a man," Jen added.

"You guys." Nat's face reddened as she waved both hands in a shooing motion. She scooted forward to the edge of her cushion. "When's breakfast? I'm starving."

Amy chuckled to herself. Though Nat had shot down the idea that Sam might be interested in her, she was pretty sure no one in the room had missed the speculative gleam in their niece's eyes.

"I thought we were waiting for your mom." Jen's gaze shifted to the closed oven door.

Nat shook her head. "I don't know what time she got in, but she's dead to the world. She looked so peaceful I didn't have the heart to wake her."

"I guess it's just us, then." Jen donned thick, padded gloves and turned to the oven.

Amy's stomach growled as she caught another delightful whiff of the casserole Jen had prepared. She moved to help her aunt get up, but Nat was already there, guiding Aunt Margaret toward a seat at the folding table they'd erected for their card game the night before.

"Biscuits or toast, Aunt Margaret?" Jen asked

as she dished out a helping of the casserole from one end of the pan.

"I'd never turn down a biscuit." Margaret hooked her cane on the back of her chair and eased herself onto the seat. "Oh, phooey. I've forgotten my coffee. Nat, would you be a dear and get it for me?"

"Sure. Want a refill? Cream? Sugar?"

"I still have a half a cup left. I'll finish it, thanks."

In no time at all, the five women crowded around the small table where, after Aunt Margaret said grace, they tucked into their food. Amid requests to pass the butter or jelly, Amy scooped up a bite of the eggy casserole. The smoky taste of the Mexican sausage blended well with the cheese and other ingredients of the dish.

"Oh, boy. This is good," she said, giving her compliments to the chef. "Using chorizo instead of regular sausage or bacon makes a nice change of pace." She took another bite and chewed thoughtfully. "Would you mind if I offered it as an option for the breakfast sandwiches we make at the bakery?"

"Not at all," Jen said with a pleased look on her face. "You think people would like it?"

Amy shrugged. "If they don't, we can always take it off the menu."

"Do you need to run that by Deborah first?" Belle asked.

Amy blotted her mouth with her napkin. "You're right. I'll talk to her." She gave her head a slight shake. Having a partner was taking some getting used to.

"So Nat had a good time at the lock-in. How about you, Belle?"

Belle groaned. "I'm too old to sleep on the floor with nothing but a sleeping bag for padding. Give me a five-star hotel any day." She rolled her neck. "Besides, they didn't want to hear from an old fogey like me."

"Don't let her kid you," Nat objected. "She was amazing. I've never seen anything like it. She totally blew those kids out of the water."

Amy felt her brows knit. She'd thought she noticed a change in Belle earlier. "Is that why you seem so—I don't know—at peace this morning? Did something happen at church?"

Belle glanced upward before she answered. "I had a—a moment, I guess you'd call it. I try not to let it show, but these past few months haven't been easy. I spent decades building my career, and in one night, it all went splat." Whistling, she traced a spiral through the air with one finger like a diving plane. "I lost everything—my houses, cars, savings. My band dissolved. My agent dropped me."

She took a breath. "Don't get me wrong. I'm grateful for what I do have." She reached for her mother's hand and gave it a squeeze. "Mama. You guys. I'd be a basket case without all of you. But the path forward hasn't exactly been clear, and frankly, I've been worried. What happened last night erased some of my concerns and replaced them with...I don't know...peace?"

"You were awesome, Aunt Belle." Nat turned to the others. "Really, she was amazing." Beginning with the run-in with the group of mean girls in the bathroom, she quickly recounted the night in every detail. When she'd finished, her gaze returned to Belle's. "Where'd you learn to sculpt like that?"

"It wasn't me. I'd never worked with clay in my life before. I'm not sure I could do it again if I tried." Belle held out her hands to show her empty palms.

Amy canted her head. The change in Belle was subtle but profound. "So what *is* next for you?" she asked.

Belle gave the deep, throaty laugh that had captivated talk-show hosts and fans throughout the world. "No clue. But for the first time in months, I'm determined not to fret about it.

Whatever happens, I know it'll be wonderful."
She flexed her fingers. "But enough about me. I
want to hear all about your date, Amy. Where'd
you go? What'd you do?"

"Yeah." Jen leaned forward, a glint in her
eyes insisting she wouldn't take *no* for an
answer. "Don't leave us hanging. Spill, girl."

Amy summoned a pensive smile. Though she
felt her heart stir with a desire to hear more
about Belle's experience, she wouldn't push. Her
cousin would share the rest of the story in her
own good time. In the meantime, she had her
own story to tell.

"You know how I like to try different
restaurants." Her gaze took in the others.
Everyone in the family knew her penchant for
checking out the competition. "Well, it's become
a thing between Max and me. He literally *needs*
to take me someplace I've never been before.
He's tried—and failed—several times. I thought
he'd have to give up and admit defeat
eventually, but I was wrong about that. Last
night, he succeeded and it was..." Letting the
suspense build, Amy took a bite of her biscuit
and chewed slowly. "Wonderful. Absolutely
wonderful," she said when she'd swallowed.

And it had been. In fact, things couldn't have
gone better, from the moment Max had escorted

her to the car and driver he'd hired for the evening to the instant he'd left her wanting more of the kisses that lingered on her lips while she watched him walk away from the front steps of her little house.

"Details. We want details," Belle urged.

"Yeah, Aunt Amy," Nat prompted.

Amy closed her eyes, savoring the memory of a night she'd never forget. "For our first stop, Max had our driver take us to a tiny restaurant called Nut and Clove in Vero. I'd never heard of it before." She scanned the faces at the table. "Have you?"

"That's a new one on me." Aunt Margaret answered for all of them.

"From the outside, you'd think it was someone's house. And really, that impression never went away. The maître d' greeted us at the door like we were honored guests in his home—a home that just so happened to be in Italy. From the flowers in clay pots mounted on the walls to the thick, rough-spun tablecloths, every item had been chosen to carry out that theme. I was half in love with the place before we even sat down."

"Hmmm. I wonder why I haven't heard of it before," Margaret mused.

"I don't know, but I'm definitely going back there. The food was incredible. Our waiter explained that they didn't really have a menu. Each night's offerings were based on availability and the creative genius of their chef." She grinned. "He actually used those words—*creative genius*. At first, I thought that was an awfully pretentious thing to say, but that was before I tasted the lentil soup." She closed her eyes. "It was the best I've ever had. Spicy-hot and meaty, it was the perfect opposite of the tropical salad that came next. The pineapple in it was so fresh and so sweet, I swore it had been flown in from Hawaii that morning."

Nat stabbed a piece of watermelon with her fork, stared at it for a moment and set it back down on the edge of her plate.

"There was some kind of fish—grouper, I think—that melted in my mouth. And then the main entrée, perfectly prepared saltimbocca."

When her aunt's expression clouded, she explained. "It's paper-thin slices of prosciutto and sage leaves wrapped in tenderized veal and pan-fried. Served with a sweet wine sauce." In this case, the chef had prepared a Marsala reduction that paired beautifully with the salty meat.

"Whoa. That sounds like the kind of meal you'd expect from a restaurant with a couple of Michelin stars," Belle said.

Amy nodded. "I know, right? And I haven't gotten to the dessert. They offered two choices: chocolate cake covered in chocolate mousse or sponge cake soaked in limoncello and topped with a lemon curd."

Belle licked her lips. "They both sound so good. How could you pick just one?"

"When in doubt, you can't go wrong with chocolate," Nat declared.

"We asked for one of each and traded bites. I honestly don't know which one was better. Both were pretty amazing." She ran a finger over her lips, remembering the contrast of the limoncello's sharp tang mixed with the creamy sweetness of the pudding.

"Okay, okay." Jen waved a hand over her empty plate. "You're a foodie, so he buttered you up with the meal of your dreams. Sweet! But you need to get to the good stuff. Where'd you go next?"

"After that fantastic meal, I didn't know what to expect. A moonlit cruise down the river? Somewhere with candlelight, an orchestra and a dance floor?"

"Oooh, like those old black-and-white movies," Nat suggested.

"Yeah." Amy let her head bob up and down in agreement. "None of that. He had the driver take us to Captain Hiram's in Sebastian." She giggled. When the driver had pulled into the parking lot, she'd had her doubts. After the sheer perfection of Nut and Clove, a crowded beach bar seemed like a huge step down.

But it had been indeed a night of surprises. Though it was as different from the hushed atmosphere of the restaurant as it could be, the popular bar with its strands of colored lights and a live band had been its own brand of perfection. She and Max had kicked off their shoes and danced the night away while a band straight out of the '90s played all their high-school favorites. Shortly before the clock struck midnight, Max had led her to a quiet spot a little way down the beach. There, they'd watched the fireworks and celebrated the New Year with a series of kisses that had stolen her breath and melted her heart.

"Awww," Belle said. "That sounds wonderful."

Nat pressed her hands over her heart. "Positively swoony," she declared.

"When are you going to see him again?" Jen wanted to know.

"In just about an hour." Amy checked the clock built into the microwave.

"You're leaving so soon?" Her aunt looked disappointed.

"I'm sorry, Aunt Margaret, but we both have

the day off, and who knows when that will happen again," Amy explained. Max had several big jobs lined up, and her work at the bakery still kept her busier than she liked. "We wanted to look at potential sites for a second storefront for Sweet Cakes while we have the chance."

"You'll be back for dinner, won't you?" Margaret asked, insistent. "Kim is fixing black-eyed peas and cornbread."

"I wouldn't miss it," Amy promised her aunt. "I could use a little luck finding the right place." The tradition of serving black-eyed peas for luck on New Year's dated back to the Civil War, when Union soldiers, who considered the plants good for nothing more than animal feed, had left fields of the lowly beans untouched in their raids on farms and plantations throughout the South.

"We could all use some good luck," Jen agreed.

Though Belle's face remained smooth and untroubled, she chimed in with the others. "I wouldn't mind a little of that myself."

"Count me in," said Nat. "And my mom," she added when the hinges on the front door squeaked and Kim stepped into the cottage.

"Hey, look who finally decided to join us. Happy New Year," Amy called. "Late night?"

"Early morning," Kim corrected. "And

Happy New Year to you all, too." She didn't stop to exchange hugs, but made a beeline for the coffeepot. "What was that you were saying when I got here? Count me in on what? Whatever it is better not interfere with my nap," Kim warned. "I'm going to need one today."

"We were just saying how much we're looking forward to the dinner you're making tonight," Nat said.

"Mmmfff. That's the only reason I'm up this early. Those ham hocks need to cook for several hours." Kim wiped sleep from her eyes on her way to the kitchen. She took a cup from the shelf near the fridge and filled it nearly to the brim. "Ahhh," she sighed after she'd taken several long swallows. "That's the ticket. I'm too old to stay up that far past my bedtime."

"Have a little too much to drink, did you?" Jen asked.

"No."

Amy chuckled when Kim treated her sister to a pointed stare.

"I don't think you can get drunk on two glasses of wine," Kim insisted defensively.

"If you didn't party too hard, why do you look like something the cat dragged in?"

"Ouch," Kim complained and looked around the table for support.

Amy held up her hands. "Sorry. You're on your own." Free of makeup, Kim's face did look a little pasty. Though her hair retained its lustrous sheen, it had lost its curl and hung, board-straight, to her shoulders. The sweats and long-sleeved T-shirt she wore were a far cry from the beautiful gown she'd worn last night.

"Oh, leave the poor girl alone," Aunt Margaret said, coming to Kim's defense. "Let her tell us about her date."

"Thank you, Aunt Margaret." Kim smiled sweetly at her aunt.

Amy smothered a laugh when her cousin waited only long enough for their aunt to turn her head before she scrunched her face and stuck her tongue out at the rest of them.

"Okay, okay." Jen hid her own laughter behind a napkin. "Let's hear all about it. Don't leave anything out."

"Yeah, Mom," Nat prompted. "I want to hear every detail."

"Well, if you insist…" Kim began.

"We do," Amy said and waited expectantly. Though Kim hesitated a few seconds longer, she knew it was just for effect. If she knew her cousin, and she did, Kim was dying to spill her news.

At last, Kim sighed. "Craig and I had such a

good time, we didn't want the night to end. After we had dinner at the Gaylord—which was fabulous, by the way—we went to a party at the stadium up in Melbourne." The multisport complex in Viera hosted spring training for high school baseball and softball teams across the nation. "A little before midnight, everyone raced out onto the field and lay down on the grass." Ignoring Belle's quick intake of breath, she gushed, "It was incredible. We watched the fireworks light up the sky right over our heads. But don't worry." Kim aimed a finger straight at Belle. "Craig thought of everything. He brought blankets and spread them on the ground so neither of us would ruin our clothes."

"I wasn't worried in the least," said Belle, though a faint crease between her eyes said otherwise.

"What'd you do next?" Nat asked.

"Weren't we talking about a new wine bar in Melbourne recently?" Kim's question prompted a round of confused questions but no answers. "We checked it out, and it was really lovely. The second floor has an outdoor patio overlooking the river. The view is incredible. We shut the place down at three, then had a long drive home."

"No wonder you're exhausted," Aunt Margaret commiserated.

"But it sounds like the evening was a success." Jen looked around the table, her gaze stopping briefly on her aunt and Nat. She cleared her throat. "How was the, um, the rest of it?"

"Craig's a pretty good kisser," Kim admitted slowly, her eyes never leaving her daughter's.

"Oh, spill it, Mom," Nat protested. "It's nothing I haven't heard before."

"In that case, I especially liked the kissing part," Kim said, her face only reddening the slightest bit.

And that, Amy thought, was something else she and her cousin had in common. She pressed her fingers to her own lips, where the feel of Max's kisses lingered.

Max backed his truck nearly to the water's edge in one of the extra-long spaces normally reserved for boaters who'd launched their boats from the city-owned ramp and needed a place to leave their vehicles and trailers. Today, a brisk wind coming off the ocean had turned the river into a sea of whitecaps and kept all but the most foolhardy from venturing out on the water. As a result, the parking lot sat practically empty.

"Are we good here?" he asked. He aimed a thumb toward the rear of the truck, where a break in the trees along the river provided a good view.

"Perfect." Amy reached for her door handle.

While Max hefted the cooler he'd stashed on the rear bench seat, she grabbed blankets to spread across the bed of the truck. In a matter of minutes, they were both sitting on the tailgate, their feet dangling above the little stretch of scrub grass and sand that ended at the water's edge. While a lone white heron worked the shallows, they assembled their sandwiches and opened the cans of soda Amy had packed for them.

"That first place wasn't bad," she said, studying the foam that danced on the top of the waves while she tried to convince herself that she could make the less-than-ideal location work.

A hank of dark hair fell onto Max's forehead when he shook his head.

"Too far off the beaten path," he objected.

"Yeah, but the building was perfect." The small storefront, which had housed a succession of businesses—including a doughnut shop and an ice cream parlor—had many of the features she'd been hoping for.

"Location. Location. Location," Max argued.

"What good does the right building do you if it's in the wrong place? You might want to consider why all those other businesses failed."

Amy sighed. He was right, of course. Though she'd ticked off many of the boxes on her list when they walked through the sturdy little building—cement block, a functional kitchen, adequate parking—it was at least a half-mile from the nearest gas station or fast-food restaurant. Foot traffic was another item on her list, and this one hadn't had any.

She and Max had taken turns rejecting the next two properties. The first housed a clothing store run by a young woman who was none too happy that her landlord had refused to renew her lease. When she threatened to sue, Amy had turned on one heel and walked straight out of the store. "It might be perfect," she told Max when he joined her on the sidewalk, "but I don't have time for their legal drama to play out. I want the new location up and running within six months."

Next, Max had followed Amy's directions to a storefront on Main Street that offered plenty of much-needed foot traffic. To their dismay, though, the shop's roof had sustained damage in a hurricane several years earlier. The place had been sitting vacant ever since.

"A total gut job," Max had declared when he'd pressed his hand to the window and looked through the glass. "You'd have to take it down to the studs, maybe more, to get rid of the mold."

Amy had shivered despite the warmth of a sunny winter's day. Once black mold gained a toehold, Florida's heat and humidity made its removal a difficult and expensive proposition. It would take years for a bakery—even a popular one like Sweet Cakes—to recoup the cost of those repairs. And that didn't even begin to count the other modifications the place would require. Trusting Max's insight, she'd turned her back on the property without taking a second glance.

"You want another sandwich?" Max asked. He'd wolfed down his first one with gusto.

"No, thanks." She eyed her second half before deciding to save it for later. "Help yourself."

Glad she'd brought enough fixings for extra helpings, she watched as Max piled cold cuts on a thick slice of bread, topped it with lettuce and tomato and pried open a packet of Italian dressing. Amy caught a whiff of garlic and oregano when he poured enough over the vegetables to drench them before he finished his creation with a second slice of bread.

"You want the rest of the coleslaw?" she asked, holding out the container.

"Nah. But I'll take one of those dill slices." He snagged the last one in the container before he leaned back, propping his weight on one arm. "My mom makes a tangy coleslaw. I still haven't gotten used to the kind they serve down here."

"She must use vinegar in hers. Maybe some mustard?" she asked. When he nodded, she suppressed a shudder. Everyone was entitled to their own preferences, she supposed, but she followed her mother's recipe and considered anything else a sacrilege. "My customers would riot if I mixed anything but mayonnaise, celery seed and a little salt in with the cabbage."

At the river's edge, the heron probed beneath the water with his long beak again and again. Watching the bird work so hard for food, Amy was tempted to rip a piece of crust from her sandwich and toss it to him. She resisted, knowing the bread would only fill him up without providing the nutrients the bird derived from his usual diet of fish and crabs.

"What's next on your list?" Max asked while the breeze ruffled the leaves in the trees.

"We only have two more to look at today." She'd been hoping for at least a dozen, but surprisingly few Realtors had been willing to interrupt their holiday weekend long enough to send her their listings. She flipped through the pages she'd taken from the printer this morning. "The closest one is a standalone building just off US 1."

"That might work. It wouldn't have the foot traffic you were hoping for, though." Max took another bite of his sandwich and chewed thoughtfully. "How big is it?"

"Not huge—about three thousand square feet. The previous tenant was an insurance broker, so it's probably configured for office space."

"No kitchen?"

"Not really. The room they probably used as a breakroom has a fridge and a small sink."

Max let out a long, slow breath. "It'd be a big undertaking. I can handle knocking out a wall or two. Drywall's no problem. Even a kitchen, as long as it's not a commercial kitchen. But I thought you were looking for a storefront. Three thousand feet is a lot more space than you wanted, isn't it?"

Amy slipped what was left of her sandwich into a container and snapped the lid closed. "The only other place is in the Riverwalk Shopping Center. The location and the size couldn't be better."

Max must have sensed her hesitation. He prodded, "But?"

"But the asking price is nearly double what I'd hoped to spend."

"Ouch," Max commiserated. "You still want to look at it?"

"We can drive by on our way back to Emerald Bay, I guess." She waited a beat while she mulled it over. "On second thought, why bother? It could be absolutely perfect, but it's so far out of my budget that trying to negotiate would be a waste of the seller's time and mine."

"Smart decision." Max's gaze met hers over the lid of the cooler. "I like that you know what you want and how much you're willing to spend to get it. We'll be patient. The right place—at the right price—will come along."

Amy allowed herself a minute to bask in the glow of Max's approval before she packed their trash and leftovers into the cooler. "I guess we ought to head to the inn, then. Diane and Caitlyn said they'd be back from Tampa by early afternoon." As much as she was enjoying the time alone with Max, she had to admit she was anxious to hear how things had gone during her little sister's last day at Ybor City Accountants.

"We'll take US 1. It'll be quicker," Max said. Earlier, they'd followed A1A north along the ocean.

Sure enough, by the time they pulled into the

inn's parking lot, Diane's sedan was parked in its usual spot. But a shiny SUV beside it drew Amy's attention. She tipped her head inquisitively. "I wonder who that is. Not someone looking for a room, I hope." It would take another week for the finish on the floors to cure completely. Then the house would need to air out for a day or so before they could hope to open it up to the public.

"Someone got themselves a nice Christmas present," Max noted. He pointed out the paper license most new vehicles sported until the permanent tag arrived in the mail. "I guess we'll find out who it is soon enough." He threw his truck in Park, shut off the engine and came around the front of the vehicle to hold her door.

As Amy stepped down from the high seat onto the crushed coquina, Max slipped his arms around her and pulled her close. At his touch, her heart hammered so loud in her chest she was surprised the noise didn't startle the parakeets from their roosts in the nearby trees. A searing heat shot through her when Max's hands settled at her waist. She held her breath in anticipation as he, ever so slowly, lowered his lips to hers. Need stirred in her belly when their kiss deepened until she wondered how long she could resist taking their relationship to the next level.

She had no doubts they'd be good together. Even now, Max seemed attuned to her every need. He'd no doubt bring all that thoughtful consideration into bed with him. But, as she'd told her cousins the day before, sex changed things in a relationship. It created a bond, one she wasn't sure she was quite ready to share with Max.

She was, however, quite perfectly content to stand exactly where she was, with his arms around her, his lips pressed against hers. As if of their own volition, her fingers threaded through his dark hair, urging him closer. He obliged, and her breath hitched when her breasts brushed against his broad chest. She inhaled deeply, drinking in his musky scent, savoring the sweet taste of the soda that lingered on his lips from lunch.

Their kisses deepened until she approached the point where she knew if she remained in his arms even one more minute, all her doubts and reservations would simply evaporate. Knowing she was going to hate herself for what she was about to do, she edged backward, putting the tiniest bit of distance between them. Looking up, she stared into dark eyes that smoldered with desire. Max's yearning made her tremble. She fought down a desire to climb back into his truck and have him drive straight to her house where, this time, she'd most decidedly ask him inside.

But she'd been burned once. Though years had passed since that long-ago day when she'd discovered her husband cheating on her, she'd vowed never again to trust lightly. She'd promised she wouldn't give her heart away until she knew for sure the man in question was worthy of her love. She doubted Max would ever intentionally let her down, but their feelings for one another were too new, too fresh to trust completely. So instead of throwing herself into his arms with abandon and following her feelings wherever they led, she took a beat.

"You are amazingly good at this, you know," she whispered.

"Less talking, more kissing," he said, his voice a low growl.

"Don't tempt me." She pushed lightly on his shoulder.

A teasing glint lightened Max's dark eyes. "If we're both enjoying ourselves, why stop?"

He'd asked an excellent question, and at that particular moment, she couldn't think of a single reason. She rose on tiptoe, prepared to indulge herself with another of Max's amazing kisses, when the sound of voices—young voices— coming from the other side of the hedge cooled her libido quicker than an ice bath chilled boiled potatoes or hard-boiled eggs.

"Sophie, wait up." Sneakered feet skidded across the pavers. "Daddy said we were supposed to get them *together*."

"Then run faster!"

Despite the incessant hammering of her heart, Amy grinned. Her brother's daughters, Isabella and Sophie, sounded just like she and Diane had when they were younger.

She broke out of Max's embrace. "To be continued?" she asked lightly.

"You name the time and the place. I'll be there," Max said. If he was disappointed at the abrupt end of their make-out session, he hid it well.

She and Max had barely straightened their clothes and hair in a flurry of motion before the two girls bounded around the end of the hedge and into the parking area. In seconds, they were skidding to a stop in front of Amy and Max.

"Aunt Amy! Aunt Amy!" Sophie wrapped her thin arms around Amy's legs. "Daddy says you're taking too long."

"Everyone is waiting for you," Isabella said with all the self-importance of an older sister.

After untangling her niece's arms from her legs, Amy sank into a squat. Her nose filled with the sweet scent of little girls when she drew both of her nieces in for a squeezy hug. "What's the hurry?" she asked, peering first at Sophie and then at Isabella.

"Daddy says he has a 'nouncement," Sophie shouted. She squirmed out of Amy's embrace.

"An announcement," Isabella corrected like big sisters did. She gave Amy a final hug before she edged toward her sister. "He says they're going to start without you if you don't hurry."

"It's a big secret, an' I'm not s'posed to tell." Sophie looked to her big sister for confirmation and grinned when Isabella nodded.

"A secret, huh? Can't you give me a hint?" Amy asked.

"No," Isabella answered.

Sophie hopped on one foot. "Mommy an' Izzie an' me baked a cake special, but Mommy says we can't have it till after. Will you hurry, Aunt Amy?" Pleading, Sophie's big blue eyes stared into Amy's.

"How can I resist when you've asked so nicely?" Amy slipped her hand in Max's. "Well, then," she said agreeably. "We'd better go see what this is all about, hadn't we, Max?"

"I think we should. We don't want everyone else to eat all the cake before we get there." Smiling, he gently tugged Amy to her feet.

"We'll tell everyone you're coming." Sophie sped off in the direction of the cottage at the end of the row with Isabella close on her heels.

"You have any idea what this big announcement is about?" Max asked as they trailed behind the girls.

"Not really." Amy shrugged. Her big brother had a flare for the dramatic. It was part of what made him such a good attorney. She snapped the fingers of her free hand. "That's got to be it. Scott's been tied up in a big case for weeks. He must have won."

"Does he usually make such a deal out of his court cases?"

"Well, no…" Max's raised eyebrow made her stop to reconsider. She snickered. "Usually I hear the verdict from the grapevine long before he gets around to telling us."

But if Scott didn't have news about his big case, what else was there? Her heart sank when she considered another possibility.

"Do you think he could have found a buyer for the inn?" she wondered aloud.

"Has he been looking for one?" Max asked.

"I didn't think he was, but maybe…" Her older brother certainly hadn't been happy about using all of their aunt's savings to refurbish the inn. Though he'd changed his mind eventually, she knew he'd breathe easier once Aunt Margaret's financial future was secure.

"A buyer. That has to be it," she said softly.

The thought should have elated her. After all, selling the inn was what they'd all been working so hard to accomplish, wasn't it? She and her cousins were whipping the old place into shape so they could put it on the market right after the family reunion. Once the inn sold, Aunt Margaret could enjoy the rest of her life without the constant worries of running a business.

But if that's what they wanted—what she wanted—why were tears gathering in her eyes? Despite all the time she'd spent painting and hanging wallpaper, not to mention the money she'd contributed for redoing the floors, she had to admit she found the prospect of selling her family home oddly depressing.

Suddenly, she didn't want to go inside, didn't want to hear whatever her brother had to tell them. She skittered to a stop, her thoughts a jumble.

"Amy?" Max had come to a halt the instant she'd stopped moving. "Is something wrong?"

"It's—it's nothing." But there was no denying the way her voice had thickened. "I'm just being silly, but I can't help thinking how much I'll miss having my cousins and Diane around when

Aunt Margaret moves to Emerald Oaks."

Max's brows dipped. He nodded slightly. "That's not silly. You all are pretty tight."

"We weren't always. Before Aunt Margaret's broken arm, we'd drifted apart. We were each busy pursuing our own dreams, living our own lives. We weren't close, not like we are now. It's just been since the accident that we all ended up here." And what would happen once the inn sold? Her home was here in Emerald Bay. It always had been, and that wasn't going to change. But what about the rest of them? Would they scatter to the four winds, relegated once more to relying on the occasional telephone call to keep them connected?

"Maybe it won't be as bad as you think. Maybe Scott wants to tell you all something else entirely."

"I hope so." She crossed her fingers. But she couldn't help the feeling that Scott's big announcement might be the beginning of the end.

Max's grip on her hand tightened. "Whatever it is, I'm here for you."

"That's good." She swallowed before she drew in a steadying breath. "That's very good." She'd been standing on her own for so long that having Max at her back felt both strange and wonderful.

"Should we go in and face the music?" he asked. "Whatever it is?"

Amy stared at the cottage where her family had gathered to hear her brother's news. She tried to force her feet to move forward and couldn't. Just as she had reached the decision that they'd have to go on without her, the curtains at the front window parted. Sophie's head appeared in the gap. The little girl waved her hand, beckoning them to hurry.

Tightening her grip on Max's hand, Amy said, "Yeah. I guess we'd better."

The atmosphere in the crowded cottage hummed with anticipation when they stepped inside. A beaming Scott hollered out, "Happy New Year!" a sentiment that was echoed by Fern, who stood at his side near the island that divided the seating area from the small kitchen. Tugging Max along in her wake, Amy waved to the rest of her family while she made a beeline for her brother. Scott wrapped her in the usual bear hug and planted a glancing kiss on her cheek before his gaze landed on Max. Amy waited while her brother gave the handyman a long, appraising look followed by the slightest nod of approval. A tension she'd barely noticed eased from her shoulders. Knowing Max had passed some unspoken test, she traded warm hugs with Fern while the two most important men in her life shook hands.

Hoping to get some insight into why they were all gathered together, she peered past Scott's shoulder to the countertop, where a long line of champagne glasses stood at the ready. Next to them, several bottles of expensive champagne rested in a large bowl of ice. She noted a bottle of nonalcoholic sparkling cider among them and smiled, glad that Isabella and Sophie were included in the festivities. Whatever they were. She continued her search for clues. Someone had stacked dessert plates and arranged forks and napkins by a cake stand. Her efforts to learn the reason for their meeting were stymied, though, by a tall domed lid that covered the cake and hid any telltale decorations.

Spying Kim and Diane in one corner of the room, she looped arms with Max and went to join them. Less than a week had passed since she'd seen Diane, but it felt like forever, and Amy pulled her into a tight embrace. "Welcome back, sis," she said. "Happy New Year. How did things go in Tampa?" she asked, hoping the trip had been successful.

"Good. I'll fill you all in on the details later." Diane returned Amy's firm squeeze with one of her own. "This is quite the party to come back to, isn't it?" She motioned to the rest of the room. Their aunt and Belle sat on the sofa with Isabella tucked in between them. Caitlyn and Nat had taken chairs on either side of the couch and appeared to be listening to their younger cousin with rapt interest. Now that Amy and Max had arrived, Sophie clung to her mother.

"Do you know what it's all about?" Amy whispered.

"I think so," Kim grinned like the proverbial Cheshire cat.

"You do?" Amy felt her eyes widen. "Spill it," she ordered. If Scott's announcement was going to put an end to the closeness they'd shared over these past few months, she suddenly wanted to rip the bandage off and be done with it.

"Uh-uh." Laughing, Kim traded knowing glances with Diane. "You'll have to wait."

But she wouldn't have to wait long, she discovered when Scott guided Fern to the middle of the room. "Isabella, Sophie—girls—come here please."

Isabella clambered down from the couch and joined her parents. Sophie, however, dawdled on the other side of the room until Fern said, "Sophie, one...two..." Before her mother reached the dreaded *three*, the headstrong youngster hurried to her mom.

Amy had just a moment to think what a nice family her brother had when he cleared his throat.

"I'm sure you're all wondering what's going on," Scott said, sounding like a courtroom lawyer. He slipped one arm around Fern. "We have some news and didn't want to let New Year's Day pass without sharing it with those who mean the most to us." With a nod to Max, he added, "And our good friends."

"We especially wanted you to know before the word gets out." Fern made a face. "I don't have to tell any of you how fast news spreads in Emerald Bay."

Laughter rippled through the room. When everyone quieted again, Scott looked down at his wife. His eyes filled with love and awe. "My heart is so full right now. I can hardly tell you how happy it makes me to say that we're going to welcome another person into our family in a few months. Isabella and Sophie are going to have a little baby brother or sister."

"You're pregnant?" Aunt Margaret asked. "Oh, my!" She clapped her hands. "This is the best news." She stared pointedly at Fern's still-flat tummy. "When?" she demanded.

"Yep, it's official. We're pregnant, Aunt Margaret." Scott's voice boomed the way it would when he made his final argument to a jury.

Fern folded her hands over her midsection. "This little one should make his or her appearance the last week of June."

At that, everyone in the room began talking at once. As one, they surged toward Scott and Fern, embracing them in a group hug before each person added their own personal well-wishes.

When Max had shaken Scott's hand and thumped the lawyer soundly on the back, he excused himself. "Don't worry about me," he said when Amy expressed concern that he might be feeling left out. "I'll help Jen with the drinks and cake. I'll catch up to you later, after you have a chance to talk with your family."

Amy lingered, enjoying the opportunity to watch the thoughtful and considerate man stride across the room, before she rejoined Kim and Diane.

"I knew it!" Kim whispered when they'd retreated once more to their corner.

Putting all thoughts of Max aside for the moment, Amy wheeled to confront her cousin. "What do you mean, you knew it?"

Kim's cat-like grin only widened.

Diane called to her sister-in-law, "Are you going to find out the sex?"

"Yes, but it's a little too early," Fern

answered. "We won't find out for another month or six weeks."

"Oh, darn," Diane whispered. Cupping her hand over her mouth, she whispered in Amy's ear. "I'm working on a baby blanket. It sure would be nice to know what colors to use."

"You knew, too?" Amy asked, incredulous. "And you didn't tell me?"

Diane gave a half-shrug. "We didn't want to say anything until we knew for sure, but Fern wasn't feeling well at Thanksgiving."

"She didn't have any wine with dinner that day. You know how she loves her little glass of wine," Kim pointed out.

"I wish you'd told me," Amy huffed, but her happiness at the prospect of having another niece or a nephew quickly overcame her pique at being left out of the loop.

Once the champagne corks had popped and the sparkling cider had been poured for Isabella, Sophie and Fern, they all toasted the impending arrival. Minutes later, Max and Jen passed around slices of vanilla cake decorated with pink flowers and blue grass that Amy guessed were Isabella's and Sophie's handiwork.

After a bit, Kim left to have a word with Nat. Seizing their chance, Amy and Diane worked their way through the crowded room to their nieces. Amy heaped praise on both girls for their cake-decorating skills, and her heart warmed when the girls beamed with pride.

"What are you hoping for, sweetheart?" she asked Isabella. "A little baby brother? Or a little baby sister?"

The leggy preteen smiled sweetly. "Mama says we should be happy as long as the baby is healthy. But I'd kind of like another sister."

"Not me." Sophie's face scrunched. "My friend Aubry has a new baby sister. She says it isn't any fun. It cries all the time."

"So you'd rather have a brother?" Diane asked, humor dancing in her eyes. All babies cried, a fact Sophie would learn before too long.

The little girl's curls bounced when she shook her head. "I asked Mommy if we could get a kitten instead." She pouted. "She said it was too late. The baby was already on its way."

Amy clamped a napkin over her mouth and spun away so fast her champagne sloshed over the rim of her glass. But it was either that or laugh in the little girl's face. And considering how sensitive kids could be, she thought a little spill might be worth it if it saved her niece from any sort of embarrassment. Laughing silently, she bent and mopped a few droplets from the floor.

The party wrapped up when, shortly after the

champagne bottles had been emptied and the last slice of cake had been eaten, Scott caught his wife in the middle of a yawn. With a tender look of concern on his face, he thanked everyone for sharing in their good news but announced that it was time for him to take Fern and the girls home. Moments later, he shepherded his daughters and wife out the door and up the walkway to the shiny new SUV he'd purchased to accommodate his growing family.

The sun had dipped below the horizon, a full day coming to a close by the time Amy walked halfway to the parking area with Max.

"Well, that was different," Max said with a good-natured smile. "Dessert and champagne, then dinner. I'm not complaining, mind you." He rubbed his stomach. "Give my best to Kim. Those black-eyed peas were awesome. If she cooks like that all the time, her catering business is going to be a huge success."

"They were good, weren't they?" Amy asked. She made a note to ask her cousin for the recipe.

"So, a new baby in the family, huh? That's something to look forward to."

"A baby and the reunion. Things are going to be pretty busy this spring." Amy stifled a yawn. Last night's New Year's Eve celebrations and a long day of looking at properties, followed by Scott's news—it was all beginning to catch up with her. Though she owed her sister a good chat, she vowed to make it an early night.

"That wasn't the big announcement you expected, was it?"

"It wasn't. This was so much better." She paused. "I guess that means I'll have to forgive Kim and Diane. They've known about the pregnancy since Thanksgiving, but they didn't say a word. Just kept it to themselves."

"You can't really blame them, though, can you? I mean, they could have been wrong. Just 'cause a woman doesn't drink or needs a nap, that doesn't mean she's pregnant. She could have been coming down with a cold." He kicked a pebble off a paver and watched it sail into the grass. "Or—and I wouldn't wish this on anyone—she could have lost the baby early on. That happened to my oldest brother and his wife. Their first pregnancy, they were so excited that they told everyone. Then, when things didn't work out, the whole family was devastated. The next time, they waited a couple of months before they told anyone." He kicked another pebble.

"They have three now. All boys and, whew—they're a handful."

"I'm sorry about your brother and his wife. I can't imagine how hard that was on everyone." Thankful she'd never had that experience, she whispered a prayer for all those who had.

They walked in silence for a few more steps before she said, "I guess I was wrong about him finding a buyer for the inn."

Max snugged one arm around her waist. Stopping, he turned to face her. "How do you feel about that?

"Honestly?" Amy took a second to turn the matter over in her mind. "I've never been happier to be wrong in my entire life."

"Well," Max said, his voice low. "That gives us one more thing to celebrate, doesn't it?"

And with that, his lips met hers.

Five

Diane

Floor plans and lists spread out on the table before her, Diane referred to the email she'd found in her inbox that morning. A cousin she'd never met—her Uncle Edward's son, Harry—had changed his mind. He, his wife and their three children were coming to the reunion after all. He thought his sister and her family might join them and hoped there'd be enough room. Diane rubbed her throbbing temples as she eyed the layout of the suites on the second floor of the inn. Those rooms had already been spoken for. They were filled to overflowing, in fact. And not only those. She and Caitlyn, Kim and Jen would all be bunking in with Aunt Margaret and Belle for the entire Memorial Day weekend.

Her focus moved on to the cottages. With some shifting around, she decided she could put Harry and his sister beside each other in Rosario and Trinidad. She erased the names of the family members previously assigned to those cabins and moved them elsewhere before she penciled Harry and his sister into the newly vacated spaces. She sat back, holding the floor plans at arm's length. They would do, she nodded. At least until she received the next batch of last-minute reservations. Or found out that Harry and his sister fought like cats and dogs and she'd need to put them on opposite sides of the compound.

Done for the moment, she carefully returned all her notes to the manila folder filled with printouts and room requests for the week of the reunion. She was about to roll up the floor plans and secure them with a rubber band when Caitlyn walked out of one of the two small bedrooms tucked into the rear of the cottage they were sharing.

"Hold on. Let me check with Mom." Standing at Diane's elbow, Caitlyn fiddled with a barely visible earbud. "It's Dad. He wants to come over and spend the weekend. He says he can be here in time for breakfast Thursday. Is that okay?"

Diane frowned as she mentally reviewed the appointments for the upcoming week. "You have

Youth Group at the church Thursday night, don't you?" she asked. Caitlyn had been excited about a special guest who was speaking at this week's meeting.

"I do, but I'd only be gone for a couple of hours."

Diane gave an indifferent shrug. "It's fine with me as long as he knows you're busy that night." Though she didn't say so, she appreciated Tim giving them a heads-up. This wasn't his weekend with Caitlyn. For that matter, it wasn't the weekend at all. But she'd vowed to do everything possible to keep the communication lines flowing between their daughter and her dad. That included making Tim feel welcome in Emerald Bay whenever he wanted to make the drive.

Caitlyn tugged on the device in her ear. "She says it's fine." Her side of the conversation came in short bursts between longer pauses. "Okay. See you then...I love you, too, Dad. Bye." After removing her earbud, she held out her phone. "He wants to talk to you."

"Okay." Diane slid the elastic around the tube of floor plans, using the few seconds the motion gave her to settle a sudden rush of nerves.

"Hey, Tim," she said, pressing the phone to her ear.

"Yeah, I just wanted to make sure you didn't

have a problem with me coming over this week. With school starting soon, it might be my last chance to spend any time with Caitlyn before spring break."

"No, it's fine. Bring your shin guards. She'll probably drag you out onto the soccer field." Soccer tryouts at Emerald Bay High started right after classes resumed, and Caitlyn was intent on making the team. She thought for a moment. Tim and his partner, Warren, closed their dental practice between Christmas and New Year's, but they were usually booked solid this time of year. "You don't have to work?"

"Warren and I worked it out so that, starting the first of the year, I'd only be seeing patients three days a week." He didn't say anything more for several long seconds. Diane was just beginning to wonder if the connection had failed when he said, "It sounded like a great plan when we came up with it. I thought I'd have more time to spend at home with you and Caitlyn. Of course, it hasn't quite worked out that way."

Diane's mouth filled with an acrid, bitter taste along with the urge to remind Tim that he was the one who'd walked out on their marriage. She deliberately swallowed both. If they had even the slightest hope of salvaging their marriage, she and Tim needed to start over with clean slates. That meant no more finger-pointing, no matter who was at fault.

Pretending to ignore his last comment, she said, "Just remember, she does have Youth Group Thursday night."

"That's fine. I've never expected her to cancel her plans, and the girl *always* has plans."

"I know." Diane laughed. Like most teens, Caitlyn and her friends were constantly on the go. "We could have put a revolving door out front, as often as she was in and out, in and out."

"Maybe I can take you both out to breakfast Saturday," he suggested. "They don't have Mom's Place in Emerald Bay, but I'm sure they serve waffles at Pirate's Gold."

She smiled to herself, thinking of all the Sunday brunches they'd eaten after church at their favorite diner in Tampa. This week wouldn't work, though. "I'll have to pass on breakfast. Everybody's going to be busy putting things in order at the inn this weekend." Now that they were finished staining and sealing, the workers planned to buff the floors a final time before they cleared out. Movers would arrive to put every-thing back in its place first thing next week. Before that happened, she and her cousins and her sister needed to give the entire house a thorough, top-to-bottom cleaning.

"I should bring my grubbies, then," Tim said, referring to the clothes he wore when he tackled odd jobs around the house.

"I wasn't asking you to help," she protested.

"You're going to turn down an extra set of willing hands and a strong back?"

"When you put it that way, how can I refuse?" Though she kept her voice light, Diane's stomach tightened. She'd have to warn everyone to be on their best behavior. Tim had fallen from grace with certain members of her family.

"Okay, then. I should be there around ten Thursday. I'll take Caitlyn to breakfast and we'll do whatever she wants after that."

"Sounds good." Feeling oddly let down, she was prepared to end the call when Tim spoke again.

"Um, one more thing."

"Yes?" Her finger hovered over the red button.

"Since Caitlyn already has her own plans for Thursday night, will you—would you like to have dinner with me? Anywhere you want— your pick. I just, um…"

Thinking hard, Diane pulled the phone away from her ear. She shouldn't be surprised, she told herself. When they'd spoken at Christmas, Tim had pleaded for her forgiveness. Why, the man had done everything short of getting down on his knees and begging for a second chance. And she'd promised to give it to him. But she'd known they couldn't fix things between them with the snap of her fingers. Or his. For one thing, rebuilding the trust he'd broken would require time. It'd be a process.

It had been her idea that they start slow, go out on a few dates and make sure they still had a future together before they jumped right back into a relationship only to find out later that it was doomed to failure. In the heat of the moment, she thought she might have actually suggested he *woo* her. Had she? She felt her cheeks warm.

"Diane?" The faint sound of Tim's voice caught her attention.

"Sorry." She pressed the phone to her ear. "Um. Sure." She couldn't very well turn him down. Not when seeing one another had been her idea. "There's a seafood place in Sebastian I've heard good things about," she suggested. "Fog Horn's."

"Great. Pick you up at six?"

The mix of relief and pleasure she heard in Tim's voice filled her with hope. "That'll work. Caitlyn and I are staying in Carmen. Just follow the path from the parking area. It's the first cottage you'll come to."

"Right. Caitlyn told me." In the pause that followed, the whispered, "I love you," was so faint Diane barely caught it.

"I love you, too," she said after the phone went dark. She stared at the screen, hoping their feelings were enough to help them rebuild the broken pieces of their marriage.

After returning Caitlyn's phone to her, she poked through the few dresses she'd kept out of storage when they moved into their temporary quarters in the cottage. Wire hangers scraped along the metal bar as she considered and discarded one possibility after another. She'd learned over the past few months that a broken heart made an excellent diet aid. The clothes that once stretched tightly across her bulging stomach now hung from her narrow shoulders like shapeless gunnysacks.

Which begged the question: What on earth should she wear on a first date...with her husband?

"How far is this place? We're almost to the bridge." Tim frowned. The road would merge into busy US 1 just before it reached the point where the St. Sebastian flowed into the Indian River.

In the passenger seat, Diane studied the passing scenery. Set back from the road on the left, a mix of one- and two-story homes with million-dollar views and price tags to match sat on manicured lawns dotted with scrub oaks, palm trees and clusters of sea oats. On her right, the setting sun glinted off the mirrorlike surface of water that stretched farther than she could see. Spoil islands provided added interest to the scene. They had been created decades ago when tons of sand had been dredged from the river to deepen the channel. Now birds flocked to build nests among the Australian pines that grew wild on the sandy spits of land.

"It shouldn't be much farther. Maybe another hundred yards on the right."

"You're sure this is where you want to eat?" Tim asked when he'd pulled into a mostly empty parking lot. A few steps beyond the hood of his car, fishing and pleasure boats bobbed in slips on either side of twin walkways. The ramps led to a square, windowless building that stood over the water on thick, concrete pilings. He pointed. "It kind of looks like a bait house."

She had to agree. No one would mistakenly call the nondescript entrance "charming." In fact, if it hadn't been for her sister's recommendation,

Diane would have driven on by without giving the place a second thought.

"Amy said not to be fooled by the exterior. She insisted Fog Horn's is very nice and the food is totally worth the drive." Diane kept a firm grip on her smile, all the while hoping her sister hadn't sent them on a wild-goose chase.

"Let's hope she's right." Tim dipped one shoulder in an acquiescent shrug. He shut off the engine. But instead of reaching for his door handle, he turned toward her. "Have I told you how nice you look tonight?"

Diane felt a warm smile tug at her lips. "You might have mentioned it once or twice." The blue dress she'd unearthed from the back of her closet no longer strained in all the wrong places but highlighted all the right ones.

"You look...different. Healthier. Have you been working on your tan?"

"Not exactly." She laughed lightly. "Belle and I've been walking several miles a day," she explained. Not even the strongest sunblock could keep out all the sun's rays, and her skin had darkened a shade or two. "I tried running with Kim—she and Amy are both runners—but I decided I'd rather walk an extra two miles than run one." She smoothed the skirt that lay loosely across her thighs. "And I've lost weight."

"I noticed. It looks good on you." Encouragement filled Tim's smile. "It's not just that, though. You're..." He tapped out a beat on the steering wheel. "You're less tense. More at ease."

"Leaving Ybor City helped," she said, willing to let him chalk her calm demeanor up to the fact that she wasn't hopping out of bed to rush off to work before dawn or returning home later and later each night. The truth was, her newfound peace probably had a lot more to do with the business venture she wanted to pursue. She eyed the chiseled jaw of the man she'd not so long ago intended to sleep beside for the rest of her life. What would he think of her new plan? Would it drive a bigger wedge between them? Or would he lend her his support?

Her lips parted, her plans for the future clamoring to get out. She managed to clamp her mouth closed despite an urge to tell Tim everything. This was not the kind of news she could just spring on him out of the blue. She'd need to lead up to it and promised herself she'd do just that over dinner.

"What do you think?" She nodded to the restaurant. "Should we go inside?"

"I suppose we should give it a chance now that we're here."

After nearly a quarter of a century together,

Diane recognized the doubt Tim hid behind his smile and gave him points for trying. "If we don't like it, we'll go back to Captain Hiram's," she promised. They'd passed the popular restaurant five minutes earlier.

Tim said, "Stay put. I'll come around and get you."

Tim was the perfect gentleman on the short walk to the restaurant, holding the door for her, guiding her with a light touch at her waist, all the things he used to do when they were first dating. A wave of nostalgia swept through her, and she thought back to those early years. The mornings when she'd fix his coffee before she'd pour herself a cup. When they'd shop for groceries together and he'd sneak a packet of expensive cheese or a jar of imported olives into the cart for them to share later. And after Nick was born, the nights Tim would walk the floor with their colicky baby so she could get a few hours' sleep.

She winced. It hadn't happened all at once, but as the years had passed, the sweet things they'd done for one another had gradually ended. Once they had Nick, their carefree shopping trips had morphed into a flurry of buckling and unbuckling five-point restraints, grabbing diaper bags and unloading the stroller. They'd managed to shop as a family until they had Caitlyn. But neither of them had wanted to face the daunting prospect of hauling a toddler and an infant through the aisles, and it hadn't made sense to hire a babysitter just so they could go to the grocery store. Instead, they'd split the task—one staying home with the kids, the other venturing out—and the days of buying special treats for one another had tapered off. Later, in her rush to get to work at Ybor City in the mornings, she'd barely had enough time to fix her own coffee, let alone Tim's.

Now, as Tim guided her up the wooden walkway to the restaurant, she realized how much she'd missed going out of her way to please him, or having him do the same for her. When and if they managed to fix everything else that had broken in their marriage, she vowed to pay more attention to all the little ways they could demonstrate their love for one another.

When they reached the entrance, she laughed when Tim said, "Here goes nothing," and opened the door.

They stepped into a waiting area that was much smaller than she'd anticipated, considering the size of the building. Diane didn't know whether to be disappointed or encouraged that no one sat on any of the wooden benches or in the sturdy chairs that lined paneled walls adorned with fishing nets and metal fish in bright colors. She was still trying to make up her mind when a young woman greeted them from the hostess stand. Behind her, a dark hallway led to what was presumably the dining room.

"Good evening," the girl said with just the right blend of warmth and class. "Welcome to Fog Horn's. Could I have the name for your reservation?"

Tim's head swiveled to Diane's. She gulped. Amy hadn't suggested making a reservation, and she hadn't even considered it.

"I'm afraid we don't have one," Tim answered for them. "Do you have a table for two available?"

"Just a moment." The girl consulted a seating chart before looking up at them brightly. "I'm afraid the deck is full, but if you don't mind eating inside, I can seat you by a window."

Tim turned to her. "I think that would work, don't you?"

"Yes, that'd be great," Diane said, wondering if Amy had been playing a joke on them after all. Despite a hostess who seemed like she'd be a perfect fit for an upscale restaurant in downtown Vero Beach, so far, Fog Horn's held all the ambience of a fish camp.

Their hostess gathered menus from beneath the stand and said, "This way, please."

She led them down a short hall that opened onto a surprisingly beautiful dining area. Throughout the space, couples and several larger groups sat at cloth-covered tables conversing in quiet tones. Glasses and silverware clinked softly beneath flickering glass globes. The faint smell of linseed oil and lemon mingled with delicious aromas as wait staff moved about the room with efficiency and grace.

Straight ahead, on the other side of an immense glass wall, colorful lights dripped from the rafters of a tin roof over a deck twice as long and just as wide as the main building. Dozens of casually dressed people crowded the bar of a tiki hut in one corner of the platform. Diane tried, but she couldn't spot an empty table among the dozens of two- and four-tops outside. At least twenty boats had been tied up to mooring cleats that lined the end of the wooden planks. Those, she supposed, explained the nearly empty parking lot. Apparently, most Fog Horn's patrons had arrived on watercraft.

"This is lovely," Diane murmured when the hostess showed them to a table beside a picture window that provided a stunning view of the river and the closest spoil island.

"It's not exactly what I'd imagined." Tim hurried to hold her chair for her.

"This must be your first visit to Fog Horn's," their hostess commented as she handed out menus. "A lot of people have the same reaction. Dale will be right with you."

Within seconds, a slender young man appeared at their table. Looking quite professional in standard-issue black pants and a matching vest, which he wore over a white shirt, Dale welcomed them to the restaurant and recited the day's specials from memory. When they'd placed their drink orders—a glass of white wine for Diane and a local IPA for Tim—he hurried off. Diane had barely glanced at her menu before their server returned bearing their drinks, as well as a silver basket filled to overflowing with a selection of bread and rolls.

"I heard from Nick," Tim said while they studied their menus. "He said his first day of classes went well this semester. Ron and Buck got snowed in in New Hampshire, so he and Matt have the quad to themselves for a few days." Nick and three of his college buddies lived in a four-bedroom apartment on campus.

"I bet he's enjoying the quiet." Their son often complained that Ron and Buck commandeered the TV in the common area, where they played video games into the wee hours. Puzzled, she said, "It's strange how the different colleges and universities start classes at different times, isn't it?" Virginia Tech, which Nick attended, had begun the new semester on the second. A friend's son attended the University of Maryland, where classes didn't resume until the end of the month, while most of the Florida schools started back up somewhere in between.

"I never really thought about it much." Tim buttered a poppy seed roll and ate half in one bite. "It won't be long before he'll graduate and be off on his own."

Having decided what she wanted for dinner, Diane set her menu aside. "Caitlyn will be right behind him. It's hard to believe she only has a couple of years of high school left."

"We'll be empty nesters before we know it." Tim sipped his beer. "Can you picture us rattling around the house alone?"

Actually, she couldn't, but not just because the five-bedroom Colonial would be too big for just the two of them. It was also on the wrong side of the state. But that was a topic she'd hoped to bring up over dessert, not at the beginning of what she hoped would be a very pleasant evening. Afraid they were drifting into dangerous territory, she was glad for the reprieve when Dale reappeared to take their orders.

"The mahi is fresh-caught?" Diane asked the young server.

"Yes, ma'am. Chef meets the boats at the docks each morning."

"I'll have the house salad, then, with grilled mahi and your house dressing on the side," she said.

"I'll take the salmon," Tim said, sticking to his usual choice.

But Dale shook his head. "If I could suggest, sir?" He waited until Tim focused a quizzical gaze on him. "The salmon is flown in daily. Chef works wonders with it. But our snapper? I can guarantee it was swimming in the ocean this morning. Blackened or grilled with a lemon beurre sauce—it's absolute perfection."

"With a recommendation like that, I can hardly pass it up, can I?" Tim's questioning gaze shifted to Diane, who nodded. "The snapper. Grilled, then." He handed his menu to the waiter.

"I hope I didn't make a mistake." Tim watched their server disappear into the kitchen. "You can never go wrong with salmon."

"Yes, but you have it all the time," Diane reminded him. Tim had made the heart-healthy fish a staple of their diet and fixed it at least twice a week. "It couldn't hurt to break out of your rut.

Try something new for a change." Thinking he'd forgotten their previous conversation during the lengthy discussion of the menu, she breathed easier.

"You're right." He drank deeply from his glass. Returning it to the corner of his placemat, he inclined his head toward her. "So, what do you think?"

"About the restaurant?" Diane asked, taking a glance about the room. "It's nice, don't you think?" She controlled an urge to fidget by buttering one of the tiny rolls from their bread basket. Instead of eating the carb-laden treat, though, she set it aside.

Tim swung a quick look around. "It is that. Much better than I expected. But I was talking about our house. Do you see us there in our golden years?"

Diane steadied. As long as Tim insisted on discussing the only home Nick and Caitlyn had ever known, she might as well be honest. Beneath the table, she pleated her napkin. "It's not something I spent a lot of time thinking about, but I've pictured Nick in a tux, anxiously pacing back and forth in front of the fireplace on his wedding day. Or Caitlyn walking down the stairs in her wedding gown."

Tim cleared his throat, his eyes growing nearly as misty as hers. "So you have thought about it."

She reached across the table and took his hand. "Yes. Sometimes." However, those images were nothing more than dreams. Now that her heart was no longer in Tampa, she couldn't relate to them anymore. Her voice softened. "But that was before, Tim. Before what…happened between us."

"Before I ruined things, you mean." Tim's voice roughened. "If I could go back in time and change things…"

"I know." There was no anger in Tim's tone, only a deep sadness that made her want to extend an olive branch. "And it's a shame for that big house to sit empty now that Caitlyn and I are in Emerald Bay. You should move in."

"But aren't you coming back?"

Was it her imagination, or had Tim's face paled?

"Not for a while," she hedged, fully aware of the tightrope she was walking. Though she didn't want to promise she'd return to Tampa when she knew in her heart she never would, this was not the time or the place to discuss her plans for the future. "As long as Caitlyn and I are here, it doesn't make sense for you to stay in the apartment."

"You mean it?" Thinking out loud, Tim drummed his fingers on the table. "Moving back home would save money. And I could lease the apartment, which was my goal from the beginning."

The muscle under Diane's left eye twitched. "You mean you didn't plan to move in there all along?"

"No, Diane. Never. I was hoping—I'm *still* hoping—we can work things out between us. But no. The apartment was never for me. I saw it as an added revenue stream. To help pay for Caitlyn's college expenses. And later, I thought we'd use the income it generated for travel." Tim had purchased the building the same year he'd opened his dental practice. He'd paid off the mortgage nearly a decade ago, so any money they made from it now was pure profit.

"Huh." His explanation would have knocked her back on her heels if she'd been standing.

"You act like this is a surprise. We talked about this."

They probably had. Or at least, *he* had. At the time, though, she'd let her job push everything else to the back of her mind. That was one of several of her own mistakes she was trying to correct. "I'm sorry I didn't pay better attention.

You'll move into the house and rent out the apartment, then?"

"I probably should." His decision made, he said, "I will. Next week."

Something behind her caught his attention, and in seconds, Dale strode into her view. This time, their waiter carried a large serving tray. Balancing it on one hand, he began doling out dishes.

Seconds later, Diane gave an approving nod to the artfully arranged plate of greens, scallions, olives and thick wedges of tomatoes that lay beneath an entrée-size serving of thick white fish. She waved her hand through the air, drawing the tempting smells toward her. "This smells wonderful," she announced.

Across from her, Tim showed his appreciation by licking his lips, a habit he'd had for as long as she'd known him. The plate Dale had set in front of him was huge, nearly as large as one of the serving platters Diane only took from the china closet on special occasions. Tim's accommodated not one but two pieces of fish fillets that stretched from one end of the oval plate to the other. A lemony, buttery sauce perfumed the air and glistened atop the fillets. Mushrooms flecked a mound of creamy risotto on one side of the perfectly grilled snapper, while on the other, a small armful of grilled asparagus spears added a bright touch of color.

"Will there be anything else?" Dale asked.

"Not for me, thanks." Diane noted the crisp edges of her fish as well as the herbs and spices that covered it. She doubted she'd even need to dip a single lettuce leaf in the miniature gravy boat that held a fragrant dressing.

"I'll have another beer," Tim said.

Dale whisked Tim's empty glass from the table and hurried off to fetch a fresh one.

"I don't know whether I should ask for a box now or just dig in." Tim held his fork poised above his dish.

Diane broke off a small piece of her mahi, which tasted even better than it looked. "Hmmm," she said dreamily. "Want a bite?"

"Are you kidding? I have more than I can eat right here." Tim waved his fork over his plate.

For a while, they concentrated on the excellent food, their comments limited to the creaminess of the lemon sauce or the tasty marinade on the artichoke hearts Diane unearthed from her salad. When Tim put down his fork some time later, she eyed what was left of his meal. Despite his protests, he'd eaten all but a few bites.

"Still regret not getting the salmon?" she teased lightly.

"Um, no." Tim placed one hand over his belly. "This was excellent. We'll have to thank Amy for recommending the place after all."

"I will. First thing tomorrow," Diane promised.

Tim's eyebrows rose. "Spending some time at the bakery, are you?"

Diane shook her head. "Hardly. I'm far too busy these days. Nat is filling in behind the counter while one of Amy's regulars is on vacation. I promised I'd drop her off, since I'm going into town anyway."

"Oh?"

"I have a meeting at the church." She'd been trying to think of a way to ease into her plans for the future. Talking about the work she was doing for the church was as good a lead-in as any, she supposed. "To look over the church's book-keeping system," she added.

Tim's gaze sharpened. "Handling the books for the inn is one thing. That's family. But you've added the church?"

"They were in a jam, and I offered to help." She blotted her lips on her napkin and set it to one side.

Dale reacted to her folded napkin as if she'd dropped the green flag at the Daytona 500. In a flash, the young waiter was clearing their dishes and offering to bring them a dessert menu.

"No dessert for me, thanks," Diane murmured. "Although I wouldn't turn down some coffee."

"I'll take some, too." Tim stared out the window. Night had fallen, and moonlight danced on the mirrored surface of the river.

"What's going on with you these days?" he asked at last after Dale had placed steaming cups of coffee in front of them and moved to another table. "No one expects you to sit and twiddle your thumbs all day—least of all me—but I can't help but sense there's something going on that I should know about."

"You're right." Diane stirred her coffee slowly. "I've been meaning to talk to you about it. I could say I didn't want to take our focus off the kids while they were here for Christmas, but…" She lowered her spoon to the saucer. "The truth is, I've been putting it off."

She took a breath. Letting him know about her plan to put down permanent roots in Emerald Bay was more difficult than she'd expected, but she forced herself to go on. "I've been helping with the books at church, and, um, it reminded me how much I enjoy working one-on-one with business owners. I missed that at Ybor City." The higher she'd risen in the company, the more her focus had shifted away from actual accounting and more to monitoring the work of the junior accountants assigned to her projects. For the last decade, she'd operated almost entirely as a supervisor.

"Yeah?" Tim absently rubbed his chin. "I remember how disappointed you were when you started at YCA. You thought you'd have more interaction with the clients."

She remembered that, too. "Ybor City says it caters to the needs of everyone. *No business too big, no business too small*, that's their motto. That was one of the reasons I went to work for them in the first place; I thought I'd be working directly with the customers. That never happened."

Her first day at Ybor City, she'd been shown to a cubicle, handed a stack of paperwork and told to itemize the expenditures for a company identified only by an account number. So much for her hopes of working directly with local business owners.

"At first, I told myself it was because I was the new person on the team. I thought maybe only the higher-ups actually held face-to-face meetings with customers."

"But you never did, did you?"

"No. I might have occupied a corner office, but I never interfaced directly with the clients. It was all corporate-this and corporate-that."

It had taken longer than it should have for

her to realize that Ybor City's goals had shifted over the years. What had started out as a mom-and-pop accounting firm had grown to the point where it no longer pursued the small-business market. The company had set its sights on serving the needs of corporations, the bigger the better.

"The companies we did business with were run by boards, not individuals. I dealt with our client's head accountant, who was someone who was drawing a salary, just like I was. I hated it."

"If you were so unhappy there, why didn't you say so? Why didn't you leave? You know I would have supported your decision."

Diane blinked. "I don't think I even realized how miserable I'd been until I walked away. I have you to thank for that." She reached across the table and took Tim's hand. His leaving had devastated her and had nearly wrecked their daughter's future, but she wouldn't lie. Some good had come of it. "If you hadn't left, if Caitlyn hadn't gotten into trouble at school, I'd probably still be at Ybor City. Still working sixty-hour weeks. Still doing a job I hated but unable to admit the truth, even to myself."

"I'm glad I could be of help, I suppose." Tim stroked her thumb with his own. "But I'm sorry for how I went about it, for how badly I hurt you and Caitlyn."

"I know. But here we are." She slipped her fingers from his grasp and clenched her hands together beneath the table. Next came the hard part. She didn't think she could share it with him while he held on to her. "And we need to figure out where we go from here."

"I'm not going anywhere," Tim insisted.

"See, that's the thing." She took a breath. "Neither am I."

Deep furrows dug themselves into Tim's brow. "I don't get it."

"I want to open my own accounting firm. Here, in Emerald Bay."

Tim's eyes darkened. "The town's not that big, is it?" he protested. "You wouldn't have enough clients to make ends meet."

"That would have been true a year ago, but things have changed," Diane explained. "The woman who's been handling the books for most of the businesses in town retired rather abruptly just after Thanksgiving. Her loss has left a gaping hole that's waiting for someone like me to step in and fill it. I've taken over the accounts for the church on a temporary basis. Apparently, someone told the owner of the hardware store. He called me last week. He's desperate for help with his end-of-the-year reports. Word has started to get around."

"I would think so. You're very good at what you do." Tim leaned forward. "But you aren't serious about staying here, are you? I'm all for letting Caitlyn finish out the school year here, but I thought the plan was for her to transfer back home. Coach said she could try out for the soccer team next year."

"You want our daughter to go back to Plant High?" Though Diane's voice never rose in volume, her pitch climbed. "Our daughter, who has no friends at that school anymore? Where the staff will be watching her every move, just waiting for an opportunity to suspend her again? I don't care what the coach says now. There's no way Caitlyn will make that team again."

Tim shook his head while his mouth opened and closed like a fish out of water.

Diane's voice firmed. "Right now, the plan is for Caitlyn to start at Emerald Bay High next week and, if all goes well, to stay there until she graduates. In the meantime, I want to open my own firm. Nothing huge. More of a boutique accounting firm that caters to local business owners. I know there's a need for it, and I think I can build a life here. For me and for Caitlyn."

"But not with me. Is that what you're saying?" Tim drained his coffee cup and signaled for the check.

Grateful that, for once, Dale wasn't Johnny-on-the-spot, Diane met her husband's imploring gaze. "That's not what I'm saying," she insisted. "I want us—you and me—to be together again. Sure, we have issues we need to work out. It's going to take both of us, working together to resolve them. But in the end, I want us to be a family again. It's just that, well, my future is here, in Emerald Bay."

"And the lives we built, our house, my practice—that's all in Tampa."

She fell silent when Dale slipped a leather presentation folder containing their bill onto the table. Without saying a word, Tim handled the bill. He stood the instant he'd tucked the receipt into his wallet.

"We can work this out, Tim," Diane insisted softly when they'd stepped outside.

The man who'd been so attentive on their way into the restaurant surged ahead of her, the soles of his shoes slapping against the wooden planks.

"Tim?" Diane called, following him down the walkway that felt more and more like a gangplank.

"I can't talk about any of this right now," he said when he sat behind the wheel. "You've thrown a lot at me tonight. I didn't see any of it coming. I need time to think about it."

Fighting back tears, Diane nodded. She stared out the window without saying a word on the long drive back to the inn.

Well, that could have gone better. Without so much as offering to walk her to her door, Tim had dropped her off at the foot of the pathway that led to the cottages.

Her breath shuddered in her chest. She really couldn't blame the man for reacting the way he had. He was right—she had thrown a lot at him all at once. Maybe she should have broken the news to him in smaller, gentler steps, but done was done. She crossed her fingers and prayed that Tim just needed a little space and some time to think things through before they spoke again.

Six

Jen

"I don't know how you do that," Kim said when Jen stepped from the pavered walkway balancing a tray of wineglasses on one palm.

"I didn't spend the past thirty years working as a cocktail waitress without learning a thing or two." Jen smiled as she handed drinks to each of the women gathered around the firepit. "You should see me behind the bar. I could give those guys from *Roadhouse* lessons."

"I'll remember that the next time I need a bartender." Kim lifted her wine in a salute to her sister.

Jen kept the final glass for herself and sank onto an empty Adirondak chair. For a couple of seconds, she watched the smoke rise in a straight column from the firepit. Temperatures had warmed into the mid-seventies in the wake of a passing front that had dumped an inch of rain on the area earlier in the day. Seizing the opportunity to sit outside during the break in the winter chill, she and her cousins had tossed a couple of logs into the pit and pulled their chairs close to the fire.

"This is why people move to Florida." Jen stretched. "Nights like this."

"It's a little chilly for me." Amy tugged the edges of a long cardigan closer.

Jen shot her cousin a sympathetic glance. "What'd I miss while I was getting the drinks?"

Beside her, Kim said, "Diane was filling us in on her dinner with Tim. It did not go well."

"Oh?" Jen straightened. "I thought you two were working things out. What happened?"

"Long story short," said her youngest cousin from her spot on the other side of the fire, "I told him I want to stay here in Emerald Bay, open my own business and let Caitlyn finish school here."

"You didn't dump it all on him like that, did you?" Jen asked.

"Not in so many words." Diane must have thought better of her protest because her shoulders rounded as she shifted uneasily in her chair. "But yeah. Basically."

"Geez. No wonder he got upset. Men are so prickly." Jen sipped thoughtfully from her wine. "They're on fire one minute and crying in the corner 'cause their feelings got hurt the next. You gotta treat them with kid gloves. Heaven help you if you have bad news—you've got to break it to 'em gently. Like that story about the guy with the dogs." Not that she could be bothered with all that nonsense, she told herself. She'd rather spend her life alone than walk on eggshells all the time.

"What guy with the dogs?" Belle asked over the rim of her glass.

"Yeah, what are you talking about, Jen?" Kim shot her a questioning glance.

"You haven't heard that story? Must be a bar thing," she mused. She'd heard some version of the same tired jokes in every cocktail lounge she'd ever worked.

When all eyes remained focused on her, she leaned forward. Holding her glass in both hands, she propped her elbows on her thighs.

"Okay," she began. "So this guy—let's call him Bernie—Bernie drops his prized Pomeranians, Peanut and Q-Tip, off at the kennel before he leaves on a business trip."

Belle hooted a laugh. "What kind of names are Peanut and Q-Tip?"

"Just pay attention," Jen shot back, though she softened the order with a smile. "Now Peanut is twelve years old and hasn't been his usual frisky self, so Bernie tells the kennel owner—let's call him Fargo—Bernie tells Fargo he's going to call in and check on the dogs every day. Are you with me so far?"

After receiving encouraging nods from the other women, she continued. "The first day, Bernie calls to ask how Peanut's doing, and Fargo says, 'I'm sorry, but Peanut died last night.'"

"Oh, no!" Amy moaned.

Jen ignored her and went on. "'What?' demands Bernie. 'That's not the way you're supposed to tell me. You're supposed to say, someone left the gate open and Peanut is missing. Sure, I'd be upset, but you'd assure me you're doing everything you can to find him. The next day I call in, you tell me you have people looking all over town for him but you haven't found him yet. Then the next day I call and you tell me you found Peanut, but he was hit by a car. That he's at the vet and it doesn't look good. Then, finally, the next day I call and you tell me that you're sorry, that the vet did all he could, but Peanut passed away.' Bernie takes a breath before he says, 'That's how you give people bad news.'"

"So true!" declared Kim. "I can't count the number of times I had to dole out information in tiny bits and pieces so I didn't upset a certain someone." She coughed a soft, "Frank," into her hand.

Diane nodded. "Teenagers can be just as touchy."

Jen sipped her wine, biding her time while the others chatted. Idly, she wished some people in her own life had shown a little more care and concern when they'd delivered bad news. The personnel manager at Card-A-Val, for instance. She'd propositioned her without so much as batting an eye. Before that, her boss at The Beau Rivage had cut her loose without a word of warning. As for the men she'd married, they were in a class by themselves.

On the other side of the firepit, Amy cleared her throat. "Isn't there, um, a little more to the story?"

Jen chuckled. Apparently, Amy had heard the joke before. She aimed a smile at the brunette and turned to the others. "Ready for the rest?"

When the group quieted, she picked up where she'd left off. "Well, Fargo was ashamed of the way he'd blurted out the news about Bernie's dog, and he vowed to do better in the future. So the next day, when Bernie called to ask about Q-Tip, Fargo said, 'I'm sorry, but someone left the gate open and Q-Tip is missing.'"

"Oh, my!" Bell pressed one hand to her chest while laughter rippled around the firepit.

At last, wiping tears from her eyes, Diane aimed a pointed gaze straight at Jen. "I should have asked you to tell Tim about my move to Emerald Bay. You would have handled it better."

Jen shook her head. "Not me. He's *your* husband. If I'd wanted to deal with one of those, I would have kept one of my own." She'd married and divorced twice and wasn't about to make that mistake again.

"Have you heard from Tim since then?" Belle asked.

Jen reeled in thoughts that wanted to wander in another direction. Her heart went out to Diane when her cousin sank lower in her chair.

"No." Diane twirled her glass until the wine spun in a circle. "He was supposed to pick up Caitlyn this morning. They had a whole day planned—shopping for school supplies, soccer practice, dinner down in Vero somewhere." Her shoulders slumped. "But he canceled. He said he had a touch of food poisoning." She made a face. "He blamed the fish he ate last night."

"At Fog Horn's?" Shock and disbelief made Amy's voice rise. "I hardly think so. I know the chef. He's militant about keeping a spotless kitchen." She laughed to herself. "I could never work for him. I don't live up to his standards."

"Don't get your feathers in a ruff," Jen cautioned. "I'm sure Tim's fine. People use 'food poisoning' whenever they need an excuse to get out of doing something they don't want to do." She stared across the fire at her cousin. "He couldn't come up with anything more original?"

"Guess not." Diane shrugged. "I ended up taking Caitlyn shopping myself. We got every-thing she needed for school, including a new laptop, because the one she used for homeschool didn't fit in her backpack."

"Ouch!" Kim murmured.

"It wasn't all bad. As long as we were out, we indulged in a little retail therapy. I found a pair of pants and a blouse I liked. A size smaller than I've been wearing." Diane danced in her chair. "Caitlyn bought three pairs of jeans and six tops for school." She gave a sheepish grin. "That girl can shop when she puts her mind to it."

"She does come by it naturally." Belle propped her feet in their red-soled mules on the edge of the firepit.

Jen felt her scalp prickle with envy. If she'd caught anyone else subtly bragging about their $900 house slippers, she'd have oh-so-casually mentioned all the starving people in the world, people who'd practically sell their souls for any kind of shoes at all. But Belle had more generosity in her little finger than most people had in their entire bodies, so instead of snapping at her, Jen pushed down the misdirected prick of spite.

"Tim had offered to help us get the inn ready this weekend." Diane worried her lower lip. The movers would arrive first thing Monday to put all the furniture in their proper places. Before then, all twenty-plus rooms in the two-story house needed a thorough cleaning. "Now I'm not sure if we can count on him."

"We should be all right without him," Belle assured her. "Irene and Eunice will be here." With the inn shuttered for the past two weeks, the housekeepers had gladly signed up to work the weekend and earn some money.

"Nat will help out, of course," said Kim. "Craig will be here all day Saturday and after church on Sunday. He might bring his nephew, but I can't be certain." Craig had stepped up his game as the doting uncle after his sister's husband died. He and Toby normally spent Saturdays working on one project or another. Lately, though, the teenager's other commitments had eaten into their time together.

"Deborah is manning the bakery all weekend." Amy stretched. "I love that she's eager to prove she can handle things on her own. That means I can be here bright and early."

"What about Max?" Jen wondered aloud. The handyman and the baker had been practically inseparable since New Year's.

"He has a job in the morning," Amy answered, looking glum. She brightened as she added, "But he said he'd try to break free later."

"Caitlyn's on tap to sit with Aunt Margaret. The two of them have some big crochet project they're working on." Diane's face softened. "I love that they're getting this time to spend together."

"Mama does, too," Belle said with feeling.

"That makes nine of us to handle the cleaning." Jen splayed the fingers she'd used to keep track of everyone who'd actually be working in the main house. "We should be able to finish all the suites and the main rooms in two days, shouldn't we?"

"We'll be lucky if we aren't tripping over one another." Belle's face crinkled into a smile.

"I have a list of all the things we need to do," Kim volunteered. "It'd probably be best if we break into teams of two and go room by room."

"Great," Belle said with a teasing look. "I want Craig on my team."

"Fat chance," Kim answered dryly. "He's all mine."

"Okay. Okay." Belle held her hands up in a sign of surrender. "I see the way things are. Then I'll take Nat. She and I need to spend some time together anyway."

"Okay, that just leaves you, Jen," Kim said after Diane and Amy paired up together. Her expression turned coy. "Guess we'll have to work on finding someone special for you next."

Something in Kim's tone told Jen her big sister had more in mind than just a helper for the weekend. She shook her head, wanting to cut the idea off before it took root. "Don't bother. I'm perfectly fine on my own."

Looking as if it had never occurred to her that her sister might not want to be in a relationship, Kim asked, "Aren't you looking for your Mr. Right?"

"Not hardly," Jen scoffed lightly. "I need to figure out what's next for my life before I complicate things with a man."

"Well, sure. For now. But don't you want someone? Sometime?"

One thing about her big sister, she was persistent when she had a bee in her bonnet. Well, two could play that game, Jen decided.

"Been there. Done that. Got the T-shirt,"

she quipped. "You do, too," she pointed out. "Remember Frank?"

"Not all men are like Frank," Kim said pointedly.

"True," Jen allowed. *Some are worse.* She should know; she was the poster girl for picking out losers. Her second husband had had a vile temper. Something she hadn't known about him until the night Larry got drunk and thought he could use her as his own personal punching bag. She'd warded off one blow, marched herself straight into their bedroom, locked the door, packed a bag, climbed out the window and kept on going. It was one decision she'd never regretted.

She did, however, regret that she hadn't confided in Kim about that period in her life. Other than the lawyer she'd used when she filed for a divorce, she hadn't breathed a word to anyone about the mistake she'd made by marrying Larry.

She eyed her sister. Kim and Craig had a good thing going, and Craig seemed like a good guy. But she'd thought Larry was a good guy, too. It wouldn't hurt to keep her guard up, to be ready to swoop to her sister's defense if things in that relationship took a bad turn. As for herself, though, she needed to make sure none of her cousins or her sister wasted their time trying to set her up on a date.

Deliberately, she softened her voice until she smoothed out all the rough edges. "I'm just not looking for anybody right now. In fact, I'd be perfectly content to end up as an old maid. Just me and a dozen cats to keep me company. They can call me The Cat Lady." She tapped the arm-rest of her Adirondak chair with freshly polished nails. "Maybe I should get one. Kind of an old-maid starter kit. What do you think?"

"Hey, I resent that!" Amy protested. "I have a cat."

"Yes, but you also have Max." Deciding it was high time to shift the attention away from her own nonexistent love life, Jen asked, "How are things going with him, by the way?"

"Good. Better than good." Amy pressed her hand over her heart. "He's wonderful," she said in a swoony tone.

"And we're all happy for you," Belle said, weighing in. "You deserve someone special in your life."

Just as Jen had hoped, the focus of the conversation quickly shifted to Amy and from there to the upcoming reunion and on to a variety of other subjects. Wineglasses emptied as the fire died down to mere embers. When an owl hooted from a nearby tree, Amy shivered. She gathered her cardigan closer.

"That's it for me," she announced. She circled the firepit, exchanging hugs and reminding everyone she'd see them bright and early in the morning.

Jen waited until she heard the door of Amy's van slam shut and saw her taillights wink out of sight before she stood. "I'm going to follow her example and get some shut-eye."

As she grabbed the serving tray she'd propped beside her chair, the others stood, too. They trooped the short distance to the cottages where they peeled off by ones and twos, eager to get a few hours' rest before they tackled the monumental task of prepping the inn to reopen.

Jen tucked her cell phone into a back pocket and leaned against the wall of the laundry room. She sucked in her stomach until the small of her back met the solid surface. Stretching, she pushed her shoulders as far back as they would go. She took a breath and held it for a ten-count before she slowly exhaled. She'd never complain about waitressing again, she promised. Not after spending the better part of a day removing sawdust from every nook and cranny in the living room, den and, most recently, the laundry room.

Peeling herself away from the wall, she walked down the short hall to the kitchen, where she spotted Craig running a wide furry mop over the walls in long, slow strokes. Dust motes danced in the air with every pass.

"Where's Kim?" she asked when she didn't see her sister.

"She ran to the store. We're out of paper towels." Craig continued to work while he spoke.

"Already?" She shook her head, unable to believe they'd burned through an entire case of wipes in a matter of hours.

"Irene asked her to pick up more spray cleaner while she was at it. Apparently, they're having to go over the sinks and toilets several times. Once or twice to remove the dust. Another pass to make the fixtures shine." He finished one wall and propped an elbow on the handle. "You need something?"

"Another mop." She pointed to the long-handled one Craig held. "Nat says she needs one upstairs."

"Tell you what..." Craig slid the business end of his mop from the ceiling to the baseboard.

"Take this one. I'll get the wet/dry vac out of the truck and finish up in here with it."

Jen weighed the pros and cons. If Craig's vacuum was anything like the industrial strength model her Uncle Eric had kept in the shed, it'd make an incredible amount of noise, and if it even had a brush, it wouldn't be nearly as wide as the one Craig currently wielded. But the trade would allow Nat to get back to work. She took the mop from his outstretched hand before he had a chance to change his mind. "I'll call Kim and ask her to pick up an extra one of these."

"No problem." Not one to waste time, he was already moving down the hall to the service entrance at the back of the laundry room.

Watching him go, Jen added another checkmark on the plus side of the tab she was running for Craig. She wasn't quite ready to stick a Prince Charming label on the man—not yet, at least—but she couldn't deny that his helpful attitude was a point in his favor.

On her way to find Nat a few minutes later, she slowed when Amy stuck her head out of the entrance to the Opal suite. Wiping her hands on a rag, she asked, "You got a minute to look at something while you're up here?"

"Sure. Hang on a sec." Jen brandished the mop. "Let me drop this off."

Her footsteps left dusty tracks on the recently finished floors as she moved down the hall to the Beryl suite where she found Nat.

"Thanks, Aunt Jen," the younger woman said, taking the long handle. "We're almost finished in here. I just need to wipe down the walls while Aunt Belle goes over the windows again. You want to see how good it looks?"

Jen peered into the smallest of the suites on the second floor. Though the front room looked perfect, Belle was still hard at work. The woman who'd wowed presidents and potentates stood atop a folding stool holding a bottle of glass cleaner in one hand, a wad of paper towels in the other. She might have a closetful of designer duds, but today, she'd stuffed her hair beneath a ballcap and donned a dingy gray sweatshirt over skintight leggings the color of a ripe tomato. Apparently unconcerned about height, she stretched to reach the upper corner of one of the gleaming windowpanes. She sprayed and swiped again.

"What the tabloids wouldn't pay for a shot of this." Jen peered through a make-believe lens.

"I'm feeling pretty feisty today. I'll take you down if you so much as reach for your phone." The scathing look Belle threw over one shoulder said she meant business.

Jen tossed her hands into the air with a laugh. "Relax. I wouldn't dare." Considering her cousin's current mood, the device would stay in her back pocket.

Leaving Belle to fret over the already spotless windows, Jen retreated to the hallway where she paused, listening to the loud whine of a motor. She nodded. Craig had wasted no time in putting the heavy-duty vacuum to work. Turning, she headed for the Opal suite, where she found Amy crawling around the perimeter of the sitting room on her hands and knees.

"You needed something?" she asked.

"I need a break." Amy dropped the rag she'd been running over the baseboards and stood. "And I want to ask your opinion on something." Wiping her hands on her jeans, she headed for a set of closed double doors at the end of the main hall. "I think we might have a problem."

Motioning Jen to stand beside her, Amy grasped the doorknobs. The instant she twisted the handles, a strong chemical smell floated out of the roomy walk-in closet.

Jen coughed and put one hand over her mouth. "But we aired out the house," she protested.

And they had. Once the final coat of sealant had dried, they'd thrown open every window sash and propped all the doors to every suite ajar. That had been two days ago. When Jen and the others had walked in this morning, they'd all breathed easily, reassured that not even a hint of the strong-smelling polyurethane lingered in the air.

"Evidently, no one thought to open these doors when they aired out the rest of the house."

"We can do that now, I suppose." But as Jen eyed shelves of linens and towels, she had the oddest sense that Amy was about to drop the other shoe.

"Yeah, well...Smell this." Amy grabbed a fitted sheet from the middle of a pile.

Jen buried her face in the soft fabric and sniffed. She instantly regretted the move when a harsh odor filled her nostrils.

"Oh, my," she said, coughing. "We can't put these on the beds the way they are." She gazed at the shelves that held at least three sets of sheets and pillowcases for each of the beds in the twelve suites on the second floor. Hundreds of washcloths and towels in assorted sizes filled shelves on the back wall, as well. She nearly groaned. "They'll all have to be washed."

Amy issued an audible sigh. "That's what I was afraid you'd say."

Jen did a quick calculation. Even with both of the washers and dryers going, it would take days to wash, dry and fold every item. She gulped. "What about the linens downstairs?" she asked. With only two suites and the family quarters on the ground floor, that closet was a smaller version of this one.

"It's fine," Amy said. "It was standing wide open when we came in this morning. We don't have to worry about the pillows and comforters, either. We put those in the storage units."

"Thank goodness for small favors, right?" Jen counted out a dozen neatly folded sheets. She hefted the stack. "I'll start with enough to put clean linens in every suite. Then we can work our way through the rest."

Amy grabbed a pile of matching fitted sheets. "Let me carry a load downstairs for you."

"This sure brings back memories." Jen raised her voice, speaking above the roar of the vacuum, which grew louder as they headed down the stairs.

"All those hot summer days we spent washing sheets and towels, making beds, sweeping floors." Amy whistled. "Of all the things we had to do, I hated working in the laundry the most."

"I didn't like any of it," Jen admitted. The endless list of chores had been matched only by her Aunt Liz's and Aunt Margaret's even longer list of rules. She'd chafed under each and every one of them.

Glad she no longer had to shout to be heard when the whine of the vacuum changed pitch and abruptly died, she added, "I couldn't wait to get away from this place." She'd struck out on her own the day after graduation.

"After you left, Mama had us pray for you to come home every night. For years, she expected to find you sitting on the front porch when she opened the door one morning."

Guilt twisted its knife in Jen's gut. Her footsteps slowed. "I never knew that. I hate that I caused her so much grief. There were so many times her wish almost came true. Turns out, life on your own at eighteen is a whole lot tougher than you'd think."

"Why didn't you? Come back, I mean?"

Amy's plaintive question floated over Jen's shoulder. She would have shrugged, but she was afraid she might lose her grip on the sheets. Instead, she said, "Some misguided sense of loyalty to my mom, I guess."

"Say, what?" Amy's footsteps skidded to a stop.

Jen turned to face her cousin. Defending the decisions she'd made as a teenager wasn't easy, but Amy deserved the truth, didn't she?

Jen took a steadying breath. "I thought I owed it to her memory to live the kind of life she'd always lived." Her mother had prided herself on her footloose existence. Whenever opportunity knocked on her door—be it a new man or a chance to jaunt off to Mexico—her mom had answered it willingly and followed wherever it led. Sometimes, she'd taken her daughters along for the ride. Most often, though, she'd dropped them off on their aunts' doorstep and kept right on going. Right up until the day she was diagnosed with terminal cancer.

"When I left here, I imagined I'd pick up where she left off. It didn't take me long to realize that my mom's lifestyle didn't suit me. I actually like having a roof over my head and knowing where my next meal is coming from. I even like following the rules." The discipline her aunts had instilled in her as a teen had served her well as an adult. "And I missed—oh, how I missed—Kim and you and the others." Jen shook her head. "But I couldn't come back here. I couldn't bring myself to admit that your mom and Aunt Margaret were right."

Amy rocked back and forth for a few seconds. When she began to speak at last, her words came slowly. "I get it. After the accident, I spent a lot of sleepless nights wrestling with the idea of running the kitchen here at the inn like my mom had. In the end, I chose to chase my own dreams. But you know what?"

Jen stared at her cousin. She couldn't imagine how horrible the months following their mother's death had been for Amy, Diane and Scott. No one was ever really prepared to lose a parent, but she'd at least had some warning before mother had passed. Amy hadn't. Aunt Liz had died in a tragic car accident, the same one that had left Aunt Margaret reliant on a cane. She swallowed. "What?"

"When I drop off the bread order each morning, I still feel a little bit guilty for not stepping into my mom's shoes." A hint of a smile graced her lips. "Or slipping on her apron."

Jen felt laughter bubble in her chest. Aunt Liz hadn't been a small woman. Her apron would have wrapped around Amy twice with room to spare. She shook her head. "Those pretty teal ones at the bakery fit you much better." She stared into Amy's brown eyes. "And if your mom were here now, she'd tell you how proud she is of you for what you've done with your life."

"I'd like to think that," Amy murmured.

"No doubt about it," Jen insisted as she shifted the stack of sheets in her arms. "We'd better get moving. These aren't going to wash themselves."

"And I have more baseboards to wipe down before Belle gives me grief about them."

"She's been on everyone's case today, hasn't she? It's not like her."

Amy rolled her eyes. "You remember how picky Aunt Margaret used to be. The beds had to be made exactly right. There couldn't be a single scuff mark on the walls or on the stairs."

Jen sighed. "She hounded us until we got the floors so clean people could practically eat off them. But what's that got to do with Belle?"

"I was thinking that, maybe, with Aunt Margaret unable to get upstairs to check on things, Belle is tapping into her inner mom."

Jen considered the theory. Amy might be right. Or maybe Belle was just in a bad mood. Whatever the reason, if her cousin didn't knock off her cleaner-than-thou attitude soon, someone was going to snap at her. Afraid that someone might be her, Jen vowed to keep her tongue in check as she resumed her trek through the house to the laundry room.

She made it as far as the entrance to the kitchen, where Craig's wet/dry vac stood silently blocking their path. Jen stopped to give the big vacuum a stern look. Big, bulky appliances that took up a lot of space weren't high on her priority list, so she'd never owned one. She nudged this one with her foot. Despite its wheels, the machine didn't budge. She put a little more muscle into her next push. This time it slowly rolled aside.

"Careful you don't trip," she warned Amy. She took an extra-wide step over the thick power cord before she proceeded to the laundry room.

"Ooof." She lowered the flat sheets onto the folding table a minute later. "I'll get started on these right away," she said after Amy had dropped the fitted sheets beside hers.

Before she could move, though, Amy grabbed her with both arms and enveloped her in a tight hug. "We've both had our own ghosts to deal with," her cousin whispered. "Now that I know about yours and you know about mine, I really hope you'll stay in Emerald Bay. We've all missed you so much."

"I can't promise, but I'm sure thinking about it." Jen returned the embrace with one of her own. She had to admit, she'd missed the closeness that came from being with family. And she wanted to feel it again. Even more so now that she was aware of how much she and her cousins had in common.

"Amy, where are you? You need to finish

Opal. We're falling behind schedule." Sounding more strident than usual, Belle's voice echoed through the house.

"Duty calls." Amy's gaze shifted pointedly toward the second floor. Letting her hands fall to her sides, she promised, "We'll pick this up later."

"I'm right behind you," she said as they headed back the way they'd come. "I want to move that machine out of the way before somebody trips over it."

Somebody like me, she added, thinking of the many treks she'd make up and down the stairs over the next couple of days.

With no desire to do a faceplant right in the middle of the kitchen, Jen looped the thick power cord around the narrow top of the vacuum. Bending over the squat, round machine, she gave it a shove. Trailing the hose, it rolled about six inches before it lost momentum and stopped. With a sigh, she uncoupled the hose, placed her hands on either side of the bulky canister and, putting some muscle into it, pushed harder. That got things in motion. Slowly, she maneuvered the heavy machine across the floor toward an out-of-the-way spot.

"There!" She congratulated herself when she'd finally wedged the vacuum into a corner.

Retracing her steps, she retrieved the hose and the brush attachment. It took some fiddling with the unfamiliar device, but she tinkered with it until she fit the hose onto the machine.

Her mission accomplished, she returned to the laundry room. In practically no time, she'd filled the soap and softener dispensers on both washers and started the first of a hundred or so loads. She waited until she heard water pouring into the deep tubs before she picked up a bottle of spray cleaner and a rag. While the washers chugged, she tackled the dirty shelf in the storage closet.

Sunlight and a burst of cool air spilled into the room when Kim opened the door to the laundry room just as Jen was finishing up. Bulging grocery bags hanging from her arms, she swung the exterior door wide and held it in place, allowing Craig to move past her.

"Well, we've got enough paper towels to last a lifetime," the man announced, barely able to see over the top of the large box he carried. "Where do you want these?"

"That case can go upstairs," Kim directed. "We'll put the other one in the pantry."

Glad she'd moved the bulky vacuum out of his path, Jen hurried to her sister's side. "Want some help?"

Liquid sloshed against the sides of plastic bottles when Kim held out one arm. "You can take these. There's more in the car."

Jen slipped the handles of several heavy bags from her sister's wrists. Opening the bags, she stared down at six or seven bottles of various cleaning products. "Did you buy out the store?"

"Pretty much," Kim acknowledged.

After dumping their supplies on the kitchen counter, they made quick work of retrieving the rest of the supplies and another case of paper towels from the car. By the time they finished putting everything away, the timer Jen had set on her phone dinged to let her know the first wash cycle had finished. While Kim went upstairs to check on everyone's progress, she crossed her fingers, hoping against hope that one trip through the washer and dryer would be enough to replace the chemical smell that clung to the linens with the scent of lavender and herbs their guests expected.

She was moving the wet sheets into the dryers when the loud whine of the heavy duty vacuum roared to life. She tossed a softener sheet on top of each load and slammed the doors. Spinning the dial on the first machine, she was rewarded by the steady thunk-thunk-thunk of sheets being tossed around in the rotating drum.

She reached for the dial on the second machine but froze when someone shouted.

"Oh, crap!"

Jen's head jerked. Had Craig fallen? Was he hurt? Shouting to make herself heard over the noise of machines, she called, "Are you all right?"

Five long seconds passed. When no one answered, Jen bolted for the kitchen. Her feet flying, she made it halfway there when the vacuum's motor issued a high-pitched whine before it died out altogether. The caution she'd learned from dealing with hundreds of bar fights made her skid to a stop before she ran headlong into a situation and made things worse. Standing on the threshold, she struggled to remain calm as she surveyed the scene before her.

Just beyond the kitchen island, Craig stood in a veritable cloud of dust. His eyes wide, he stared in disbelief as a few of the larger clumps settled to the floor around him. Instantly reminded of the snow globe she'd found in her Christmas stocking one year, Jen blinked.

"What the..." A mix of wonder and frustration filled Craig's voice. His gaze dropped to the vacuum, and he shook his head.

"What happened?" Jen asked.

Craig idly shoved the machine with one foot. "Somehow the hose got connected to the wrong side of my Shop Vac. When I turned it on, it blew all this out." He gestured to the cloud that ever so slowly drifted to the floor. Craig brushed his fingers through his hair. The move set off another snowstorm. "Was this somebody's idea of a joke?"

Jen's stomach dropped. She was responsible for this mess; she had to be. Not wanting to suck in a lungful of dust, she took a shallow breath. "I, uh, I might…"

Her voice ground to a halt as she scanned the walls and windowsills Craig had spent hours cleaning. A fresh coat of dirt and grime covered every surface. Her mistake would take hours to correct.

She groaned and forced herself to face the man who had every right to be angry. She'd dodged enough flying fists in her day—mostly in the bars she'd worked in—to know she should keep a wary eye on Craig's body language.

"It wasn't a joke," she said, prepared to run at the first sign of trouble. "The—what'd you call it—a Shop Vac? It was in the way. When I moved it, I must have put the hose on wrong. I'm sorry." When Craig's hands remained loosely at his sides instead of clenching into fists, she shuffled forward a step. "I'll help clean up the mess," she offered.

As dust and dirt continued to rain down on him, Craig shot her a quizzical look. "Don't you know anything about wet/dry vacs?" He toed the offending machine.

"Not hardly. Uncle Eric had one, but he never let us girls touch it. My first husband was a mechanic. He probably had one at the shop, but he didn't believe in bringing his work home." Which explained why the check-engine light on her own car glowed red until the vehicle up and died on her. "My second husband didn't believe in work. Period." More to the point, he didn't think he should be the one doing it.

"Well, that's not right. They're very useful to have around. Broken glass. Spilled milk. They'll pick up just about anything. They're pretty simple, too." Pointing out the various parts, Craig launched into a five-minute lesson on the workings of the bulky device. "Attach the hose to the front, and the vacuum sucks up just about anything. Wet or dry. Attach the hose to the back and, well..." He laughed and pointed over his shoulder. "That's the result."

"You'd think they'd label the holes *in* and *out*," Jen said when he'd finished. "Otherwise, how's somebody like me supposed to know?" Though, to be honest, until five minutes ago, she'd thought *in* was the only option.

"A fair point," Craig conceded. He disconnected the hose from the back of the machine and reattached it to the front. "Now I better get to work before Kim accuses me of loafing on the job."

Jen let her gaze run over the walls. "You're sure you don't want my help?"

"Nah, I got this." He flipped the switch on the top of the machine, and it whined into action. Seconds later, he was running the brush over walls he'd already vacuumed once that day.

Watching the tall man work, Jen gave him high points for keeping his cool when others would have struck out in anger. The man was definitely a keeper, she decided, and wondered if he had any idea that he'd passed all her tests with flying colors.

Seven

Margaret

"What is that amazing smell?" Diane toed her dusty shoes off in a corner of the cottage she and her daughter were sharing.

From her spot at the kitchen table where she nursed a cup of coffee, Margaret tipped her head toward Caitlyn. The girl deserved all the credit for the enticing aromas that wafted through the small cottage.

Excitement mingled with pride in Caitlyn's voice when she said, "I made spaghetti, Mom. And garlic bread. There's salad, too. Aunt Margaret showed me how."

"I did nothing of the sort," Margaret protested. Her great-niece had been perfectly capable of following the directions on the side of the pasta box. The girl hadn't needed Margaret's help with slicing the two loaves of bread from the bakery or in dousing them with butter and garlic, either. As for the sauce, well, she might have shown Caitlyn how a pinch of oregano and a bit of sugar improved the flavor of even the best of the store-bought brands, but that was the extent of her efforts. Caitlyn had done all the rest. She'd even filled a motley collection of containers with wildflowers she'd gathered from the nearby gardens.

Diane padded over to the stove in her stockinged feet. "If it tastes half as good as it smells, I can't wait for dinner." She reached for a spoon. After dipping up a small portion, she blew on it before she took a taste. "Mmm." She smacked her lips. "This is every bit as good as the sauce I make." She gave the tiny kitchen a second look. "But honey…"

"Did I make a mess?" Caitlyn cast a worried look at the nearly spotless kitchen.

Margaret held her breath. Caitlyn had worked all afternoon to prepare a special dinner for everyone. She hoped Diane wouldn't say anything to dampen the girl's enthusiasm.

"You've made enough for an army!" Diane gushed. "What are we going to do with all this food?" She waved a hand toward the two trays of garlic bread that were ready to run under the broiler.

Margaret exhaled easily. She should have known better than to doubt her niece. Diane had always been such a devoted mom.

"We thought, after how hard everyone's worked the last couple of days, you all might enjoy a nice meal," Margaret explained. Yesterday, while she and Caitlyn crocheted until their fingers went numb, Diane and the rest of the family had worked from sunup until well after dark with only a couple of sandwiches to sustain them. They'd all rolled out of bed at the crack of dawn this morning, downed coffee and day-old pastries from Sweet Cakes and hurried off to work as though their lives depended on it. Margaret and Caitlyn had agreed that it was high time her mom and the others put their feet up and ate something substantial.

"Aunt Margaret and I cleaned off the picnic tables out back so everyone can eat outside." Caitlyn nodded toward the sliding glass door at the back of the cottage. Beyond it, two long picnic tables stood in the shade of a towering oak tree.

"You did?" Diane's brow furrowed as her attention swung to Margaret. "You were careful, weren't you, Aunt Margaret?"

Margaret did her best not to squirm beneath Diane's piercing gaze. "I only supervised. Caitlyn wouldn't let me lift a finger. She did all the running back and forth."

Diane wrapped her arms around her daughter and squeezed her tightly. "Thank you for fixing dinner and taking care of Aunt Margaret these last two days. You've been a big help."

"She took care of herself." With a coy smile, Caitlyn added, "I mostly supervised."

Margaret nearly choked on the laugh that rose from deep inside her chest. She blotted her lips with a napkin while Diane chuckled at her daughter's little joke.

Sobering, Diane asked, "Do I have time for a quick shower before we eat?"

"Sure. I need to let everyone else know to come here anyway." The family had been gathering for most meals in Margaret's slightly larger cabin. Caitlyn punched a few buttons on her phone. "A half an hour good?"

"Perfect." Diane waited until her daughter was staring down at her phone before she blew her aunt a kiss.

Though she had enjoyed every minute of the last two days she'd spent with her grand-niece, Margaret's heart swelled when Diane followed up the air kiss by mouthing a quick *Thank you* before she dashed out of sight.

"Okay." Caitlyn laid her phone on the table and slid into a chair next to Margaret. "I sent out a group text. Everyone except Aunt Belle will be here in thirty minutes. She said to start without her."

Margaret clucked her tongue. Her daughter did love her creature comforts. Even as they spoke, Belle was probably treating herself to a long, hot shower. If she knew her daughter as well as she thought she did, Belle would rather spend the next hour applying lotions and oils than join them for dinner.

"We'll fix a plate and set it aside for her," Margaret decided.

A scant thirty minutes later, Kim, Jen, Nat and Amy crowded into the small cottage. By then, Caitlyn had arranged steaming bowls of pasta and sauce on the counter, buffet-style. Tall glasses of iced tea and a pan piled high with freshly toasted garlic bread stood at the end next to the salad. Soon everyone had helped themselves and carried their food outside, where candles flickered from the Mason jars the teen scattered about the picnic tables.

"Ooof, it feels good to sit down." Amy placed a full plate on the table and slid onto the bench.

"I don't think I've worked this hard in ages."

"Oh, my aching back. I'll be putting some liniment on it tonight for sure." Her hands pressed just above her hips, Kim arched backward. She rolled her shoulders, trying to shake out the kinks before she took her place at the long table.

"Not that stinky stuff you used on us when we were kids," Nat objected. "It'll smell up the whole cottage."

"Are you using the kind with camphor?" Jen's nose wrinkled. "You should use mine. It's made with sunflower oil. Practically no odor and it works like a charm." She twirled spaghetti around her fork and took a bite. "Hmmm. This is heavenly."

"At least tomorrow should be an easy day," Margaret pointed out. "You won't have to do anything but tell the movers where to put the furniture."

Amy stopped eating long enough to give the others a doubtful look.

"Moving is never easy," Nat murmured.

"Truer words were never spoken," Kim agreed. She dug into her meal. Between bites, she said, "When I tell Craig what he missed, he's going to be sorry he had to leave. But he had to get ready for an early meeting with the Town

Council tomorrow." She chased a bite of garlic toast with a sip of tea. "This is excellent, Caitlyn."

"Well, I'm glad Max couldn't stay. More for us," Amy said. "Anyone else want seconds?" She carted her plate inside for a refill.

Between bites of the simple but filling meal, the women praised Caitlyn's efforts. It pleased Margaret to no end when, by the time the last bit of sauce had been mopped up with a crust of garlic bread, the teen's cheeks had turned rosy from all the attention.

"Can I get your plate for you, Aunt Margaret?" Jen asked, after declaring that Caitlyn should leave the cleanup to her and the others.

"Thank you, honey. I'd appreciate that." Margaret angled slightly to the side so Jen could remove her empty dish. She glanced toward the door of the cottage. "I thought Belle would be here by now. She's got to be hungry, and I'm sure she's used up all the hot water."

Amy's mouth twisted to one side. "Maybe she's trying to wash away that bad mood of hers."

The warning look Diane shot her sister lasted less than a second, but Margaret caught it. "She's been grumpy?" she asked.

"That depends on what you call *grumpy*," Amy said, patently ignoring her sister's hard stare. "She's been bossing us around like a drill sergeant."

Margaret frowned. "That's not like Belle," she mused aloud. Though if anyone had a right to be in a bad mood, she supposed her daughter did. Not so long ago, Belle had been preparing for a coast-to-coast tour to celebrate her brand-new album. Then, without warning, her world had come crashing down. The tour and the album had been canceled with devastating financial consequences. Not only that, but both her record label and her agent had dropped her. The combination was bound to make anyone a little testy.

Diane cleared her throat, a move that apparently caught Amy's attention, because she shifted uneasily.

"I, uh, we've all been stressed. I shouldn't have said anything, Aunt Margaret," Amy apologized. "I'm sure she'll be all right now that we have the house ready for the movers tomorrow."

"I hope so," Jen muttered. "She was riding everyone pretty hard today."

"Oh, hush. She wasn't that bad." Diane glanced pointedly at her aunt.

"Now, girls." Margaret let her gaze drift from one of her nieces to the other. "You don't have to pull any punches with me. I'm fully aware of Belle's perfectionist streak. Where do you think she got it?" She aimed her index finger at her own chest. How many times had she scrubbed the kitchen floor a second time because she'd missed a tiny spot? Or fluffed the cushions on the front porch because they weren't quite fluffy enough?

Kim's brows knitted. "You know, now that I think about it, somebody ought to check on her. She was still working when the rest of us came back from the house."

Margaret felt her face pinch. "Belle didn't stop when the rest of you did?"

Diane slowly lowered the plate she held. "She said she needed to finish one more thing, and then she'd be right behind us. She's probably enjoying some much-deserved alone time."

Margaret felt her pulse quicken. Anything could have happened to Belle after the others left. A door might have slammed shut, trapping her in any one of the dozens of rooms in the house. She could have fallen and could be lying at the foot of the stairs with a broken leg...or worse. Or maybe some crazed fan had tracked her down and even now was holding her at knifepoint.

Don't let your imagination run wild.

Margaret shook her head. People in Emerald Bay guarded and respected Belle's privacy. The town was probably the one place on earth her daughter was absolutely free to come and go without worrying about anyone snapping a picture that might end up on social media. Still, a little concern wouldn't hurt. After all, what would have happened to her if Kim hadn't discovered her lying on the ground the night she'd broken her arm?

She turned to Caitlyn. "Sweetheart, would you run down to Regala and make sure your Aunt Belle is there?"

Caitlyn glanced at her mom for permission. When Diane nodded, the teen stood quickly. "I'll be right back," she promised before racing around the corner of the cottage.

Margaret dawdled outside over her tea, letting the others clear the dishes and clean the kitchen. Quiet conversation and the metallic rattle of silverware drifted from inside the cottage while the younger women stowed the leftovers, wiped down counters and washed and dried dishes. Before they finished, Caitlyn jogged into view.

"She's not in the cottage, Aunt Margaret," she said, barely breathing hard. "She must still be at the inn. There's a couple of lights on there."

Caitlyn grabbed the glass she'd left on the table and downed a sip or two. "Want me to go check on her?"

Though her unease deepened with the news, Margaret summoned a brave face. If Belle had been fussing at her cousins all day, she was apt to snap at Caitlyn, too. That was the last thing Margaret wanted to have happen. No. If anyone was going to check on Belle, she should do it. After all, she'd had the most practice in dealing with Belle's occasional mood swings.

"Thanks, honey." She pushed to her feet. Grabbing her cane, she leaned heavily on it. "I'm sure she's fine. Your mom is probably right—she just wants a little alone time." She smiled at the girl. "All this cooking and such wore me out today. I'm going to turn in early."

"I'll walk you to Regala," Caitlyn offered.

"Oh, I don't think that's necessary. I can make it on my own." She wasn't lying to the child. She fully intended to crawl into bed and read for an hour or two. First, though, she wanted to check on her daughter, and that was something she thought she should probably do by herself.

But Caitlyn was already shaking her head. "We fixed a plate for Aunt Belle. My mom wouldn't like it if I let you carry it all the way to Regala."

Margaret heaved a sigh. The child was right, of course. Trying to tote Belle's dinner to the cottage was just tempting fate. She'd already done that once when she'd tried to repair a downspout on her own, an escapade that hadn't turned out so well. She rubbed a spot in her arm where she still felt an odd twinge. *Better safe than sorry.*

"All right," she said, addressing her grand-niece. "But first I have to run the gauntlet or they'll never let me hear the end of it."

Caitlyn narrowed her eyes in that way teens had of asking if someone was off their rocker without saying a word. "The gauntlet?"

"Call it what you will—the gauntlet, the hug brigade—it all boils down to the same thing. When you live in the South—even if it's in Florida—you can't leave without giving and receiving a hug from every woman in the house." She motioned toward the cottage behind her where pots and pans were being put away.

Caitlyn hooted a laugh. "That's rich, Aunt Margaret." She shot a look at the interior of the room. "I'll meet you around front," she said with a wicked grin.

Margaret went inside, where she bid good night to her nieces. Rather than giving her a tight squeeze, though, Amy held her at arm's length.

"You won't be upset if I'm not here tomorrow, will you? I really feel like I should check in at Sweet Cakes. I don't want Deborah to think I've abandoned her."

"Of course not," Margaret assured the younger woman. "You have a business to run."

"I'll be back as soon as I can—at least by lunch," Diane said when it was her turn to say goodnight. "School starts tomorrow, and I need to make sure Caitlyn's first day goes smoothly."

"I'm going to miss having that child underfoot." While Caitlyn was homeschooling, Margaret had grown used to hearing the girl tromp downstairs for a midmorning snack. She supposed, between school and soccer practices, their daily crochet lessons were on hold for the time being.

"Do you think you can handle the movers without us?" Amy worried her lower lip.

"Please. Even without you, there are five of us. And the movers will do all the real work. All we have to do is supervise." Margaret laughed softly.

The wonderful sound of her nieces' laughter echoed in her ears as Margaret handed Caitlyn a foil-wrapped plate outside the cottage a moment later. They walked the short distance to Regala, where Caitlyn insisted on coming inside.

"Want me to stay with you while you get ready for bed?" she asked after placing Belle's dinner in the small fridge.

"Oh, pshaw!" Margaret scoffed. "I'm perfectly capable of changing into my nightgown. Run along now." She waved the girl toward the door. "You have a big day tomorrow. Your mom said it's your first day at Emerald Bay High. You must be looking forward to making new friends and meeting your teachers."

"I hope my classes are interesting." Worry created frown lines on Caitlyn's face. "It'd be nice to have some of the kids from Youth Group in my classes, but I'll see them at lunch anyway." She paused, as if remembering that returning to public school had been her idea. "And I'll get to play soccer." She kicked an imaginary ball. "I can't wait to meet the coach and find out about tryouts. I'm lucky Emerald Bay plays spring soccer. My old school only had a fall season."

"Well, then, I won't keep you. You need your beauty sleep." Margaret shuffled a step or two closer to the door.

Caitlyn laughed again. "That's funny, Aunt Margaret. It's not even seven o'clock yet. I won't go to bed for *hours*."

Hoping the girl would take the hint, Margaret cupped one hand over her mouth and pretended to yawn. "My bedtime is a bit earlier than that."

"Aren't you going to make me run the gauntlet?" Her arms open wide, Caitlyn moved close enough for a hug. She propped her head on Margaret's shoulder and whispered, "Thanks. I had fun today."

Feeling the girl's arms around her stirred Margaret's favorite memories of the days when Belle and her cousins had been Caitlyn's age. She gave the girl an extra squeeze before she prodded her toward the door. This time, Caitlyn took the hint and didn't linger. Once the latch clicked behind the teen, Margaret slowly counted to thirty before she hobbled forward. She opened the door just wide enough to peek outside. After making sure the coast was clear, she stepped onto the pavered walkway that led to the inn.

Ten minutes later, she heard Belle singing in another part of the house as Margaret let herself in through the employee entrance. So much relief pulsed through her at finding out she'd been worried about nothing—her daughter was obviously alive and well—that she felt light-headed for a moment.

She took a deep, steadying breath. Pressing one hand over her heart, she acknowledged how scared she'd been. Though she'd never admit it to the others, she'd been afraid that she'd find

Belle nursing a sprained ankle in the front room or crumpled at the foot of the stairs. Or worse, be unable to find her at all on the first floor and have to call on Kim or Jen to search the rooms upstairs. Silently, she cursed the leg that hadn't healed properly after the accident and made it next to impossible for her to manage even a short flight of stairs.

"Enough!" she told herself. She'd had nothing to be afraid of. Belle was here, safe and sound. Her forehead wrinkled. So why was she still here instead of enjoying the night off with her cousins?

Determined to find out, she waited until Belle reached the end of the song before she called, "Belle? Belle, where are you?" Margaret tried not to wince when her voice seemed to grow louder as it echoed across the bare floors and bounced off the walls.

"Mama?" Shock and disbelief registered in the single word.

"Yes," Margaret hollered in return.

"What are you doing here?" Footsteps echoed from somewhere in the back of the house.

"I could ask you the same question." Margaret hobbled past the tiny office built into the back of the staircase and down the hallway. She rounded the corner into the living room just in time to see Belle emerge from the Emerald suite with a bottle of glass cleaner in one hand and a trash can overflowing with crumpled paper towels in the other. Her daughter had tucked what was left of the roll of towels under one arm. Belle's green eyes widened when they landed on her.

"Mama, you didn't walk all the way over here by yourself, did you?" Belle peered over Margaret's shoulder as if expecting the rest of the family to materialize behind her.

"I most certainly did. I might be eighty and need this infernal cane, but I'm not dead." Margaret started to make her point by swinging the cane but stopped herself. It wouldn't help her case one bit if she lost her balance and ended up on the floor. She propped one hand on her hip. "The real question is, what's going on with you? Why didn't you come to dinner with the rest of the family? And why are you working when everyone else quit hours ago?"

"You know me, Mama. I won't stop before the job is finished."

Margaret supposed a leopard could change its spots, but of all the teenagers who'd spent their summers working at the inn, her daughter had always been the least likely of the bunch to volunteer to work an extra shift. No, something else had to be going on, and hoping to get a clue form Belle's appearance, she took a closer look. Several strands of her daughter's red hair had escaped her baseball cap and trailed down her back in thick tangles. The woman who never left the house without looking like she was headed to a photo shoot hadn't applied so much as a drop of foundation. Something that looked an awful lot like dirt smudged one of her cheeks. Her polish was chipped, her lips chapped and dry, and she certainly hadn't paid some designer to put those holes in her jeans. But what bothered Margaret most was the fevered look in her daughter's eyes. Alarm shot through her when Belle swayed slightly on her feet.

"When did you eat last?" she demanded.

"I don't know." Belle's brows knotted in concentration. "This morning? I had a banana, I think."

Margaret scoffed. "We haven't had any fresh fruit at the cottage in two days." With the move back into the main house just around the corner, they were making do with whatever was on hand.

"Okay, not a banana then." Belle paused. "I ate something. I must have."

"How about water? Have you had enough to drink?"

"I, uh…" Another strand of hair tumbled from beneath her ball cap when Belle shook her head.

"Are you trying to make yourself sick?" Margaret asked, though she didn't expect or wait for an answer. "How many times have you reminded me how important it is to stay hydrated? Especially when you're working hard. Like you've been doing today." And Belle had been working hard. The dust that streaked Belle's sweatshirt proved it. "Go to the kitchen right now and grab a bottle of water from the fridge."

"Yes, ma'am." Belle stuffed the window cleaner and the roll of paper towels in the trash can, which she carefully placed on the floor before she trotted off to do her mother's bidding. She returned less than a minute later carrying a half-empty bottle. Raising it as if she was giving a toast, she said, "Thanks for the reminder, Mama. I'll be all right now. I have a couple of things I need to finish up here before I meet you at the cottage. Can you make it there on your own?"

While Belle twisted the lid on her water bottle, Margaret let her gaze travel the room. A reddish hue lit the evening sky beyond the sparkling windows. Someone had recently run a dry mop over the hardwood floors, which gleamed beneath the overhead lights. As far as she could tell, not a speck remained of the dust that had coated the walls and the wide slats of the plantation shutters. She cleared her throat. "I think you've done enough. Why don't you call it quits for the night?"

Belle cast a fretful look over her shoulder. "I'm not quite finished with the Emerald suite. And I still need to do Diamond and the family quarters."

"I thought Kim and the others took care of those." At dinner, Kim had shown her the checklist she'd used to keep track of everyone's progress. Margaret would have sworn every room on the list had a bold X beside it.

"They did a good job, I guess." Belle bounced on the balls of her feet. "But I found a few spots on the windows, so I'm going over them again."

Her daughter had always been particular about her clothes and her hair. When it came to her music, it wasn't at all unusual for her to go over the same passage a dozen times or more until she got it exactly right. But housework? Belle's attention to detail had never extended that far. Whatever was going on with her, Margaret would bet her last dollar it had nothing to do with a speck or two of dust on a couple of glass panes. Forcing herself to remain calm, she exhaled through her nose. "And this can't wait?"

Belle retrieved the trash can and the paper towels she'd left on the floor. Her tone turned so brusque it bordered on snippy. "Once the furniture's in place, it'll be harder to get the windows spotless."

"True," Margaret said, slowly. "But they can wait long enough for you to take a break, don't you think? Come. Sit with me for a minute." She moved toward the stairs where, keeping her feet on the floor, she carefully lowered herself onto one of the steps. She patted an empty spot beside her. "C'mon."

Belle released a dramatic, long-suffering sigh before she turned ever so slightly in the direction of the Emerald suite. Margaret held her breath. Was her daughter actually going to turn her back on her and walk away? Just when she was certain that was exactly what Belle planned to do, she seemed to catch herself. Margaret's tummy gave a happy little shimmy when her daughter joined her on the step.

"Now." Margaret folded her hands over the top of her cane. "Amy and the others told me you were harping at them all day. And here you are, washing the same windows and wiping down the same window shutters they've already cleaned. I can't believe you're that upset about a little bit of dirt. So why don't you tell me what's really going on?"

Belle swept her hat from her head, letting the rest of her long red curls cascade onto her back. She gave a wry smile. "You always did know when something was bothering me."

"Well, of course I do—I'm your mother, aren't I? When you were a baby, I could tell whether you were hungry or needed a diaper change just by listening to your cries. Whenever you were afraid that you'd failed a test at school, you'd get a tiny little crease between your eyebrows. No one else noticed, but I always saw it." Margaret ran one finger lightly down the center of her daughter's forehead.

"I could never hide my problems from you."

"I hope you never do. Troubles are always lighter when two carry the load. So what's the problem?" A fresh concern rose in her chest. "You're not ill, are you?"

"No. I'm not sick." Belle stretched. "I think I'm actually in better shape than I've been in a long time. Must be all the running." She and Kim had been running five miles along the beach each morning. "It probably helps that I'm eating better, too. That no-carb diet helped keep the weight off, but I have a lot more stamina now."

Margaret exhaled. As long as people had their health, a roof over their heads, food in their bellies and faith in a higher power, little else mattered. Belle's faith had always been an unshakable rock. She said she was healthy. She had a place to live and plenty to eat. What if that wasn't enough for her? After all, for the last three decades her daughter had lived the life of the rich and famous. If an expensive piece of art caught her eye or she liked a particular dress by a top designer, she'd never been forced to stop and consider the cost. She simply bought it. Was that the problem? "Is it money, then? I know you were worried about that when you first got here."

"I wish it were that simple, but no." Belle shook her head. "Selling the Twombly paid off all my creditors." The pricey piece of art had been a very worthwhile investment. "Between finding buyers for the house in Positano and the apartment in Paris and leasing the condo in New York, I'm in the clear. Not rich. Not like I was. But I can afford more than a bologna sandwich once in a while."

"Your father loved those." Margaret smiled at the memory. Whenever they'd eaten dinner at the diner, Eric had ordered a fried bologna sandwich, fries and a vanilla milkshake.

Belle shuddered. "I know I used to like it when I was a kid, but as an adult, I can't think of anything I'd want less."

"I can. How about Spam?" On the rare occasions when Liz and Paul took the night off, Margaret had usually opened a tin of the canned meat, sliced it thin and fried it in a little butter. Eric had rated it right up there beside his beloved luncheon meat. "You and your dad used to fight over the last piece."

Belle clamped a hand over her mouth and pretended to gag. "The way Daddy ate, it's no wonder he had a heart attack."

"If we'd known as much about cholesterol and heart disease then as we do now, I never would have let him eat that stuff." Margaret swiped a tear from her eye. "Even if he fussed about it."

"I can't believe he's been gone so long. I still miss him so much."

"Me, too. Every day." More tears threatened. This time, Margaret succeeded in blinking them away. "But I'll see him again soon."

"Let's hope that's not for a good long while yet."

Margaret leaned against her daughter when Belle stretched a comforting arm around her shoulders. Thinking of her husband, she let the silence stretch for a minute or two before she straightened. She'd come here to find out what was bothering her daughter, not to wallow in her own grief. She patted Belle's thigh. "Now are you ready to tell me what's bothering you? Or are you going to make me pry it out of you?"

"The Lord and I are having a bit of a set-to." As if she was afraid to face her mother, Belle looked away.

Shock rippled through Margaret. Of all the things she'd considered might be troubling Belle, her daughter's faith hadn't even made it onto the bottom of her list. "What about?" she asked when she could catch her breath.

In a move that prevented her from facing Margaret, Belle bent to touch her toes. "I've been blessed, you know. So blessed. I have this amazing talent, which I've always considered a gift from God."

Hearing a hesitant note in her daughter's voice, Margaret swallowed. "Go on," she prodded.

"But I keep thinking of that parable in the Bible. You know the one—where a rich man gives his servants some talents to hold for him while he goes on a journey. Two of the servants invest what they were given, but one buries his in the ground for safekeeping. When the rich

261

man returns, he rewards those who made investments and doubled their talents, but…"

"But he was furious with the one who simply saved his," Margaret finished. Pastor Dave had preached a sermon based on the story last spring. He'd said the parable was about more than a rich man's concern over his money.

"Right. I've always tried to be like the first two servants. I've used my talents the best way I knew how. For a long time, it looked like I'd have plenty to show for all I'd been given. The cars, the houses, the fat bank account—I had it all." She took a deep, shuddery breath. "And I lost it all. I'm afraid that when the time of reckoning comes, I won't have anything more than the talent I started out with."

For a long moment, Margaret forced herself to ignore a pressing need to reassure her daughter. To say all the things a mother was supposed to say in times like these. That Belle had been given more than her voice. That everyone loved her. That she'd always be a star in her mother's heart. In the depths of her soul, though, she knew Belle didn't need platitudes, no matter how well-meaning they were. But while Margaret sat and gathered her thoughts, her daughter grew restless.

"I guess that's it. I'm doomed," Belle said, her

irritation showing after several minutes. She started to push herself off the steps.

"Hold on." Margaret placed a restraining hand on her daughter's thigh. "I needed a minute to think. This isn't just some trivial question. You aren't asking if you should wear the pink shirt or the blue one. Or if your shoes match your outfit. You've raised an important issue. It deserves more than an off-the-cuff answer."

Like a cup of coffee that had been left on the table for a while, Belle's bluster cooled. Settling back down on the stair, she focused on Margaret. "Well?"

Margaret refused to let her daughter's insistent stare rush her. She bided her time, waiting until she knew what she wanted to say, what she *should* say.

"I think the point of the story is more about what the men did with their talents rather than the results," she said, measuring each word. When Belle's brow creased, she explained. "It's true that the first two men doubled the amount they were given and the last man, the one who buried his talent in the ground, dug it up and gave it back to the wealthy owner. But what if he hadn't? What if he'd taken that talent to the money lenders like the rich man suggested?

What if, instead of earning some interest, the money lenders lost his investment? Would the rich man still be angry at him?" She shook her head. "I don't think so. I think the rich man would have patted the poor servant on the back and said, 'Better luck next time. The important thing is that you tried.'"

Margaret knew she'd touched a nerve when Belle's forehead smoothed. She continued. "Life is a series of trials and errors. No one wins all the time. Sometimes, we bet on a sure thing, only to have it fail. I think the wealthy man understood that. What he couldn't abide was his servant's fear and laziness."

"I've been accused of many things," Belle said, clearly considering the matter. "Being afraid to take a chance is not one of them."

"No." Margaret smiled. "You're one of the bravest people I know."

At that, Belle laughed out loud. "I'm not brave. I'm just as afraid as the next person. I just hide it better. You remember the first time I ever sang a solo at church?"

Margaret nodded. She remembered that day like it was yesterday. She and Eric had sat in the first pew and held hands. "You wore your favorite jean skirt and a yellow shirt with ruffles down the front. You sang "His Eye Is On The

Sparrow." The choir director had chosen something else—she didn't think you had the vocal range. But you proved her wrong. There wasn't a dry eye in the church when you finished. Including your father's."

"I bet you didn't know I was so scared before church that morning that I threw up. Twice. And that's not the only time. When I auditioned for Juilliard, I was shaking so hard, I thought the judges would think I was a tap dancer. I still get butterflies every time I step on stage."

"Oh, honey!" It was a good thing she hadn't known about the vomiting. If she had, she would have kept Belle home that day. "The thing is, you never let your nerves hold you back. You've never buried your talent out of fear, like that servant did. You stepped up to the mic and sang."

"I still failed, Mama." Despair strained Belle's voice. "I've lost...everything. My home. My savings. The cars. It's all gone."

Margaret blew air across her lips. "You can't take any of that stuff with you to heaven when you go."

"True. But—"

"But nothing." For emphasis, Margaret tapped her cane on the floor. "Material gain is not what's important. Instead, think about the lives you've touched. By following your dreams, how many young women have you inspired to follow theirs? How many nervous eleven-year-olds have watched you and said, 'If she can make it, there's hope for me'? If you've touched even one person, given them hope, inspired just one, it's worth more than all the cars, the houses or the money."

Margaret took a breath. Belle believed in sharing the wealth, in reaching a helping hand down to those who were trying to climb the ladder to success. Didn't she invite an unknown talent up on stage with her at practically every performance? Hadn't she donated heavily to their church, to Juilliard? If that wasn't sharing her talent, she didn't know what was.

"That's..." Belle paused. "That's humbling."

"Are you more at peace now?" Margaret asked.

"I..." Belle seemed to be weighing all her mother had said. "I don't think the Lord and I are through figuring things out yet. I think there's more I'm supposed to do, but I don't know what it is. But, yeah, my mind and my heart are resting a little easier than they were."

"Good. Caitlyn made spaghetti for dinner. We fixed a plate for you. It's in the fridge at the cottage when you want it." Which probably wasn't right this minute. Margaret's gaze dropped to the small pile of cleaning supplies Belle had left on the floor. Supper could wait. Her daughter had some more wrestling with the Lord to do, and if she did her best wrestling while she cleaned, so be it.

"I'll leave you to it, then." Content that Belle would find the answers she was looking for, she retraced her steps to the little cottage that was serving as their temporary home.

Tired of pacing from the bedroom through the living room and back again, Margaret sank onto the rocker by the cottage's front window. She hooked her cane over the back of the chair, gripped the armrests with both hands and peered through the glass at the main house. The setting sun cast the rear deck in shadow, but she could tell the movers had at least made some progress.

They certainly should have. The crew of ten had arrived shortly before seven this morning. It was well past five now, and they'd been crawling over the property like hardworking ants all day. With so many hands, they'd made light work of emptying the storage units before lunch. They hadn't dawdled or stretched out under the palms for a nap after eating the sandwiches and cookies Amy had dropped off, either. No, sirree. They'd gone straight back to work.

She'd lost sight of them after that, and her frustration had been building ever since. She thought everyone had been working inside all that time, but a couple of hours ago, the workers had removed the temporary covering over the back deck. To her surprise, all the furniture and items that had been stored there had already been moved inside.

From where she sat, she couldn't see around to the front of the house. Had that porch been cleared off as well? She had no idea. Nor could she tell what shape the interior was in. Had the movers simply carried the dressers, tables, sideboards and lamps inside and scattered them about willy-nilly? Or had they put everything in its proper place?

The suspense was killing her, she admitted. She had half a mind to walk over to the house and see how things were progressing for herself. She would have gone ages ago if Belle and the others hadn't made her swear to stay put. On the family Bible, no less.

Fiddlesticks.

Margaret fumed while her anxiety grew. She

had every right to be at the inn along with the others. More, to be perfectly honest. After all, the Dane Crown Inn had been her home since she was a youngster. She and Liz and Shirley and Edward had grown up playing hide-and-seek in the rambling, two-story house. Later, while friends and family had looked on, she and Eric had exchanged their wedding vows in front of the big fireplace right there in the living room. After they'd had Belle, she and Eric had moved into Regala, but she'd spent most days greeting new arrivals and bidding a fond farewell to departing guests, helping Liz prepare meals in the roomy kitchen, and overseeing the staff, including the *girls* who now considered themselves her boss.

And soon—too soon, as far as she was concerned—those same girls expected her to trade her stately home with its airy living room, various sitting rooms and cozy family quarters for a tiny one-room apartment in an assisted living facility. To go from watching the sun rise over the ocean from her very own front porch each morning to staring at the same four walls day in and day out. In a building where someone else would monitor her comings and goings like she was a child, no less.

She shuddered. How was she supposed to do

that? To go from running the inn on her own to letting someone else choose what she ate at any given meal? Was she supposed to give up her independence just because she'd celebrated her eightieth birthday?

Her bottom lip quivered. She'd given her word to Belle and the rest of them, though. Together, they'd struck a deal. She'd agreed to spend what remained of her savings on restoring the inn to its former glory. In exchange, her daughter and her nieces were pulling out all the stops for one last family reunion before they put the Dane Crown Inn on the market. Her only condition had been that they find a buyer who'd keep the doors of the inn open. Once they did, she'd have no choice but to move into Emerald Oaks.

But she could pray—and, oh, how she prayed—that the girls couldn't uphold their half of the bargain or find a new innkeeper for her family home.

"Mama?"

A hand landed on her shoulder. Margaret jerked, her eyes flying open.

"I'm sorry, Mama. I didn't mean to disturb you. I thought…" Belle seemed flustered. "Do you want to come and see how nice the house looks?"

"Oh, my." Margaret's hand fluttered to her chest. "Are the movers finished already?" She'd been so lost in her memories and hopes for the future that she hadn't even seen her daughter coming down the path to the cottage.

"Yes, ma'am. They'll be pulling out of the parking area any minute."

Hoping Belle wouldn't notice her tears, Margaret scrubbed at her cheeks.

"Do you want to walk over to the house now? Or would you like to finish your little nap first?"

Glad her daughter had assumed she was sleeping, she reached for her cane. "I'm ready." Her head was bursting with a hundred questions. Questions she couldn't answer without taking a good, hard look at the house.

"I'm sorry you had to stay in the cottage all day." Belle held the door for her mother.

"I didn't mind." *Much*, Margaret added silently.

"It's just that, well, we were afraid one of the movers would bump into you and knock you down. They were moving so fast and carrying such heavy items that we all had trouble keeping out of their way. Remember the tall chifforobe in the Beryl suite?" Belle didn't wait for an answer but rushed on. "The guys nearly ran Diane over when they were bringing it upstairs. She had to take the steps two at a time to get out of their way."

Margaret smiled at the image of Diane hot-footing it up the stairs. "She made it home in time to help out, then. Everything must have gone smoothly at the school?"

"I think so. She said she'd heard from Caitlyn. She liked most of her classes and had lunch with Toby and his crowd."

"Sounds like a good first day." Margaret's smile changed to a full-fledged grin when she followed Belle into the roomy kitchen. Off to one side, the sturdy banquette sat precisely where it belonged with the long trestle table the family used for informal gatherings right in front of it. Someone had lined up exactly the same number of chairs as always on the opposite side of the table. Margaret crossed to the one at the head of the table. Running her fingers over the top rail, she felt for her late brother's initials. Their father had given Edward the rough side of his tongue for taking a knife to the wood. Years later, Margaret was glad he had—it gave her some-thing to remember him by.

Marveling at how wonderful the floors looked, she moved into the family quarters where, again, everything was as it should be.

"Who made the beds?" she asked, eyeing the tidy comforter and the throw pillows she kept on Eric's side of the mattress.

"That'd be Jen. She's been a bed-making demon. The movers would barely slide the box springs over the frame before she'd be standing at the door with an armload of fresh bedding."

"She made all of them? In every suite?"

"Yes, ma'am," Belle assured her. "You want to see the rest of the house? I think the others are anxious to see your reaction. Craig and Max, too. They've been a big help this afternoon."

"I must remember to thank them," Margaret murmured. She followed Belle, who headed for the staircase.

Margaret couldn't help herself—she gushed like a schoolgirl when they made their way past a spot in the hall where a long-ago guest had once dropped a heavy briefcase. The accident had gouged the flooring. For the last several years, she'd hidden the scar beneath a rug, but that was no longer necessary.

"Did you see this?" she asked, beckoning the small crowd of people who lingered at the foot of the stairs. "There was a mark right here." She toed the spot. "I think it was here. The refinishers did such a good job repairing it, I can't tell."

"The floors are fantastic," Nat agreed. "I love

the contrast of the dark stain against the white walls."

"They look even better with all the furniture in place," Diane said.

Margaret scanned the faces of her nieces, her grand-niece and the two men who'd lent a hand to her family today. Judging from their expressions, everyone was quite pleased with how the day had gone. Tired as all get-out but pleased nonetheless. She made the rounds, giving hugs to each of them and thanking them for all their hard work.

"Ms. Margaret, if you want anything moved, anything at all, Max, here, is your man." A serious expression on his face, Craig slapped the handyman soundly on the back.

"And what, exactly, will you be doing, Mr. Mayor?" Margaret peered up at him, her face a mask of innocence.

"He'll be helping Max." Kim prodded Craig with her elbow.

"Ouch. I mean, yes, ma'am." The tall man rubbed his side, but a sidelong grin announced to anyone who wanted to know that he'd only been teasing. "That's what I'll be doing all right."

Margaret shook her head at the antics of the couple. After the misery her first husband had put her through, Kim deserved someone who treated her like a queen. And Craig, who'd lost his wife in such a tragic accident, needed someone steady and strong. The two of them seemed like a good fit, and she hoped things would work out for them.

"All right." Margaret pulled herself straight. Summoning the eagle-eyed stare she'd brought into play whenever she'd inspected her nieces' efforts when they'd worked at the inn, she asked, "Where do we start?"

"How about the living room?" Nat suggested.

"Lead the way," Margaret directed.

And, beginning there, they trooped through the ground floor. The grandfather clock kept perfect time in the exact spot where it had stood for as long as Margaret could remember. In the front parlor, Diane broke off from the group and crossed to one of the club chairs that flanked the couch. Margaret nodded approvingly when she angled the chair a smidge closer to the piano. The recliners in the game room had been lined up to give their guests the perfect view of the wall-mounted television. In the three downstairs suites, the beds and furniture were arranged precisely as she remembered.

"How in the world did you get everything right?" Margaret asked when they'd completed their tour of the first floor.

Like an excited schoolgirl, Nat waved her cell phone in the air. "Mom and I took pictures."

"Smart girl!" Margaret said.

"I'll take more when we finish putting everything away."

Margaret nodded. To make the furniture light enough for the movers to manage, they'd removed the dishes from the sideboards, emptied desks and taken books out of the bookcases. All those items would need to be put away. It would take most of the week to unpack the games in the game room, arrange the knickknacks on the end tables in the parlors and scatter doilies over the dressers in the bedrooms. She was certain the piano would require retuning after a couple of weeks wrapped in a tarp on the front porch. To say nothing of the myriad other little things that went into creating a warm and inviting atmosphere for their guests.

Guests who had reserved the Lapis and Jasper suites on the second floor. Margaret eyed the stairs and wished she could check out those rooms as well.

"Do you want to see if you can manage to get up them?" Jen asked. "I'll be glad to help you."

"Or Craig and Max can carry you," Kim suggested.

At the thought of the two men carting her up

the stairs like a sack of grain, Margaret shuddered. "No, thanks. If I can't make it under my own steam, then I'll just have to take your word for it that everything upstairs is as perfect as it is down here."

"I can do better than that," Nat insisted. "This won't take but a few minutes." She dashed up to the second floor with all the grace and speed of a young deer.

"Let's have a glass of sweet tea while we wait," Kim suggested. "I, for one, am dead on my feet. I'm sure I'm not the only one."

When the rest agreed, they moved to the kitchen, where Margaret slipped into her usual spot at the table. Ten minutes later, she felt a twinge of envy when she heard Nat practically skipping back down the stairs.

"Here, Aunt Margaret." Nat plopped down on a chair beside her. Turning her phone on its side, she scrolled through picture after picture of the upstairs suites. In each, the movers—under the direction of her nieces—had placed the beds, dressers, tables and nightstands exactly where they belonged.

Warmth spread through Margaret's chest. "Oh, girls. This is the best. The floors are just lovely. Everything else is perfect. I couldn't be happier with the way things turned out."

"We still have a lot of work to do." Kim flexed her arms and stretched. "But I think I speak for us all when I say the look on your face makes all our effort worthwhile."

Eight

Kim

"Hey. Where are you headed?" Kim asked, spotting her sister coming down the stairs.

"Laundry. It never ends." Resignation freighted Jen's words. "You?"

"Kitchen," she said when her sister hit the last step and joined her in the hallway. She straightened the runner on the narrow table in the hall as they walked past it. "I'm anxious to get Royal Meals off the ground."

Three months ago, who would have believed that she'd be starting her own business? Not her. Before she came to Emerald Bay, she'd been estranged from her children, weeks away from an eviction notice and barely putting food on the table with the series of temp jobs she'd taken

279

since the big layoff at Connors Industrial. Yet, here she was—reunited with Nat and Josh, surrounded by people who loved her and whom she loved, living in the one place she'd always called home, and a business owner to boot.

"That's right." Jen snapped her fingers. "Your first delivery is Friday, isn't it? How many customers do you have now? Twelve?"

Warmth shot through Kim. Her sister had remembered. And she wasn't the only one. Diane had wished her luck before leaving to run some errands this morning. Belle had drawn a crown mounted on a plate—the logo Nat had created for Royal Meals—on the bottom of her note reminding everyone that she and her mom were taking Maude Anders out to breakfast. Craig had even sent flowers, along with encouragement for what he called "kick-off week." All of which was more support than she'd ever have received from her ex. Frank had never cared one whit about her passions as long as they didn't interfere with his. But Frank was her past. Craig and her family—and Royal Meals—were her future.

"How are things with the Smiths?" In addition to taking over the laundry, Jen was helping Margaret with the hostess duties. "Are they comfortable in the Lapis suite?"

"They love it," Jen said. "Mr. Smith said he'd never felt quite so at home. And Bernice—she hates to be called Mrs. Smith—Bernice loves the view." A strategically placed club chair provided comfortable seating for guests who enjoyed looking at the beach from their quarters on the second floor.

"They weren't upset that we moved the Jenkinses downstairs?" The two couples were making a leisurely trip to Key West from their homes in New Jersey. Their reservation had requested adjoining suites.

"If they were disappointed, they haven't said anything about it. But Mrs. Jenkins's ankle brace makes it nearly impossible for her to manage the stairs." The retired schoolteacher had tripped over a curb and sprained her ankle while she was on a walking tour of St. Augustine last week.

"And they're happy in Diamond?" Aunt Margaret had insisted on giving the Jenkinses the best set of rooms on the first floor.

"Who wouldn't be? But it's a good thing they're only staying here a couple of days. Otherwise, we might need to install an ice maker in their room. I must have refilled her ice pack a dozen times yesterday while the others were out." Hampered by her bum ankle, Mrs. Jenkins had opted not to accompany her husband and the Smiths on a shopping trip to the outlet malls in Vero Beach. "Not that I'm complaining... much," Jen added with a grin.

"It sounds like they're enjoying themselves." From her room at the top of the stairs, Kim had listened to the two couples drinking and playing cards in the game room until the wee hours. "What are they doing today?"

"They haven't stirred, near as I can tell. Yesterday, I overheard Mr. Smith say they were going to the Mel Fisher Museum after lunch. Then they're supposed to go snorkeling. He's sure they'll find a cache of gold doubloons."

"Yeah?" Kim laughed. "Like they're easy to find." Though coins and artifacts from the shipwreck of a Spanish fleet in 1715 washed ashore from time to time, it had been years since anyone had made a significant discovery. She rubbed her fingers together. She couldn't fault the Smiths or the Jenkinses for trying. Not when the price of gold was through the roof. Add in the historical value, and a single doubloon might be enough to pay for a new car.

"We ought to go on our own treasure hunt one day," Jen suggested.

Kim brushed the comment aside. She'd had her fill of those when she was a child. Which didn't stop her from keeping her eyes peeled for a sparkling emerald or the flash of a gold coin buried in the sand when she went for her early morning runs along the beach.

"You told them we aren't serving a hot breakfast?" Kim wanted to offer their guests a hearty breakfast like her Aunt Liz had when she ran the inn's kitchen. For now, though, getting her catering business off to a good start was her top priority.

"Anyone who'd turn up their nose at Amy's sweet rolls can just find themselves another place to stay," Jen said sternly. Two steps into the kitchen, she gave a mock salute. "Duty calls." She turned down the short hallway that led to the laundry room.

"Same here." Reaching the center island, Kim opened the thick binder that contained the paperwork for Royal Meals. She leafed through the notebook until she found the menu section. Her task for the day was to finalize her choices for the first week and gather all the necessary ingredients. That would leave her three days to cook, pack and deliver a delicious heat-and-serve meal to each of her customers.

Lost in thought, she ran one finger down the list of entrees and side dishes that had won her family's highest praise. Which main dish should she choose to kick off her business? Her heart pounded as she scanned the paper for the umpteenth time. The first delivery for Royal Meals had to be awesome. Not just good but spectacular.

Her finger stopped at lemon chicken. Was that it? Would that set a high enough bar? Everyone raved about the dish, but was it good enough? She ran a hand through her hair and sighed.

With its golden-brown crust and lemony, glistening glaze, the entrée certainly qualified as "food fit for a king." Plus, the black, disposable serving containers she'd chosen would showcase the dish beautifully. With an ample scoop of homemade mashed potatoes on one side and a pretty arrangement of flash-fried green veggies on the other, the combination definitely appealed to the eye. As for the aroma, when her clients removed the see-through lid and took their first whiff of the tantalizing mix of citrus and butter, their taste buds would go bananas.

At least, that was the hope.

But maybe she should start with something more impressive. Thick slices of a pork roast stuffed with spinach and cheese, perhaps. Or maybe even beef Wellington.

She shook her head. While some people might call pork "the other white meat," a variety of reasons made it a risky choice for kicking off a catering business. As for the beef Wellington, a layer of prosciutto would prevent the Duxelles—a savory blend of mushrooms, shallots and thyme—from turning the puff pastry into a soggy mess, but the thinly sliced ham had its limits. Plus, the recipe called for pricey tenderloin, which would strain her budget nearly to the breaking point. The smarter choice would be to wait until Royal Meals was solidly in the black before she added such expensive fare to the menu. And the one thing she knew, the one thing she was certain of, was that she needed to make smart choices if her fledgling business was going to succeed. So chicken, then. She drew a circle around the item on her list of possible dishes and drew in a satisfied breath.

Though she'd prepared the dishes often enough that she felt certain she could make each one blindfolded, she leafed through the journal where she kept all her favorite recipes. Using the calculator app on her phone, she carefully calculated the number of chicken breasts and lemons, the cups of broth and heads of broccoli she'd need in order to end up with enough servings. After recording the totals on her shopping list, she repeated the entire process, just to be sure. She blew out a breath when her figures matched.

Feeling like she'd taken one step in the right direction and needed to make another one, she grabbed the slip of paper. She carried it into the large walk-in pantry where, with Belle's help, she'd reserved one set of shelves for Royal Meals. Nat had put her own spin on things by plastering Kim's shelves with cute warning signs that threatened anyone caught pilfering with a stay "in the dungeon."

Late last week, Kim had stocked her area with all the basics—sugar and flour, several kinds of pasta, bread crumbs, spices and herbs. For the next fifteen minutes, she carefully cross-checked the ingredients required for her first delivery against those she had on hand. Pleased that she knew exactly what to buy on her trip to the grocery store this afternoon, she returned to the counter, where she drew lines through several items on her master list.

Her next task was to inspect the various pots, pans and utensils she'd use when she started cooking. Moving to the wall of cupboards, she opened one of the doors. Feeling more confident by the minute, she located a half-dozen long, flat baking pans in the exact same spot her Aunt Liz had always stored them. She reached for one. But instead of the polished metal's smooth surface, her fingers met a gritty substance.

"Yuck!" she exclaimed when she pulled out the first pan on the stack. She stared down at a film of dirt and dust that marred the non-stick surface.

"Son of a…" She stumbled over the final word. "How?" she asked the empty room.

She hadn't thought she needed to remove the dishes, pots and pans while the workers refinished the floors. After all, the entire kitchen had been swathed in plastic from the time the workers revved up the first sander until the last of the flooring crew had left the building. So how on earth did gritty, nasty sawdust seep beyond the barrier to coat the baking sheets? Looking down, she spotted a layer of grime lying atop the shelf liner she'd recently installed.

An uneasy feeling swelled in her chest. Determined not to panic, she forced herself to take a breath. It was just one shelf. *One shelf.* She could remove these pans, wash and dry them and replace the shelf liner in no time.

Unless…

She opened the door of the next cabinet. Peering at the saucepans arranged by size and shape, she felt her whole body begin to tremble. Dust coated every lid. It collected in tiny piles along the handles. She pulled out a stew pot. The pan left its outline on the dusty shelf liner.

"No, no, no," she whispered.

In quick succession, she opened the rest of the cupboards that lined the wall. Only a light dusting coated the mixing bowls, but the small appliances stored on a top shelf were positively grimy.

Praying that someone had done a better job covering the cabinets where they kept the dishes, she moved to the other side of the island. She brushed her fingers over the bottoms of the drinking glasses that were stored, upside-down, on the shelves closest to the refrigerator. She exhaled slowly when all she felt was smooth, cool glass. She held one up to the light. It sparkled. In quick succession, she examined the everyday dishes and the few serving platters they kept within easy reach. Try as she might, she couldn't find a single speck of dust in the bank of cabinets they used most often.

Not that it mattered, she reminded herself. No matter how much dirt had or had not seeped through the plastic seal, the end result was the same. She'd have to remove every item, wipe down the shelves and lay new liner throughout the kitchen. And then everything—from the shot glasses in the liquor cabinet to the hand-cranked ice cream maker stored above the stove—would need to be washed and dried and put back where it belonged before anyone so much as made a piece of toast.

Panic gripped her belly when she thought of the time the task would take. Time she didn't have. She'd promised her customers they'd get their first Royal Meals delivery on Friday. Over the next four days, she needed to shop for the items on her grocery list; make two dozen mini apple pies from scratch; slice, dice and artfully arrange twenty-four individual salads. Only then could she prepare an equal number of servings of lemon chicken, mashed potatoes and seared vegetables. Finally, she'd need to fill and seal the food in serving containers, label them and store them safely until it was time to make her deliveries. Which it would take most of Friday to accomplish.

She did not have time to do all that and tear the kitchen apart, too.

But what choice did she have? She couldn't ignore the grime and hope it went away. Any health inspector worth his salt would shut her down in a heartbeat the instant he saw so much as a speck of gritty sawdust on the pots and pans. Which would put her out of business before she even got started. Besides, she would not, could not, risk making someone sick. Not in her kitchen.

There was nothing for it—she'd have to postpone the opening of Royal Meals. That meant calling each one of her customers, apologizing profusely for the delay and offering them a substantial discount for the inconvenience. Which was money out of her pocket. And money, like time, was also something she couldn't afford to waste.

Where was a gold doubloon when you needed one?

"Ahhhhhh!" Frustration churned her stomach, and she groaned. Marching to the counter, she ripped her carefully constructed timeline from the notepad, scrunched it into a ball and pitched it toward the trash can.

"Problems?" Her hands gripping the bath towel she'd been folding, Jen appeared in the doorway wearing a worried frown.

"Stupid sawdust!" Kim exclaimed as if Jen should know what she was talking about.

"I'm not sure I'm following." Tucking the short edge of the towel under her chin, Jen folded the thick terrycloth in thirds. She turned it and repeated the process lengthwise. "What's the problem?"

Kim heaved a sigh. "The problem is somehow sawdust found its way inside the plastic barrier. Everything inside the cabinets on this side of the kitchen is covered in it." She gestured across the room toward the sink and stove. "Those are okay."

"Really?" Disbelief turned Jen's tone dry. Stuffing the folded towel under her arm, she opened the nearest cupboard. The platter she pulled out looked dull despite the bright sunshine that streamed through the windows. She ran the white towel across the surface and stared at the clean swath it left behind. "Crap. You say this is everywhere? What about the cups and plates in the dining room?"

Kim's heart rate stuttered. The Jenkinses and the Smiths had helped themselves to sweet rolls and coffee yesterday. Had she poisoned their guests? For an instant, her world turned dark. There was something she needed to remember, but a roaring noise in her head made it difficult to think.

Calm down.

Propping her hands on her knees, she bent at the waist. Deliberately, she forced herself to take several deep breaths. Her heart rate slowed. The darkness receded, and finally, her memory cleared. Relief weakened her knees. She sank onto a chair.

"All the dishes and cups from the sideboard were in storage. I unpacked and washed them all myself last week." Once she and Jen and their cousins had cleaned the house from top to bottom—except, apparently, the kitchen—the women had spent the rest of the week emptying the boxes of knickknacks and table linens, framed photographs and, yes, the dishes from the dining room.

"And the plates we've been eating off all week?"

"They're okay. They were better sealed, I guess."

"Thank goodness for small favors."

"It doesn't matter. They'll all have to be washed anyway. We can't risk not doing it. I can't, at least." She shuddered a breath. "I tore this kitchen apart and put it back together when I first got here. Even with Diane's help, it took all day. I don't have that much slack time built into my schedule. I won't be able to open Royal Meals this week after all."

Fighting tears, she shook her head. What had she been thinking, trying to launch her own catering business? She wasn't a businesswoman. Not a boss. She was an admin, or at least, she had been until Connors Industrial had merged with a larger company and she'd lost her job. She should have seen that coming. Just like she should have known Frank was a con artist. Her entire life had been a series of bad decisions.

Going into business for herself was just another one of them.

"Not so fast. Before you postpone, let's think about this," Jen protested.

"You're right. You're so right. I shouldn't postpone. I should quit altogether." Sure, she'd be out the money she'd spent for licenses and special equipment and a few groceries. But what was a couple hundred dollars compared to falling flat on her face?

"Whoa! Take a breath. That's not what I meant at all." Jen fixed her with a hard gaze. "How'd you go straight to quitting? Don't you want to run a catering business? Isn't that your dream?"

"Yeah, but I'm not ready. I don't know enough. I'm not even a chef."

"No, but you're a darned good cook."

Kim tugged at her apron and scrunched the skirt between her hands. "Some cook I am. Would you like a side of sawdust with your lemon chicken?" she asked in a mocking tone.

"Hold on. This is not your fault. Plus, you didn't serve sawdust to your customers. You double-checked to make sure everything was spic-and-span before you started. Doesn't that sound like the kind of thing a smart, savvy business owner would do?"

"I guess," Kim said, but she didn't think she'd convinced anyone. Least of all herself.

"You know I'm right," Jen insisted. "Look at how meticulously you've planned everything." She retrieved Kim's schedule, placed it on the counter and smoothed out the wrinkles. "You've put months into getting ready for this moment. Are you really going to let a little sawdust stop you in your tracks?"

"I don't think I can—"

"I don't think you can let us all down," Jen interrupted. "You know we're all rooting for you. Think about this for a minute. Do you want Nat or Caitlyn to think it's okay to quit the first time things get a little bit difficult?"

"Well, no." Thinking of herself as a role model forced Kim to admit she might have overreacted a tad. "Okay. I won't quit, but I still have to postpone the opening. There just aren't enough hours in the day to take care of this mess and do all the other things I need to do."

"Let's think about that." Jen walked to the chair closest to Kim's and sat. "You were planning to get groceries today, cook for the next three days, make deliveries on Friday, right?"

Kim blinked. Jen had been listening—really listening—when she'd reviewed her plans. "Yes," she said slowly.

"So you have a list of what you need at the store."

"I don't know what good that will do, but yeah."

"Why couldn't Belle and Aunt Margaret do the shopping for you while they're out this morning? That way, you and I can get started on all this." Jen swept a hand through the air.

As much as she appreciated the offer, Kim felt her shoulders droop. "We'll never finish in time."

"We won't if we don't try." Jen put her hand on one hip. "You could use a change in attitude, Big Sis."

Kim studied the floor. Her sister made a valid point. She raised her eyes to Jen's. "You really think we can pull this off?"

"What's the worst that can happen?"

"We don't finish and I have to delay the opening after all."

"It's early yet, not even nine o'clock. Let's see how far we get today, and then we'll know for sure, but I think we can do it." Jen's gaze swept over the kitchen as though she were taking inventory. "Let me put another load of towels in the washer. Including this one." She hefted the one she'd used on the plate. "After that, I'll be at your command. Meantime, you call Belle and tell her exactly what you need her to pick up. Better yet, snap a picture of your shopping list and text it to her."

"Good idea." As Kim whipped her phone out of her back pocket, she felt the first faint stirrings of hope. Maybe, just maybe, with her sister's help, she could get Royal Meals—and her dreams—back on track.

The clear blue winter sky had darkened to a deep velvet by the time Kim slid the freshly scrubbed ice cream maker onto a high shelf and closed the cabinet door. "That's it." She climbed down from the stepstool. "I can't believe we did it."

She surveyed the bedraggled group of women who'd dropped whatever they were doing this morning in answer to her sister's all-hands-on-deck text. Jen had been a godsend—summoning the others and then working all day without complaint. Amy, who'd been looking at property with Max, had pulled an abrupt U-turn in the middle of busy US 1 and sped to the inn. She'd been washing dishes ever since. Diane had returned to the inn after walking out of a meeting with the owner of the hardware store in town. She'd returned to the inn and dashed upstairs, where she'd shucked her suit in favor of jeans and a sweatshirt. Standing beside Amy, she'd spent the entire day rinsing and drying everything from vegetable peelers to crockpots. Nat, meanwhile, had taken charge of the shelf liner, measuring and cutting like a pro, while Belle and Kim had spent hours hauling dirty cutlery and cookware out of drawers and off shelves and putting it all back once it was clean again. Even Aunt Margaret had gotten in on the act. Determined to keep the inn's guests out of the kitchen—and out of their hair—she'd doled out coupons good for lunch at the Pirate's Gold Diner to the Smiths and the Jenkinses.

Kim knew she'd never be able to thank her family enough for all they'd done. Determined to try, she began, "I could never have accomplished all this without your help."

"That's what family is for, isn't it?" Margaret asked from her seat at the kitchen table.

"We're here for you," Belle insisted, while Amy nodded.

"Besides, I have a vested interest in this catering business." Diane shoved the sleeves of her sweatshirt a little higher. "My taste buds are already looking forward to Friday."

LEIGH DUNCAN

Kim grinned. She'd offered to provide meals for the family in exchange for using the kitchen. "I'll do my best," she said before turning to Jen.

"Thanks for the tough sisterly love," she whispered in Jen's ear. "You kept me from making a big mistake."

"Aw. I just gave you a little push." Jen prodded her ribs. "You would have figured it out on your own, eventually."

Footsteps sounded from the stairs seconds before Caitlyn, who'd taken one look at the beehive of activity in the kitchen when she'd come in from school and made herself scarce, appeared in the doorway. She rubbed her tummy. "I'm hungry. What's for dinner?"

Kim checked the time. It was after seven. The teen was probably famished. For that matter, they all were. "How about something simple, like pancakes and eggs?" She reached for a skillet.

"Don't you dare," ordered Amy. "We are not messing up this spotless kitchen."

"Okay." Kim snatched her fingers away from the cabinet. Thinking, she rubbed her hands together. "Why don't I order pizza then?"

Caitlyn didn't need to be asked twice. "I want veggie," the teen piped.

"That sounds good, but I'd like a salad," Belle said.

298

"Vegetable pizza and salad," Kim noted.

"Anyone like pepperoni?" Amy asked.

Jen raised a hand. "I do."

"Anything's good with me," Diane said. "How about you, Aunt Margaret?" She turned to face her aunt.

"Don't worry about me. I can pick off the toppings if I don't like them," Margaret said.

"Get one plain cheese, okay?" Belle said over her mother's head.

"Got it. Three large pizzas—one vegetable, one pepperoni, one cheese. And salads," Kim recited. Her budget might be limited, but it would stretch far enough to cover dinner. After all, it was the least she could do to repay everyone who'd interrupted their own plans in order to come to her aid.

Nine

Belle

*B*eyond the deck, a soft breeze sighed through the stands of bird-of-paradise that dotted the yard. The orange trees near the rear of the property had bloomed. As the sky darkened, the air carried the sweet, citrusy scent of the blossoms. A bull alligator bellowed from the river, his mating cry informing everyone for miles around that they weren't the only ones enjoying the change in the weather.

"I can't believe how warm it turned. Pretty sweet for the middle of winter, isn't it?" Glancing at the others gathered around the table on the back porch, Belle plucked at the navy blue T-shirt she'd paired with lightweight seersucker pants. In January, no less. Though she'd never regret trading her snow galoshes for flip-flops, her cashmere coat, scarf and wool sweater for short sleeves and cotton tees, or her long johns for capri pants, she fretted that the clothes she'd worn last year were just a touch snugger than they should be.

"Don't put away all your winter sweaters just yet," Diane cautioned from her seat on the other side of the glass-topped table. "You know what they say—if you don't like the weather in Florida, just wait five minutes. It'll change."

"I heard a cold front is supposed to blow in by next week," Jen offered.

Belle crossed her fingers. Rain usually accompanied a change in the weather. She hoped the approaching front would hold off at least until Jason left. Or would he find Florida's January heat wave too stifling? The last time she'd checked, New Yorkers were digging out after a record-breaking snowfall. It rarely snowed in Florida, unless orange blossom petals counted. Those fell from the trees in flurries when the wind blew hard. They did have sand, though. Miles and miles of white, sandy beaches.

She felt a chill that had nothing to do with cold air and everything to do with Jason's plans for the weekend. If the warm weather lingered, he'd expect to spend at least one afternoon at the

LEIGH DUNCAN

beach, wouldn't he? Which meant she'd have to
wear a bathing suit. More to the point, he'd *see*
her in said bathing suit. She tugged again at the
T-shirt that felt as if it had shrunk two sizes since
the day she'd picked it up in a little boutique in
Soho. Sucking in her stomach, she straightened
as the French doors opened and Kim walked
onto the porch holding a shallow pan with
scalloped edges between thick oven mitts.

"What's this?" Belle asked, praying the dish
contained some fat-reducing miracle food.

"It's a seafood dip—crab and shrimp baked
with three different cheeses. If you like it, I want
to add it to the menu for Royal Meals."

Not exactly diet food. Belle suppressed a quiet
groan.

"Sounds heavenly." Amy leaned forward to
get a better look. She drew in a deep breath.
"Hmmm. It smells yummy."

"Careful, the dish is hot," Kim warned. She
lowered the pan onto a trivet in the center of the
table and, peeling the gloves from her hands,
blotted her forehead. "I'll be right back with the
crackers and another pitcher of sangria."

"I'll get that for you, Mom. You've been on
your feet all day." Nat sprang from her chair.
Gently but firmly, she steered Kim into a vacant
seat.

"Could you grab a couple of carrots while you're up?" Belle asked, while she tried her best to ignore the tantalizing aroma wafting out of the casserole dish. Determined to distract herself while the others took turns helping themselves to the dip, she turned to Kim. "How'd your first set of deliveries go?" Once they'd scoured the kitchen from top to bottom, her cousin had worked in the kitchen from sunup to sundown, making sure every item on her menu was sheer perfection.

"It wasn't a complete disaster," Kim allowed. "Although there were a couple of last-minute hiccups that had me pulling my hair out one minute and questioning my sanity for going into business at my age the next."

"Oh?" Belle's interest flared. "That sounds only a little bit ominous. Do tell."

Kim glanced toward the kitchen where her daughter bustled about. Her voice dropping to a near whisper, she leaned forward. "Nat insisted on taking pictures of each of the dishes on today's menu. She said she needed them for the website, but I had to stop what I was doing every five minutes so she could get the right shot. It really put a crimp in my schedule."

"Her photography is top-notch." Belle had studied the girl's posts on social media. "Plus, the photos she took of the inn are simply stunning." She waved a hand, turning down Amy's offer to spoon dip onto her plate.

"She's very talented. I can't wait until she finishes the website for Royal Meals." Kim's eyes tracked her daughter's movements through the panes of glass in the door. "I just didn't plan on how much of my time it would take. Now that I know, I'll allow for it going forward."

Belle checked on Nat. At the counter, the younger woman hefted a tray that held a pitcher and two bowls. "She's coming," she warned.

Kim put a finger to her mouth. "Hush. Don't say a word. I don't want her to think I'm complaining."

"Don't worry. Your secret's safe with us," Amy said.

When Nat stepped onto the porch less than a minute later, the girl hurried to the table. "What'd I miss?" she asked as she handed the pitcher of sangria to her mom.

"Nothing," Belle assured her niece. "Your mom was telling us about her first-day hiccups."

"But I saved the best for you, honey." Kim patted the empty chair next to hers before she filled her glass with the fruity blend of wine and spice.

"So what happened? We'd already loaded

your car when I left to take the Smiths and the Jenkinses to the airport." Nat passed the bowl of crackers to Amy and a smaller one filled with baby carrots to Belle.

"My car battery died," Kim said in measured tones. "And no one else was here." She made the rounds of those at the table, starting with her daughter. "You were on the airport run." She nodded to Diane. "You'd gone to the school." Attendance had been mandatory at an organizational meeting prior to the start of soccer team tryouts next week. Kim's focus shifted to Amy. "You and Jen were at the bakery."

"And I'd taken Mama to her hair appointment," Belle finished. She rolled one of the carrots around on her plate. Too late, she'd realized she should have asked for celery instead and saved herself a few more calories.

"Right." Kim pulled a face. "So there I was, with a car full of perishable food and a dead battery."

"Oh, no!" Amy clamped a hand over her mouth, muffling her next few words. "What'd you do?"

Mirth twinkled in Kim's eyes. "I did what any self-respecting gal with a boyfriend would do." She took a drink and returned her glass to the table. "I called Craig."

"And he came?" Diane wanted to know.

"My hero." With a sly smile, Kim pressed her hands together against her lips like she was praying. "He walked out of the middle of a town council meeting to bring me a set of jumper cables."

"No, he didn't." A mix of shock and admiration filled Jen's voice. And no wonder. In a small town like Emerald Bay, the only thing worse than walking out of a council meeting was showing up at church on Easter Sunday with booze on your breath.

"He did!" Kim laughed. "It's a wonder none of the council members had a heart attack. He got here just like that." She snapped her fingers. "Then, once he gave me a jump, he followed me to my first two stops, just to make sure I didn't have any more problems."

"He's a keeper," Belle said, not entirely sure she kept the sharp note of envy from her voice. Craig treated Kim like a queen—his latest actions proved how much he valued their relationship. Amy had apparently found her Mr. Right, too. Not only was Max a good-looking guy who fit in well with the rest of the family, he was taking time away from his own business to help Amy search for a second location for her bakery.

That made two of her cousins who'd struck it rich in the dating game.

Would she be as lucky with Jason?

Other than the not-so-little matter of dropping her from Noble Records, the man seemed heaven-bent on impressing her at every turn. From the wonderful dinner they'd shared at Georgio's to the amazing night they'd spent sightseeing in New York, he'd been well on his way to proving himself to be one in a million, even before Christmas. As for his gift, well, nothing could top that.

This weekend, though...

Belle broke one of her carrots in two. This weekend was most likely a turning point in their relationship. Not that she was going to sleep with Jason. Not that or anything even close. But this *was* technically their third date, the point where most couples decided whether to move forward or cut their losses and call it quits. And here she was—practically penniless, her career in tatters and living with her mother.

Some catch, huh?

"How's your car?" Belle gave her eyes a quick brush when Diane's question reeled her attention back to the ongoing conversation.

"It's fine." Despite the reassurance, Kim's

brow creased. "I must have left the lights on or something, because the battery is practically brand-new. I replaced it before I left Atlanta. I stopped at the auto shop after I finished with the deliveries and had Mike check the levels, just to be sure. He said everything's good." The tension eased from her face, and she held her glass high. "It might not have been the most auspicious start, but it was a start. Here's to Royal Meals!"

"The beginning of something great," Jen added. Glasses clinked as everyone toasted Kim's success.

Joining in the celebration, Belle continued to hold her sangria aloft. She motioned to the others before she turned to Kim. "Do you have any idea how much I—how much we all—admire you? Going into business for yourself at this stage of your life isn't easy, but you've done it. We are all so proud of you!"

When Kim's face turned a lovely shade of pink, Belle allowed herself one tiny sip of wine. She scooched back in her seat, listening while the others heaped compliments on their cousin. Kim deserved every bit of their praise.

But did she have enough courage to follow her cousin's example?

Belle clenched her teeth and swallowed against the uncertainty that washed over her.

Lately, she felt like she was at a loss on so many fronts. After talking with her mom, she'd spent countless hours praying about how best to handle the gift she'd been given. She hadn't gotten so much as a whisper of a response. Okay, maybe she did feel a pull in one direction, but following it meant navigating some pretty murky depths with very little chance she'd succeed. It was going to take an awful lot more than just a tiny tug on her heartstrings to make her take that leap. A bright neon sign with a flashing arrow that said, "This Way," would be nice, she thought.

If that was her only worry, it'd be enough to encourage her first gray hair to take root, but she remained solidly on the fence about the inn's future. Over the past few months, the people she loved most in the world had gravitated to the inn. What would happen to them if and when they sold the place? Her mom had agreed to move to Emerald Oaks, but would she really be happy there? Kim's catering business was just getting off the ground—where was she going to find another commercial kitchen? Diane and Caitlyn had been through so much this past year, it seemed unfair to uproot them again and make them find another place to live. For that matter, where would she go? Even if her career did take off again—a slim possibility, at best—could she really jet off to who knew where and leave her mother sitting alone in the assisted living facility?

"Earth to Belle. Come in, Belle."

Belle snapped to attention. She felt her face redden when she realized everyone at the table was staring at her. "What?" she grumbled.

"Amy asked why you weren't having any of this delicious dip," Jen said.

"Why are you torturing that poor carrot, Aunt Belle?" Nat asked. "What did it ever do to you?"

Belle stared at her plate. Lost in her thoughts, she'd broken the tiny carrot into a hundred pieces. Reaching for a napkin, she wiped a few flecks of orange pulp from her fingers.

"Sorry," she apologized. "My thoughts are all over the place tonight. I'm afraid I'm not very good company. I should turn in." The last thing she wanted was to step into the limelight on this, Kim's night to shine. Her chair legs scraped against the deck's wooden planks as she pushed away from the table.

"Hold on." Kim's hand grasped Belle's wrist. "You've done so much for everyone else, and we never get a chance to help you. What's going on?"

"Yeah. Anything in particular bothering you?" Jen asked.

"Nothing," Belle insisted. Traitorous tears filled her eyes. "Everything," she whispered.

"Oh, it's like that, is it?" Diane's voice was steeped in sympathy. "I've been there."

"We all have," Jen said pointedly. "So out with it."

The way her cousin's gaze locked with hers told Belle no one would let the matter drop until she came clean. But where did she start? There was so much. Her career. Her soul. Her home. Her relationship with a man who may or may not be *the one*.

Not ready to discuss the former, not even with her cousins, she latched onto the one topic she could discuss. "I'm nervous about Jason's visit," she said, hating the way her voice trembled.

"You? Nervous?" Diane's eyebrows lifted.

"Don't laugh." Belle bent under the heavy mantle of worry on her shoulders. "I might look fine on the outside, but inside, I'm a basket case."

"When's he get here?" Nat wanted to know.

"His plane lands in Orlando at nine."

"I checked his rooms myself. They're spotless." Jen spoke with some authority. She'd been helping Margaret more and more with the hostess duties and took her new role very seriously.

Belle breathed a quick, "Thank you," glad to have one less thing to worry about. Not that her worries were in short supply. She cast about, hoping to rid herself of another one. Though darkness had fallen while they lingered at the table, the moon shone down on the long line of arborvitae that stood between the cottages and the parking area. The trees had grown bushy, unkempt. She cleared her throat. "Um, do you think we could get Miguel and his guys to trim the hedges before Jason gets here?"

Kim only shook her head. "The gardeners don't work on weekends."

"I was afraid you'd say that." Belle gave a dissatisfied sniff. "I guess I could get up early and do them myself."

"Are you nuts?" Amy sucked in a horrified gasp. "Don't you remember when Daddy and Uncle Eric would trim those bushes? It took them all day back then, and they're a lot taller now. You'd need a ladder."

"Besides, the grounds look a lot better than they were when we first got here. Remember how overgrown everything was then? Miguel and his crew have done a fantastic job with the landscaping," Kim said.

Belle turned her glass in a slow circle. "But Jason didn't see the before. He'll only see the now. Everything needs to be perfect so he's not disappointed."

"It's not going to be perfect," Jen insisted. "I mean, think about it. We've put a huge amount of work into the place, but the exterior still needs paint. The landscaping is a work in progress. I think the best you can hope for is charming." Her eyes narrowed, and her focus seemed to sharpen to a laser point. "Besides, he's not coming to see the inn. He's coming to see you."

"Which is another part of the problem," Belle said with a moan. "Except for our spa day on New Year's, I haven't had a facial in months. My hair needs a trim, but I can't afford a trip to New York to see my stylist. To top it all off, I've gained five pounds! Nothing fits right anymore." To demonstrate, she plucked at the T-shirt that strained across her chest.

The soft but insistent touch of Kim's hand on her arm forced Belle to pay attention. "I remember you wearing that shirt when you first got here. I loved it then, and I love it now. If you've gained weight, it's muscle mass from all the stair work you've been doing."

"And the running. Don't forget that," Diane added.

Belle traced the outline of one thigh with her free hand. Her cousins were making a valid point.

313

In New York, she'd hired a personal trainer who put her through intense workouts that hadn't burned as many calories as the five-mile runs she took along the beach every morning. Or the twenty treks she made up and down the stairs each day.

Amy cut to the chase. "It's time you found out what Jason really wants. Does he want to be seen with 'the Belle Dane'?" She enclosed the words in air quotes. "Or does he like you for yourself?"

"That is the question, isn't it?" Belle said wistfully. "He told me once that I was the reason he took the job in New York in the first place. But will he love the woman who looks positively frightful until she has her morning cup of coffee?"

"You need to ask yourself the same kinds of questions," Diane cautioned. "Why are you dating him? Because he's a nice guy from Queens who made it good? Or because he has the power to restore your career?"

Belle flinched. "Do you really think I'm that shallow?"

"No," Diane said firmly. "Do you think Jason is?"

Thinking of their secluded table at Georgio's and the steps he'd taken to protect her from the paparazzi the night they'd played tourist, she said, "I don't think so, but I guess we'll find out soon enough."

"If he doesn't want you for yourself, he's not the man for you, Aunt Belle," Nat said.

"Believe me, you're better off finding that out now than later," Kim added with a comforting tap on Belle's arm.

"I couldn't have said it better," Amy agreed.

They fell silent for a few beats before Kim yawned. "Sorry. I think the week—and the wine—are starting to catch up with me."

"I guess that's my cue. I'd better turn in. I have to get up early to pick Jason up at the airport in the morning."

Wine sloshed against the sides when Kim picked up her glass. She leaned to clink the rim against Nat's. "To a weekend of discovery."

"I'll drink to that." Belle hoisted her own glass and took a sip. But just a sip. Because, while she'd taken her cousins' advice to heart, there was no sense in being foolish.

Even at nine o'clock on a Saturday morning, the Orlando Airport lived up to its reputation as one of the busiest airports in the country. Belle felt an uncomfortable bead of sweat trickle down her back while she struggled to follow the directions mounted on large green signs over the roadway without hitting—or being struck by— any of the hundreds of other drivers who were intent on escaping the crowded airport as quickly as possible.

"I should have taken Nat up on her offer to drive," she muttered when she narrowly made it onto the ramp that led to Passenger Arrivals on the second level of one of four terminals. At least Nat knew the lay of the land. Belle didn't, and she'd quickly realized how much things had changed in the twenty-plus years since she'd last made an airport run on her own. Now there were more roads, more cars, more everything. But wanting to have those first few minutes alone with Jason, she'd opted to drive herself.

She hoped that didn't turn out to be a big mistake.

Spotting Jason's long, lean figure exiting the baggage area up ahead, Belle tightened her grip on the steering wheel. Cars, trucks and vans crowded all four lanes of the pickup zone, but traffic had practically come to a standstill in the two inside lanes, where arriving passengers hurriedly loaded their assortment of suitcases and backpacks into waiting vehicles. It didn't help that police officers patrolled the areas closest to the doors with a religious fervor. Blowing whistles and shouting at drivers to, "Move along! Move along!" they added to the cacophony of screeching tires, blowing horns and rumbling engines.

Her turn signal flashing, Belle eased to the right, where a space barely the length of the sedan had opened between a van and an oversized SUV. She prayed the SUV's driver would let her cut in, and when he slammed on his brakes rather than ramming into the back of her car, she gave him a friendly wave. She shouldn't have bothered. All she got for her efforts was a not-so-friendly blast from his horn. Undaunted, she searched for another hole in the ebb and flow of traffic, determined to make it all the way to the curb before she came even with the spot where she'd last seen Jason.

She'd crept a few inches closer when a tap on her passenger window made her jump. Red curls spilled over her shoulder as she swiveled toward the unexpected noise. Recognition settled her nerves the instant she spotted a man's torso on the other side of the glass. She breathed a sigh of relief while she simultaneously popped the lock. Two seconds later, the car filled with Jason's spicy, manly scent as he slid onto the seat beside her. In quick order, he stowed one duffle between his feet and tossed a leather coat along with a smaller bag into the back.

"Whew! This place is a madhouse!"

Jason's deep timbre sucked up all the oxygen in the car and sent shivers down Belle's spine. Or was it the quick kiss he'd planted on her cheek? Either way, she struggled to hear the rest.

"I'd never have agreed to let you pick me up if I'd known it was this busy. I'm so sorry. I should have insisted on hiring a car and driver."

"Welcome to Orlando." Belle hid a sudden bout of nerves behind a soft laugh. Arriving at the airport wasn't the best introduction to the city. "Did you have a good flight?"

Without waiting for an answer, she goosed the gas pedal. The car surged forward twenty feet before she had to brake for a passenger van that had stopped dead ahead in the middle of the travel lane.

"It was all right. A bit bumpy toward the end. The pilot said we were skirting a storm, but it felt like we flew right through it." Jason's seatbelt clicked into place. "It's been a while since I've flown commercial, and I'd almost forgotten how hectic it is. Even in First Class." He shoved his bag to the side to give his feet more room.

"It's good to see you." As much as she'd been looking forward to drinking in Jason's presence, she forced herself to peer into the side mirror and watch for a chance to merge into the exit lane.

"You, too. It's been too long. I was hoping to get down here earlier, but things have been their own brand of crazy at the office." He heaved an unhappy sigh. "I don't mind saying you left some pretty big shoes to fill."

Belle tried not to grimace. She hated that Jason had to deal with the fallout, but leaving Noble Records hadn't exactly been her choice. Rather than dredge up the past, though, she focused on the present. "Your timing is actually perfect. Well, except for the rain. But that should clear off by this afternoon." She'd woken to gray skies and intermittent downpours, the leading edge of the storm front Jen had mentioned.

"Even more reason why I hate that you had to come and pick me up."

"Oh, but I wanted to." She flashed Jason one of her best smiles before she gestured to the cars that swerved left and right, jockeying for position like performers in some weird form of dance. "It's worth all this for the chance to have you all to myself for a while. I'm not sure how much alone time we'll have once we get to the inn."

"Expecting a crowd?" Jason asked.

"Just the usual. Besides yours, four of the suites are occupied this weekend, but our guests normally have places to go and things to do during the day. The rest are family. Mama will be there, of course." She ran down the list of her cousins and their daughters, who were all too eager to check out the new man in her life. When she finished, she said, "Consider this your only warning: There will be hugs."

She tapped her fingers on the steering wheel while she waited for Jason's reaction. Meanwhile, apparently oblivious to the others around him, the van's driver nonchalantly walked to the back of his vehicle, where he opened the lift gate. He beckoned a woman and three school-age children who stood at the curb loaded down with a variety of suitcases and backpacks. Belle held her breath when the group began threading their way through the crush of vehicles.

"I think I can handle a hug or two. Especially from your mom."

Jason might have said more, but his words were lost when the driver of the SUV behind them laid on his horn in earnest. Unable to do anything but wait and watch until the woman and her children reached the van, stowed their belongings and climbed in, Belle only tsked.

She did, however, follow closely when the van finally began to move. With the traffic in motion once again, her grip on the steering wheel relaxed as she left the chaos of the arrivals area behind.

Her relief didn't last long. The instant her car emerged from the covered pickup area, rain pelted the roof and sluiced down the windshield. The pounding rain and the steady swish of the wipers turned the car into a cocoon, a noisy one.

Forced to raise her voice, she suggested, "Would you like to stop for a bite to eat before we head back?" It was usually a ninety-minute drive to the inn, but the rain would probably slow them down.

"Thanks, but I'm good." Jason's deep voice sent another delightful shiver down her back. "I grabbed a breakfast sandwich on my way to the airport."

"There's water in the console if you want it." Belle gave a quick nod toward the two bottles that sat in the cup holders.

"Now that, I'll take you up on." He lifted one of the bottles, unscrewed the cap and took a long swallow.

Realizing they hadn't made any specific plans for the weekend, she asked, "Anywhere in particular you want to go or anything you want to do while you're here?" She mentally crossed her fingers while she prayed visiting a theme park wasn't high on his list as she exited the airport proper onto the Beachline, which ran in nearly a straight line from Orlando to Cocoa Beach.

"Not really. I wouldn't mind catching some rays." Jason peered between the swish of wiper blades, but there wasn't much to see besides rain and the red glow of taillights. "If the weather clears up, that is."

"Tomorrow should be beautiful," Belle assured him. "A little cooler than it has been the past few days but much warmer than New York."

"Great! That gives me two whole days to thaw out." Jason gave an exaggerated shiver. "How about dinner tonight? I read about a place down in Vero Beach that sounds good—Citrus Grillhouse?"

Belle couldn't help it—she stiffened. Known for trendy food and impeccable service, Citrus wasn't exactly the kind of place she could wander into after a day at the beach. Going there meant being on display, and *that* required a full day of primping. A day she'd much rather spend getting to know Jason better. She cleared her throat. "Dinner sounds great, but would you mind if we chose someplace where we'd be a little less likely to be noticed?" She glanced his way just in time to see a flicker of understanding light his gray eyes.

"Someplace like Georgio's?" he asked.

"Georgio's, Florida-style." She grinned. "There's a quirky place in Vero Beach we like. Waldo's. My family and I have been going there practically forever. The food's good. Best of all, they know me and will respect our privacy."

Jason held up a hand. "No need to explain. All I want to do is spend a quiet weekend with you. Where we go and what we do—that's just window dressing."

"That's exactly how I feel." Finding out they wanted the same thing sent a reassuring burst of warmth through Belle's midsection. Though taking her hand off the wheel probably wasn't a good idea, she risked it long enough to give Jason's hand a quick squeeze.

A semitruck thundered past, its tires kicking up a heavy spray of water. With both hands on the wheel again, she made a snap decision. She'd been planning to drive straight to the coast and follow scenic A1A south to Emerald Bay. But the relentless rain hid the world behind a thick curtain. Under the circumstances, it made sense to take the quickest, if not the prettiest, route back to the inn. Hoping the skies would clear by the time they reached the turnoff for Emerald Bay, she flipped on her turn signal and merged onto the exit for I-95.

If anything, the storm only grew worse the farther south they drove. At one point, the rain pounded on the roof and hood of the car with such vengeance that she and Jason had to shout to be heard above the racket. Rather than fight it, they fell silent. As much as she'd looked forward to spending this time alone with Jason, Belle had to admit she was glad they'd given up on trying to talk. Driving through near white-out conditions required all her concentration.

"Finally," Belle breathed when the rain eased. "I was beginning to think…"

One glance at Jason and she forgot whatever she'd been about to say. Poor thing, she thought, noting his chin resting on his chest, his closed eyes, his breathing soft and even. Her expression shifted into a soft smile. He'd probably pushed back the covers and rolled out of bed in the middle of the night in order to take the first flight out of LaGuardia this morning. No wonder he'd fallen asleep. And that was just as well. Though the intensity had lessened, the rain still came down in sheets that made it impossible to see much more than the spray of water coming off the tires of the vehicles in front of them.

An hour passed before Jason woke with a start when she stopped for a light. "Whoa!" His head swung. "Where are we?"

Belle smiled. "We're nearly there. Another couple of miles."

He stretched. "I can't believe I went out like that. I wanted to keep you company."

"Believe me, with all this rain, you didn't miss anything. I thought you probably needed the rest—you said you'd been going at it pretty hard lately."

"I have." His smile turned sheepish. "I hope I didn't snore too loudly."

"I wouldn't have heard it if you had." She lifted her fingers from the wheel long enough to point at the storm clouds overhead. When he remained doubtful, she let her smile deepen. "Don't worry. You didn't make a sound."

"That's good." He reached for his water bottle. "I'd hate for something like that to ruin my chances."

It'd be so easy to reassure him, she thought. After all, he was bright and personable, he made her laugh, and oh, boy, was he easy on the eyes. Plus, he obviously cared for her...a lot. But she had to be fair, had to make sure she was getting involved with him for all the right reasons and, perhaps even more important, none of the wrong ones. As Diane had suggested, she needed to be sure she didn't see him as her ticket back into the recording studio. She wasn't exactly certain how to do that, but until she knew in her heart that she liked him—or even loved him—for himself, she couldn't let their relationship move beyond a casual friendship.

"We're here," she said, slowing when she spotted the familiar sign for the Dane Crown Inn at the side of the road.

Hampered by his seatbelt, Jason leaned forward.

Seconds later, she braced for his reaction as she turned onto the crushed coquina drive that led to the parking area. Once called "the jewel of the Treasure Coast," the inn had lost its sparkle long ago, and though she and her cousins had spent the last three months working on the place, they had even more to accomplish if they were ever going to restore the inn to its former glory.

The main house came into view, giving them their first glimpse of a wide wrap-around porch on a sprawling, two-story structure that sat on a low rise. The grounds in front gradually sloped down to sand dunes and the beach beyond them while palm trees and other tropical plants adorned the back of the property that stretched clear to the river. Belle offered up silent thanks for the cloudy skies that cast a favorable light on the inn. In the midday gloom, she could barely tell that paint on the green shutters had faded or that the white porch rail was chipped in places.

"Home, sweet home, such as it is." Steering away from the parking area, she braked to a stop near the front steps.

"This is…"

Belle stilled, waiting for Jason's reaction.

"This is beautiful." Interest flickered in the gray eyes Jason turned toward her. "This is where you grew up?"

Was that admiration she heard in his voice?

"Born and raised." Belle felt tension roll off her shoulders. "My grandfather came here in the early Sixties. He and my grandmother built the inn. Of their four children, two left to make their own way in the world, but my mom and her sister stayed on. They married and raised their families right here. I grew up working in the inn along with my cousins."

"I envy you. Hardly anyone has roots like that anymore."

She shook her head. "You have that, too. Didn't you grow up in Queens?"

"Not really, no. Our house was just the place where my parents spent time when they weren't touring with the band." Jason's parents were key players in a well-known rock band. "But you, you have this amazing heritage." He gestured out the window.

"Yes, well." She blinked, unable to tell him the Dane Crown Inn would become some other family's heritage before too much longer. She glanced at the sky. The rain had stopped for now, but the clouds overhead looked dark and threatening. She made a note to check the weather reports. Though Florida's weather changed on a dime, this storm looked like it might stick around for a while. "Let's get inside while we have the chance."

They gathered Jason's belongings from the car and dashed along the walkway. In honor of his first visit to her family's inn, she led them up the steps and across the wide porch to the main entrance. Belle wasn't at all surprised when her mother greeted them at the front door.

"Welcome to the Dane Crown Inn," Margaret said before Belle had a chance to make introductions. "You must be Jason. We're so glad to have you join us this weekend."

"Thank you for having me, Mrs. Clayton." Jason extended a hand. "Belle has told me so much about you and your beautiful home. I'm glad to finally meet you and see this place in person."

"Oh, posh. Call me Margaret. Please."

Belle bit her tongue when, in a motion she'd probably learned at her mother's knee, her mom grasped the man's hand and drew him in like an angler reeled in a catch. Slipping her free hand around Jason's shoulder, Margaret leaned to greet him with a warm, welcoming hug. "We're delighted to have you," she said, relinquishing her hold on him just as smoothly.

Jason gave her mom a long, contemplative study before he turned just enough for Belle to see the twinkle in his gray eyes. "You never told me your mom was so beautiful," he chided. "It's easy to see where you got your good looks."

Though she'd probably heard some version of the compliment before, Margaret's blue eyes sparkled. "You give me far too much credit, I'm afraid," she demurred despite the color high in her cheeks.

"Hey, Belle." Footsteps clomped in the hallway. "You want me to move the car for you?" Jen asked.

Belle hid a grin behind one hand. She didn't doubt for a minute that her cousins had been chomping at the bit for the chance to meet Jason. Sure enough, she spotted Kim trailing along right behind her sister.

"That'd be great," she told Jen. "But first..." She took a breath. "Jason, this is my cousin Jen.

And her sister, Kim. Jen, Kim, this is Jason. Oh, and this is Nat, Kim's daughter," she added when the younger woman stepped into view.

While the trio exchanged hugs and greetings with Jason, Diane and Caitlyn emerged from one of the back rooms where they'd undoubtedly been waiting for the right moment to put in an appearance. Another round of introductions ensued. When it was over, Jason quietly asked, "Is that everyone?"

"Except for Scott and Amy, Diane's brother and sister," Margaret answered before Belle had a chance. "Scott is an attorney. Amy is probably at Sweet Cakes—she owns the bakery in town."

Belle nudged Jason with her elbow. "I hope you're good with names. There'll be a test later."

"Wait, wait." Jason held up a hand to signal his eagerness to rise to the challenge. Starting with the most senior member of the family, he ran down the line. "Margaret, Kim, Jen, Nat..." He correctly matched every name and face without asking for a single hint. "I'll look forward to meeting Amy and Scott soon," he finished.

"Perfect." Belle gave his arm a delighted squeeze.

For some reason, the whole interchange struck Kim and Jen as hilarious. Their good humor quickly spread to the rest of the people in the hallway.

"Let's get you checked in, Jason," Margaret said when the laughter died down. "I'm sure you'd like to freshen up after your trip."

Jason patted Belle's arm where it rested on his upper arm before he tugged at the bulky sweater that was more suited to a New York winter than Florida's warmer temperatures. "I wouldn't mind changing into something a little cooler."

"In that case, we've put you in Topaz on the second floor. It's a two-room suite with a private bath and a balcony with an ocean view. Coffee and a continental breakfast are available in the dining room starting at six each morning. We also put out complimentary light refreshments from four to six in the evening. If you need anything, anything at all, please let us know. We all want to make your stay with us as enjoyable as possible." Leaning against her cane, Margaret indicated the other women with a sweeping gesture.

With a glance, Margaret signaled Caitlyn. "Honey, would you take Jason's bags to his room?"

"Sure." The teen darted forward. "These two?" she asked, pointing to the totes at Jason's feet.

"Just the big one. The smaller bag is for Belle." He turned to her. "I thought you might want your fan mail."

"Oh?" Belle's eyebrow quirked. In the past, Noble Records' in-house publicity team had handled all the correspondence delivered to their offices. Now that she'd severed ties with the record company, she supposed it was only right that they sent the mail directly to her.

"I'll put that one in your room, Aunt Belle," Caitlyn offered.

"Thanks, sweetie. That'd be great."

"I'll go move the car before it starts to rain again." Jen shot Belle a surreptitious thumbs-up sign as she skirted Jason and dashed out the door.

Belle waited patiently while her mom went over a few details about the inn with Jason. When they'd finished, Margaret pressed a key into his hand and pointed toward the stairs.

"I'll take you there," Belle said, just in case any of her cousins had planned to subject Jason to the third degree while they showed him to his suite.

When they reached the upstairs landing, Jason took one look at the hallway that ran the width of the building and whistled. "This place is a lot bigger than it looks from the outside."

Belle nodded. "The front of the house can be deceiving. We have a dozen suites upstairs, another three downstairs, plus the family quarters. Because this area of Florida is called the Treasure Coast, my grandparents named each suite after a gemstone. Topaz is one of my favorites, but if you're unhappy with it for any reason, just say the word. Kim and Nat have the rooms at the top of the stairs. Diane and her daughter are staying in Beryl and Onyx, but none of the other suites up here are occupied this weekend."

"Good to know. But I'm sure everything will be fine."

"We'll see soon enough," she said, just as Caitlyn stepped out of a room midway down the wide corridor.

"I left your bag on the luggage rack and hung your coat in the closet, Mr. Jason," the teen said.

"Thank you, Caitlyn."

Belle smiled when she caught a flash of green when Jason shook the girl's hand. Caitlyn slipped something into her pocket a moment later.

"You're welcome, sir." Caitlyn turned to Belle. "I opened the drapes and checked the towels. Was there anything else I was supposed to do?"

"Sounds like you've covered everything," Belle said, offering the girl the same reassurances her mother and her aunt had given her when she was Caitlyn's age. Nevertheless, she scanned the suite with a practiced eye after she jiggled Jason's key in the old-fashioned lock. A quick sweep told her that not a speck of dust marred the surfaces of the furniture in the sitting room, where royal purple drapes hung in neat folds on either side of the French doors that opened onto a small balcony. Plush chairs sat at an inviting angle on either side of a small pedestal table centered on a thick Oriental carpet. Beyond the sitting room, a half-dozen pillows done up in various shades of purple had been artfully arranged on the big four-poster. Though the room, with its warm beige walls and dark floors, looked perfect, Belle held her breath as she peered up at Jason. "Will this do?"

As far as she could tell, Jason didn't notice the gift basket brimming with fruit and chocolate on the table. Or the painting of a Spanish treasure ship that hung on the wall. In fact, his eyes never left hers as he murmured, "The rooms are fine, Belle. But I didn't come here for the rooms. I'm here because this is where you are."

Warmth shot from her chest, producing a tingling sensation that spread to the tips of her toes and fingers. "I'm glad you came," she whispered.

"I've been looking forward to this moment for weeks," he acknowledged as he closed the distance between them.

Belle caught her breath when Jason slipped his arms around her waist and drew her close. In a move that ignited a yearning for the press of his mouth against hers, he slowly traced her lips with one thumb. Finally, just when she thought she couldn't wait another second, he lowered his head to hers. At the first swipe of his tongue against her lips, she opened to him, and for several long moments she lost herself in the pleasurable sensation that came from being well and truly kissed.

"Do all the guests to the Dane Crown Inn get such a warm welcome?" Jason asked when they finally broke apart.

"Only the very, very special ones." A delicious shiver passed through her when Jason traced her chin with his fingers. But as much as she longed to stay right where she was and indulge in another kiss, she stepped out of his embrace. She'd promised herself she wouldn't let things go too far with the man, not until she could say for certain that she was drawn to him for no other reasons than his wit, intelligence and

personality. Oh, and his handsome features—
those were a definite plus, she admitted. But a
promise was a promise, and she intended to keep
this one. "Why don't you get unpacked and meet
me downstairs?" she suggested while she put
some added distance between them.

"I won't be long," Jason assured her, the
longing in his gaze a perfect match to what she
was feeling.

"Good." She already missed the feel of his
arms around her. She forced her reluctant feet to
take her to the door. "I'm going to grab a cup of
coffee. Want me to get you a cup?"

Jason hesitated. "I think I'll stick with water
for now."

Caitlyn, bless her heart, had arranged several
bottles of Perrier beside the gift basket. As the
door closed behind her, Belle glimpsed Jason
unscrewing the cap of one and taking a long,
deep drink. Her own mouth suddenly dry, she
swallowed and pulled the door shut.

Belle checked her image in the mirror some
thoughtful soul had hung near the foot of the
stairs where guests and family alike could give

themselves a last-minute once-over on their way into or out of the inn. She frowned at the mess Jason's kisses had made of her lipstick. Grabbing a tissue from a box on a table under the mirror, she did damage control. Next, she ran her fingers through her hair and tamed a few loose curls. Finally, knowing her cousins lay in wait, ready to offer their opinions, she took a steadying breath.

"Well?" she asked, striding into the kitchen where—just like she'd expected—Kim, Nat and Diane had clustered around the island. "What'd you think?"

"I was all set to read him the riot act for not keeping you on at Noble Records, but he's just too darn nice," Diane complained with good-natured grace.

The service entrance door slammed shut. Keys jangling from her fingertips, Jen burst into the room. "He is awfully good-looking," she said while she hung the keys to the car Belle had used on the key rack. "Remind me—what's he see in you again?" she teased.

"Don't pay any attention to her." Kim shot Jen a look filled with sisterly disapproval. "The question is, what do you see in him? Besides the fact that he's obviously a good kisser."

Belle's hand shot to her mouth. Had she missed an errant spot of lipstick?

"So I was right." With a self-satisfied smirk, Kim pulled Belle's hand away from her face. "Your lipstick is fine. These guys bet me five bucks the two of you weren't upstairs smooching." She stared at the rest of the group. "Next time we go to Sweet Cakes, you can buy my lunch."

"Oh, you!" Belle balled her fist and lightly punched Kim's shoulder. "You're right, though. The man knows how to kiss."

"Hush." Diane shushed them when, drawn by the commotion, Caitlyn rounded a corner into the kitchen and hurried to her mom's side.

"Look," the teen said in a stage whisper. "My first tip. Can I keep it?" She brandished a twenty-dollar bill.

"Wow! That's more than I ever got for carrying bags," Jen said.

"It is a bit much." Diane looked to the others for support. When Kim only shrugged indifferently and Jen rolled her eyes, she gave in. "I guess it's all yours," she told her daughter.

"Awesome!" Caitlyn returned the money to her pocket. "I'm gonna get a new pair of shorts for tryouts next week." She aimed a sly grin at Belle. "I could use some new cleats, too. So if he needs anything else, just let me know."

Kim chuckled. "I think Jason has a fan."

"Well, I'm glad he passed the first test, at

least." Belle glanced toward the closed door to the family quarters. "Did Mama say anything?" She felt a surge of anxious energy. Next to her own, her mother's opinion mattered the most.

"Relax. Aunt Margaret was quite taken with him. She said you could invite him to the reunion if you want."

"She said that?" Belle's mouth gaped open. If her mom was already thinking that far ahead, Jason must have made a positive impression indeed. She barely had a chance to appreciate the nearly giddy relief her family's acceptance of him triggered before she heard heavy footfalls on the stairs.

Pushing away from the counter, she said, "I guess I'd better find out what we want to do, 'cause it isn't looking too good for the beach." A fresh onslaught of rain pattered the windows and splattered into the puddles on the back deck. "Great," she grumbled.

"Look on the bright side." Kim grinned. "You won't have to wear that bathing suit after all."

Not until tomorrow, Belle thought as she left the kitchen. She found Jason wandering through the living room.

"Hey." She tried not to stare at the black T-shirt that hugged Jason's chest in all the right places. "Are you hungry? Kim said to let you know lunch is at one, but I can rustle up something before that if you want."

Jason waved a dismissive hand. "Please tell her not to go to any trouble on my account. I usually work through lunch. I probably won't want much before dinner."

"That works for me, too," Belle said. Muscle mass or not, she was determined to lose the extra five pounds she'd gained since her arrival in Emerald Bay. "Any idea what you'd like to do this afternoon?"

Jason glanced at the gray world beyond the window panes. "I guess the beach is out."

"Afraid so." Reading disappointment in the slight slump of his shoulders, she offered, "I checked the weather while you were settling in. Tomorrow is supposed to be beautiful. We can spend all morning at the beach and still leave for the airport in time for your flight. Today, though, we have a couple of options. We could take a drive through town or go to Vero and see a movie. We could…"

"I wouldn't mind a tour of the rest of the house. From the little bit I've seen, it's pretty amazing."

Jason's compliment stirred the pride Belle felt for her family home. "Sure," she said easily. "Let's start in the sunporch." She led the way to the front of the house, where French doors and tall windows flooded the room with light, even on a gloomy day like this one. A pattern of green vines twined over white cushions on rattan furniture that Kim had recently repainted a bright white. Potted ferns and palms added to the room's tropical feel.

"When we were kids, my cousins and I would throw our sleeping bags down on the floor and camp out in here at least once a month. This is where a lot of our guests like to take their coffee in the mornings. They like watching the sun come up over the ocean." Almost as an afterthought, she added, "And the birds. Not too long ago, a flock of monk parakeets decided to make their home in the palm trees at the back of the property. They're cute little things. Always darting about."

She pointed to two tall posts in the yard. "We started filling the bird feeders with their favorite foods so our guests can enjoy watching them."

Jason ran a hand over the back of one of the chairs. "I can see why someone would like spending time in here."

From the sunporch, they moved on to the library, where tall, built-in bookcases held a wide variety of novels and a more modest selection of biographies and history texts. Jason walked to a collection of books with black and red spines. "Helen March?" He took one of the thrillers from the shelf. "She's one of my favorite authors. Is someone else here a fan?"

"You might say that." Belle grinned. "She stays at the inn once, sometimes twice a year."

"Holy cow. Helen March stays here?" Jason looked around as if he hoped to spot the famous author walking through the halls. "I'd love to meet her."

"Sorry to let you down, but she's not here now. Whenever she gets to the end of a book, she rents one of the cottages for a month or so and holes up out there while she finishes it. She mostly keeps to herself. When she's on deadline, she hangs a Do Not Disturb sign on the door, and even the maids know not to interrupt her. Mama swears she often hears Helen typing away into the wee hours."

Jason scanned the titles on the shelf. "Drat. I've read all these. Do you know what her next book is about?"

"Not a clue." Belle gave her head a rueful shake. "Like I said, she likes her privacy." She wouldn't promise, but the next time Helen visited, she'd ask the author to sign a copy of her latest book for Jason.

They moved rapidly through the three first-floor sitting areas where overstuffed couches and chairs offered plenty of options for individual guests or small gatherings. In the spacious kitchen, Kim paused her lunch preparations long enough to give Jason an overview of her catering business.

"Do you have any plans to expand the services here at the inn?" he asked when she finished. "Add a lunch or dinner service?"

Kim's mouth twisted. "I'm hoping, once I get Royal Meals on a firm footing, to start serving a hot breakfast. Nothing too crazy—a different casserole each day. Maybe omelets on Sundays. But lunch and dinner?" Her gaze sought Belle's. "I don't think that's in the cards, do you?"

"Not before the reunion. After that..." Belle left the thought hanging. After the reunion, they'd put the inn on the market. It didn't make sense to hire wait staff and kitchen help if they'd have to let them go in a few months.

"Hmmm." Jason rubbed his chin. "I would think it'd be a good opportunity for another revenue stream."

Belle felt the tiniest bit of tension ease from her shoulders when Jason let the matter drop after Kim replied with a noncommittal, "I'll have to think about it." So far, no one outside the family knew about their plans to sell the inn, and they'd all decided to keep the matter between them for the time being. She slipped her arm through Jason's. "A hungry teenager is going to race into this kitchen looking for lunch in a couple of minutes. We'd better let Kim get back to work."

"Where to next?" he asked.

They ended up in the game room, where Jason walked straight past a video screen and game consoles to a cabinet mounted on the far wall. He peered through the glass doors at a stack of boxes. "Do you play Scrabble?" When Belle nodded, he asked, "Are you any good?"

"My cousin Diane—Caitlyn's mom—is a very competitive player. She won all kinds of tournaments when we were in school." Belle brushed one foot over a floorboard. When she was growing up, her parents had hosted Game Nights at the inn once a week. At the time, she'd fussed and fumed about not being able to practice her music for a couple of hours. Now, though, she understood the value of the nights they'd spent munching popcorn and playing Hand and Foot or board games like Scrabble. She'd even managed to hold her own against the likes of Diane. "I've beaten her a time or two," she admitted.

"Let's make it interesting, then. A penny a point?"

"Only if I can trade my points for kisses." She'd meant it as a joke, but in truth, she could think of worse ways to spend an afternoon than trading kisses with Jason.

"You're on." He grabbed the box and began setting up the board and tiles.

Soon they were arguing over whether *unmuzzle* actually counted as a word. After Belle found it in the Scrabble dictionary, she delightedly added the points for a triple-word score. They both laughed at the end of the first game, which Jason lost when he tried to use Shiraz and couldn't defend his use of the proper noun.

"Double or nothing?" Jason asked, arranging the tiles for their next match.

"Sounds good to me," Belle agreed. With kisses at stake, she had determined to beat the pants off him. Maybe not literally, but winning did present interesting opportunities.

"As nice as this place is," he said, sliding his allotment of tiles onto the rack, "I'm surprised the inn isn't bursting at the seams."

"It wasn't always like this." Tucking the compliment away to share with her cousins, Belle questioned the wisdom of using her turn to get rid of some of her seven consonants in the hope of obtaining a vowel or two. "Be glad you didn't see it last fall. Vines and kudzu had nearly taken over the gardens. Everything needed work. My mom—bless her heart—was doing the best she could, but it takes more than one person to run a place this size. Even with help."

Jason exhaled. "You'd never know it from the look of the place now." Having lost the previous game, he laid down the first word this time.

Belle studied the board. Building off of Jason's *U*, she spelled *plucky* and drew five replacement tiles. Rearranging her pieces to take the best advantage of the *A* and *O* she'd drawn, she continued. "Over the past few months, my cousins and I have given the inn a kind of a makeover. New carpets, paint and wallpaper throughout. The floors have all been refinished. We're having the exterior painted next month."

"I wouldn't even know where to start with a project that big. I'd need to hire a contractor." Jason's next word landed on a red square and gave him a healthy lead.

Belle mulled her options. "It helped that my cousins and I grew up working here as maids and bellmen. We knew what things were supposed to be like."

"You must love the inn a lot to work that hard on it."

"I do," Belle admitted with a sigh. She arranged three tiles on the board. "I love being here, being home again. I didn't realize how much I'd missed it. I'd never lived anywhere else until I went to Juilliard. After that—well, you know what a musician's life is like. You go where the work takes you. Always following that next gig. If you're lucky enough to make it to the top, you work harder and harder to stay there. You're always on the go. Cutting a record in New York one month. Flying out to L.A. to record a soundtrack the next. The touring and the personal appearances are endless. Now that that part of my life is over, I feel like I've come full circle. I'm back where I started—making beds and taking care of guests and singing in the church choir on Sundays."

At that last bit, an urge to confide in him stirred in the pit of her stomach. She glanced up, wanting to gauge his reaction, and felt a flash of alarm. Jason's hair was as damp as if he'd just finished a race. His skin had taken on a decidedly unhealthy pallor.

"Jason?" she asked hesitantly. "Are you feeling all right?" He certainly didn't look all right. Was he coming down with something? She'd chalked his nap in the car up to sheer exhaustion, but maybe it had been more than that. Maybe he'd picked up some sort of bug.

He gulped hard enough to make his Adam's

apple bob. "I think that rough flight is catching up with me."

How long had this been going on? Had he spent the last few hours putting on a brave front…for her? This wasn't a sold-out performance where the show had to go on, no matter what. The man was obviously under the weather, and he needed to take care of himself. She racked her brain for a good enough reason to let him excuse himself. She gave her fingers an imaginary snap when she thought of one.

"Um, would you mind if I take a rain check on this next game? I really ought to look through the mail you brought. In case there's a check for a million dollars in one of those envelopes." She grinned to show she wasn't at all serious. "Maybe you'd like to rest while I do that?"

"That's not a bad idea. I'm sure I'll be much better company after a short nap." In a movement that made beads of sweat break out across his forehead, Jason braced his hands on the game table and stood.

"Can I get you anything? A cup of tea?" According to her mother, sweet black tea and dry toast or soda crackers cured almost every ailment.

Jason blanched. "I'll, uh…Could you send some up to my room?" A pained expression twisted his features. Without another word, he moved quickly to the door, leaving Belle to wonder whether she should have offered to walk upstairs with him.

Careful not to slosh hot liquid from the mug onto the tray, she brought tea and several packets of saltines to his room a short while later. When he didn't answer her knock, her concern mounted. Wanting to make sure he hadn't collapsed or fallen, she tried the knob. The door sprang open at her touch, and she stepped into the darkened suite. Gagging noises came from the bathroom. The sound prompted her own stomach to gurgle uneasily. She shushed it with a hard swallow before she crossed through the sitting room to the bedroom. After leaving Jason's tea and crackers on the nightstand, she pulled back the covers on the big four-poster and plumped the pillows. Then, not wanting to intrude any more than absolutely necessary, she made her way out of the room as quickly and quietly as she'd come.

The rest of the day and through the evening, she made frequent checks on Jason. Relief flooded her each time she found him sound asleep with the covers pulled up to his neck. Once, when she'd replenished his tea and checked that he had plenty of water, his eyes blinked open.

"Would you like me to call a doctor?" she asked when he roused long enough to take a few sips of water. "Or there's a walk-in clinic in Sebastian. I could take you there."

Looking positively green, Jason waved a hand. "Food poisoning," he whispered with a groan. "I'm pretty sure it was the sandwich I ate this morning."

"At the airport?" She pictured hundreds of sick passengers and wondered if she should alert the authorities.

He hiccupped. "My driver gave it to me. He said he bought it from a food truck on his way into the city."

Belle drew in a shocked breath. How long had that sandwich been sitting in the car before Jason ate it? She let her breath out slowly. Pointing fingers wouldn't help either of them. Whatever had caused him to fall ill, she just needed to help him get on the road to recovery.

"Things happen," she whispered. "But I'm so sorry this happened to you now."

She laid the back of her hand on his forehead. Though his skin felt damp, she didn't think he had a fever. In her realm of experience, that meant he probably didn't have a stomach virus and should start feeling better once he purged the tainted food from his system. "Rest. Drink as much water and tea as you can. I'll check in on you again in a couple of hours."

His eyes were already drifting shut. Quietly, she padded out of his room and pulled the door closed behind her.

Looking up from the display on her phone, Belle gave Jason the once-over as he eased down the stairs shortly after noon the next day. He moved like a person twice his age, but she counted it as a good sign that his skin had lost its greenish tinge. His cheeks lacked their usual healthy glow, though, and she wondered if he should even be out of bed.

"I would have brought you up something to eat." Belle shut down the live stream of a church service in Fort Pierce.

"I couldn't stay in bed one more minute. As comfortable as it was." He paused, listening. The ticking of the grandfather clock in the next room rose over the constant, low roar of the ocean. "Where is everyone?"

"Our guests were up and out early this morning." Injecting a note of cheer into her voice, Belle ran down the list. "The McFaddens were going to breakfast and then making a day trip to the outlet mall in Vero Beach. The Woods are into antiquing. They were headed to Arcadia. The Archers and the Grangers are spending the day with friends in Cocoa Beach."

"And your family?"

"Church, then out to lunch."

A frown creased Jason's brow. "You didn't go with them?"

"Someone always stays behind in case some of our guests return early." Belle didn't say as much, but she would never have left Jason to fend for himself after the day he'd had. "Do you think you're up for some coffee? A little something to eat?"

"You've done so much for me already. Running up and down the stairs all day and into the night." He glanced over his shoulder at the staircase. "I didn't imagine that, did I?"

When Belle admitted that she had checked on him from time to time, Jason's sheepish expression said he wouldn't mind at all if a hole opened beneath his feet and swallowed him whole. "I'm so sorry to put you through that."

"I was glad to do it. Besides, we haven't lost a guest yet." She gave a lighthearted laugh. "I wasn't about to let it happen on my watch."

"Still, I've been enough of an imposition."

When she started to protest, he held up a hand. "I don't want to put you to any more trouble, and to be frank, I don't think I'm up to standing in those lines at the airport." As if to prove his point, he leaned on a nearby chair. "I just got off the phone with Sunny."

"Your intern?" Belle recalled the fresh-faced girl who'd greeted her on her last visit to Jason's office.

"Yeah. She's been promoted to my personal assistant. She's arranged a private flight back to New York for me."

"Oh?" The news surprised her, but when she thought about it, Belle had to agree it was a good idea. Even if the airlines gave Jason the VIP treatment, it could take up to two hours to make it through security and onto the plane. "What time?"

"Five, but don't worry. A car and driver will be here to pick me up at three."

Belle steadied herself against the wave of disappointment that coursed through her. Jason's unexpected illness had upset all their plans for the weekend. She'd thought they'd at least get to spend an hour or two together on the drive back to the airport. Now they wouldn't even have that. Rather than complain about it, though, she determined to make the most of

LEIGH DUNCAN

what little time they had left. Squaring her shoulders, she asked, "How about something to eat, then?"

"Didn't your mom say there'd be coffee in the dining room?"

"There is. And there's hot water for tea. I'm not a great cook like Kim, but I can make a mean scrambled egg if that sounds good to you."

Jason pressed one hand to his stomach. "Not egg. I may never eat eggs again. I feel like I could handle some coffee and maybe something plain. Toast? An English muffin?"

"I think we can do better than dry toast. When Amy heard you were ill, she insisted on making a pan of gingerbread. She swears it's good for an upset stomach," Belle suggested.

"I'll try it, I guess." Jason's legs wobbled like they were about to give out on him.

"Tell you what—why don't you sit on the front porch. It's a beautiful day. We can watch the ocean until it's time for you to leave. I'll fix a tray and join you." She'd skipped breakfast earlier and could use a bite of something. Soft and moist, Amy's gingerbread would do them both some good.

When Jason agreed with her plan, she watched as he slowly moved down the hall to the door. *The poor man*. She tsked. He carried himself like someone whose body had failed them and wasn't quite ready to trust it again. Hopefully, he'd feel better after he had something to eat.

Twenty minutes later, Belle brushed a few crumbs from her jeans while Jason crumpled his napkin. "Please thank Amy for me. That cake was just what the doctor ordered."

"I'm glad you're feeling better. I was worried about you," she admitted. "Are you sure you can't stay another day? We could just lay about like...tourists. Let you get your strength back." No one would mind if he stayed on for an extra day or two.

"I wish I could. And I mean that sincerely." He stared deeply into her eyes. "But I don't have a choice. I have an early morning meeting with someone Noble Records is interested in signing."

"Oh?" She might not be performing right now, but she still kept her finger on the pulse of the recording business. "Anyone I know?"

"June Martin. You know her?"

Belle nodded. The girl had charisma, drive and talent. It was no surprise Noble wanted her. "She was going to open for me in L.A. before..." She'd started to say "before my career landed in the toilet" but quickly finished with, "before I left New York."

Jason's gaze narrowed until it was sharp enough to make her squirm. "How are you handling all this? Really."

Belle took a beat. If she was going to have any kind of relationship with Jason, it had to be based on mutual trust and honesty, even if the truth didn't paint her in the most favorable light.

"I'll admit, it took me a minute to come to grips with everything that happened," she said slowly. "I was pretty low there for a little while. But being here—home with my family—it's been the best thing in the world. As for what comes next, I'm still exploring options, but a couple of ideas look promising."

"Anything you want to bounce off me?" Jason leaned forward expectantly. "I might not be able to help, but I'd be happy to listen."

She shook her head. "I'm not ready yet." Though she'd considered discussing her future with Jason yesterday, her gut told her she needed to get a grip on the next chapter in her life on her own. Right now, everything was in flux. Her heart felt pulled in one direction while her head insisted that success lay somewhere else entirely. Until she sorted it all out for herself, she didn't want anyone—not even Jason—to steer her one way or the other.

"I understand," he said. "It's a big decision.

But I hope I'll be one of the first to know when you figure things out." He paused. "So what can you tell me about June Martin?"

"I see what you did there," Belle said with a warm smile. "And I appreciate it." One of the things she liked most about Jason was that he didn't push, didn't demand. "June is a good kid, from all I've heard." At twenty-six, she'd already paid her dues and was poised on the brink of stardom. "She flew in so we could meet face to face before she agreed to do the show. That was her idea, and she struck me as levelheaded and determined." Her talent went without saying. "She'll do good things for Noble Records."

"You think?" Jason looked doubtful. "I'm getting awfully tired of working with these newbies who expect instant fame and fortune." He crossed his ankles.

"That won't be June," Belle assured him. "Her cousin is also in the business—Katie Saldana," she said, dropping the name of a well-known songwriter. "The two of them are tight, and Katie's been around long enough to know how things really work. She'll help June keep her head on straight."

Metal glinted in the distance. Belle shielded her eyes with one hand and peered in that direction. Her stomach sank when a black limo turned onto the driveway from the main road.

"I guess your car is here. Are you sure I can't convince you to stay longer?" She tried and failed not to let her disappointment show. Their time together had passed too quickly.

Jason stroked her hand with long fingers. "You don't know how much I was looking forward to spending this weekend with you. I hate like anything that I ruined it."

"It's not your fault," Belle protested. "You didn't sign up for food poisoning. No one does that." She flipped her hand over and grasped his. "You just have to promise me one thing—next time, no breakfast sandwiches from unknown sources."

"You mean there'll be a next time? I get a redo?" Jason asked as if he couldn't believe what he was hearing.

"Of course I want you to come back…as long as you promise."

She'd barely gotten the words out of her mouth before Jason raised his hand in a three-fingered salute. "I swear," he said. He paused, then added, "If things go the way I hope they do, one day when we're old and gray and sitting in these very rockers on this very porch, I'll turn to you and say, 'Remember that time I got so sick and you spent the whole weekend taking care of me?'"

The image was so sweet that tears immediately sprang to Belle's eyes. Smiling, she blotted them with her napkin. "I'll hold you to that," she whispered.

"Tell the driver I'll be right down. I just need to grab my bag."

Before Belle could offer to get it for him, Jason had pried himself out of his chair and disappeared into the house. By the time he returned, the limo sat, its engine idling, in front of the inn. The driver, looking sharp in a black suit and chauffeur's hat, stood at attention at the base of the steps.

Belle started to scramble to her feet and walk Jason to the car. She remained where she was when he rested his hand on her shoulder.

"Much as I want to wrap my arms around you and hold you close, don't get up. This is the image I want to carry with me until the next time we see each other." He brushed a handful of loose curls over her shoulder.

Belle peered up at him. "Okay, but I haven't forgotten all those Scrabble points you owe me." Yesterday, they hadn't had a chance to finish their second game, but she'd trounced him in their first match. That had to be good for at least one kiss. "I fully plan on redeeming them sometime soon." She loved the way Jason's laugh rumbled in his chest as trotted down the steps.

He handed his duffle to the waiting driver. While the man stowed his bag in the trunk, Jason paused, his arm resting on the frame of the open car door. "When will I see you again?" he asked.

"You know where to find me," Belle answered and blew him a kiss.

As the car disappeared into the flow of traffic on the main road a few minutes later, Belle ran her fingers over the rocking chair's wide armrest. Though it was much too soon to commit to spending their lives together, the idea of having a future with Jason did hold a certain appeal. Except, she reminded herself, there was one small problem with his vision of the years ahead. By the time she and Jason were old enough to sit and reminisce about their past, the Dane Crown Inn would no longer belong to anyone in her family.

And with that thought, a deep sadness that was only partly due to Jason's departure settled on her shoulders.

Ten

Diane

*D*iane stepped into Sweet Cakes' bustling kitchen. Despite the other bakers in the room, she flung her arms around her sister. "I've missed you," she cried, clinging to Amy, not wanting to let go.

"What? We see each other practically every day," Amy argued.

Despite her sister's protest, Diane felt Amy's arms tighten around her. "I know, but we're never alone together anymore. There's always someone else around," she complained. Finally relinquishing her grip, she added, "I miss our sister time."

"I do, too," Amy admitted softly. "I love being around Belle and Kim and Jen, but sometimes, I want you and me to hang out, just the two of us."

"We used to be able to do that more." The

hour or two she and Amy would sneak off for breakfast or lunch had been the highlight of every trip she and Tim and the kids made to Emerald Bay. Those sisterly retreats had stopped, though, when she'd moved her daughter here. At first, it had been a matter of necessity—she'd needed to keep such a close eye on Caitlyn that she hadn't wanted to leave the teen alone. Even after her fears for the child had eased, she'd felt guilty for wanting some alone time with her sister.

"Now it almost feels rude to leave the others behind."

"My thoughts exactly," Diane commiserated. It warmed her heart to hear Amy voice the same thoughts she'd been having. "That's one of the reasons I volunteered to handle the shopping list for the reunion. I knew we'd have a chance to spend time together without slighting anyone else."

"Good thinking." Amy untied her Sweet Cakes apron and hung it on a nearby hook. "Deborah, I'm taking an early lunch," she called. "I'll be in the café if you need me." Her voice dropped to a nearly silent whisper. "Please don't need me."

Diane let herself be dragged along when her older sister linked arms with her and steered them out of the kitchen.

"It's quiche day," Amy announced when she paused to place their orders at the counter. "Lorraine, onion or cheese—name your poison. Lunch is on me."

Diane glanced into the display cases designed to look like treasure chests. Her mouth watered at the delectable array of eclairs and cupcakes, Danish pastries and cookies stacked in neat rows on the other side of the glass. Tempted to order one of everything, she firmed her resolve.

"I've always loved your Lorraine," she said, choosing the eggy dish loaded with smoked bacon, Gruyere cheese and caramelized onions.

"Coffee? Tea?"

"Tea. Iced. Unsweetened." The calorie-laden pie with its flaky crust was going to do enough damage to her diet without adding extra sugar.

"Make that two, Sherry," Amy said to the gray-haired woman who stood behind the counter. "We'll be over there." She pointed to a small table at the back of the dining area.

As they settled in, Diane took a notebook and pen from the zippered tote bag that contained all her notes about the upcoming reunion.

"Leave that for now." Amy gently but firmly closed the booklet. "Let's catch up first. We can take care of that other stuff later."

"That works for me." Diane slid the spiral notebook aside. "I have a lot to tell you."

"Same here," Amy said with a laugh.

"Oh?" Diane let her eyebrows rise along with her voice. "You first. Is there anything new about a certain hot handyman?"

Amy pressed one hand to her heart even as she shook her head. "No news on the Max front, I'm afraid. Except, well, he and I found the perfect spot for Sweet Cakes 2 yesterday."

"Do tell!" Diane demanded.

"I was beginning to think I'd have to give up on the idea of expanding the bakery. At least for a while." Amy removed the packets of sugar from a small holder in the center of the table, straightened them and returned them to the holder as she talked. "Max and I must have looked at a dozen places. Every one of them had some fatal flaw. One was the size of a warehouse. I rejected it right away. The overhead and taxes would destroy our profit margin. The next one was so tiny customers would have to line up on the sidewalk."

"Oh, joy—they'd either swelter in the heat or get drenched in a thunderstorm." Diane frowned. Neither option was good for business.

"That's the way I saw it. We ruled that one out. A storefront in Sebastian's walking district looked promising until we discovered it had a problem with black mold. Max said it'd be cheaper to raze the place and start fresh, but that meant spending the next year dealing with contractors and building permits. Thanks, but no thanks." Amy arranged the silverware on her napkin, aligning the bottom of the knife, fork and spoon. "I didn't want to look in Vero, but we had to. We didn't have any other choice."

Diane grimaced. The added distance meant extra gas and insurance costs. To say nothing of the time Amy or Deborah would have to spend on the road each day.

"We couldn't find anything there, either." Her sister's lips turned down at the corners. "I was ready to throw in the towel and try again in a year. But then my broker left a message on my phone Sunday."

"He had something for you?"

"Yeah. You know The Bath Cottage in Sebastian?"

"I do. I used to love that store." Wooden beams overhead and tongue-and-groove flooring helped create a cozy feel in the shop on one end of the main shopping district. The cottage had been a great place to buy handmade soaps and specialty bath products. But several years ago, the business had changed hands. After the new owners replaced the more unique items with products Diane could buy for less at Walmart, she hadn't gone back.

"They're closing. Max and I went to look at the building yesterday. It's a wee bit larger than I wanted, but the location is perfect."

"I'll say," Diane agreed. With nearly two dozen mom-and-pop businesses clustered around a small lake, the area attracted plenty of shoppers. Plus, there wasn't another bakery anywhere close by.

"Last night, Deborah and I put in an offer. I expected a counter, but the owners accepted it. We close on April first."

"That's..." At a loss for words, Diane simply screeched with delight. She hugged Amy around the neck. "That's fantastic news," she said when they broke apart. "I'm so happy for you!"

"It's such a relief," Amy breathed. "Max says he should be able to make all the mods in a matter of weeks. We should open for business the first week in May. Assuming I can get all the permits in place by then."

"Wow!" Diane fanned her face with one hand. It was a lot to take in. "What does Deborah think?"

"She'll be in charge of Sweet Cakes 2, so she's even more excited about it than I am. We've run the numbers, and we're pretty sure we can turn a profit even if we close the Sebastian shop at noon each day. That'll let Deborah get back to Emerald Bay in time to pick her son up from school and take him to practices and such."

Diane took a quick look at the jewel-toned chairs and nautical touches that highlighted the bakery's Emerald Bay location. A seascape painted on the walls featured a treasure chest that spilled precious gems onto the ocean floor. "Have you thought of how you'll decorate the new place?"

Her sister nodded. "Deborah and I discussed it with Max. We'll repeat the murals and use the same style tables." She ran a hand over the layer of shiny resin that covered an arrangement of seashells and driftwood. "I think we'll stick with standard bakery display cases, though. The custom ones we have here are pricey. We need to be turning a profit at the new place before we take on that expense."

"That won't take long." Diane glanced pointedly at the line of customers who patiently waited to place their orders.

"That reminds me," Amy said. "I wanted to thank you for meeting me here. We always have a big lunch crowd when we make quiche. I didn't want Deborah to have to handle the crush on her own. She's been doing that a lot lately."

"I didn't mind. Honestly," Diane assured her sister. "I had some, uh, some errands to run anyway. This way, I get to eat." She grinned.

Amy's eyebrows knitted. "You've been doing that a lot—running errands, that is. What could possibly keep you that busy here in Emerald Bay? We don't have that many places to shop, and now that you're out of work, I know you aren't buying out the stores."

"True." Diane gave a self-deprecating laugh. She'd been hoping to talk about her plans with Amy privately, and this was her chance. "I'll tell you everything over lunch," she promised when she spotted Sherry on her way to their table with a tray.

Moments later, Diane broke a bite of crust off her slice of quiche. "You've outdone yourself, Amy. This is delicious." The flaky piece had melted in her mouth. Wanting nothing more than to devour her food, she forked up a bite of the eggy custard.

"Okay, less eating, more talking," Amy said. "So spill. What's going on with you and Tim?"

With a heavy sigh, Diane lowered her fork to her plate. She always could count on her sister to cut to the chase. She gave her lunch a last, longing glance before she admitted, "He's giving me the silent treatment—we haven't spoken since that night we went to Fog Horn's." It didn't matter how many times she reminded herself that Tim had struck the first blow; she couldn't watch their twenty-plus years of marriage go down the tubes without turning weepy.

"Oh, Diane." Compassion shone in Amy's eyes. "I'm sorry to hear that. I thought the two of you were going to be able to patch things up."

"I did, too. But when I enrolled Caitlyn at Emerald Bay High, or maybe it was when I told him she wasn't transferring back to Plant High— it doesn't matter which—one of them was the final straw. Either way, that's when he realized I wasn't coming back to him."

"You're not...ever?" Amy's breath hissed when she sucked air in through her front teeth.

"I'm not saying we won't get back together. I haven't given up on our marriage." Diane blotted her eyes on her napkin. "But I know it'll take a lot of work for me to forgive him, you know? He has to earn my trust again."

"How's that going to work if he's not talking to you? Or with you here and him there?"

"That's the sixty-four-thousand-dollar question, isn't it?" No longer hungry, she pushed her plate toward the center of the table. "But I know we can't go back to the way things were before. For one thing, there's Caitlyn. She's beyond happy at Emerald Bay High. She's made a lot of friends at church. It sounds like she's nailed a spot on the soccer team." Tryouts would continue for another week, but after the second set of drills, the coach had put Caitlyn at the goalie position and kept her there. "She has two and a half years of high school left, and I think she should finish them out here. I want her to graduate from Emerald Bay High. Like I did."

"It's a good school. She could do a lot worse," Amy agreed. She paused long enough to take another bite of her quiche. After she swallowed, she said, "You can't build your whole life around Caitlyn, though. Like you said, in a couple of years, she'll be off to college. Then graduate school. A job. She'll be her own person then. Who knows where she'll end up."

"I know. It's not just Caitlyn. *I* love it here. I love living in a small town. Going for walks on the beach each morning. Hanging out with Aunt Margaret. Most of all, though, I've missed you and Belle and Kim. And Jen," she added, almost as an afterthought. "I feel like I've been so wrapped up in trying to get ahead at work that I lost sight of what's important. Now that I see things more clearly, I want to stay here, to be a real part of the family again."

"And we want you to." Reaching out, Amy patted Diane's arm. "But…"

"*But.* I hate that word. No matter what you want to do, there's always a *but.*"

"But," Amy repeated as if for emphasis. "What will you do for money? You can't live at the inn forever."

Diane drummed her fingers on the tabletop. She wanted, needed Amy's support for her plans. Would she get it? Cautious, she eased into the subject. "I've been giving that a lot of thought, too. For me, the best thing about being an accountant is that it gives me the chance to help people have control over their finances. Working one-on-one with the owners of small businesses—that's the part of the job I missed the most when I went to work for Ybor City." She stopped to gather her courage. "It's time for me to make that dream come true. I've decided to open my own accounting firm."

Diane felt a twinge of disappointment when, instead of offering her enthusiastic support, Amy's eyes narrowed to thin slits. "Aren't you worried about stepping on toes? Emerald Bay is a small town. We already have one bookkeeper."

"You mean Sharon?" Diane gave her head a sad shake. The former math teacher had started a bookkeeping service after she retired from the classroom. A recent stroke, though, had called an abrupt halt to her second career. "I've spoken to her husband. He says Sharon's going to need to focus on her health for the foreseeable future. I hate that it happened this way, but that leaves the businesses in town with a real need. One I can fill."

A half-smile crept across Amy's lips. "Would you be interested in handling the books for Sweet Cakes?"

The knowledge that she had her sister's approval sent warm tingles straight down Diane's spine. "I'll even give you the family discount," she promised.

"In that case, what are your plans? How can I help you get started?"

Diane flexed her fingers while Amy's support gave her an extra boost of self-confidence. "Those errands you mentioned earlier?" She hiked an eyebrow. At Amy's nod, she continued, "I've been talking to some of Sharon's clients. She didn't have that many—a dozen or so. The church, the hardware store, both surf shops in town." She rattled off the rest, her plans spewing out like water from a burst pipe. "A couple already signed on with an agency down in Vero, but the rest are willing to give me a chance. It's enough to make the whole idea viable. I won't need much for startup costs, and I have that covered. I didn't exactly have a golden parachute with Ybor City—more like bronze or tin—but it'll be enough to see me through the first six months, even after I pay the insurance premiums for the inn."

"Whoa, girl!" Amy held up a hand to stanch the flow of Diane's words. "You lost me somewhere back there." She brushed a stray hair from her face.

"Sorry." Diane felt her face color. "I did get a little carried away, didn't I?"

"Yeah, but that's okay. You have every right to be excited about all this. It's a big step." Finished with her lunch, Amy placed her knife and fork on her plate. "But, um, did I hear you right? Something about insurance?"

Diane shifted, recrossed her ankles and focused on the problem that had occupied a large portion of her time ever since they'd received notice that the inn's insurance company would not renew its policy. "My biggest concern lately has been finding a new carrier. I've contacted every agency in the state. I finally found a company willing to write a policy for the inn—assuming it passes an inspection next month, that is. But rates are out of sight. It's going to cost triple what we were paying before."

"We have to pay it, though, don't we?" Amy asked, her expression serious. "If something happens and she doesn't have coverage, Aunt Margaret could lose everything."

"Don't I know it," Diane grumbled. "That's why I was planning to use part of my severance money to pay the premiums."

"Wait." Amy lifted two fingers from the tabletop. "Don't we have money set aside for the painters? Couldn't we use that?"

Diane slowly shook her head. "Everything has to be in tip-top shape during the inspection or the insurance company will back out. So painting isn't optional."

"And if we paint, we can't afford the insurance premiums. Bummer." Amy scrunched her napkin into a ball.

"It's okay." Diane struggled to look relaxed and at ease while she sought to reassure her sister. "It's time for me to do my part. After all, everyone else has. Belle sold that fancy artwork of hers. You brought Deborah on as a partner and used some of that money to refinish the floors. Now it's my turn." She blew out a breath. "I'm just glad it's working out for this year. I don't know what we'll do if we can't find a buyer for the inn before the time to pay next year's premiums rolls around."

"I guess we'll cross that bridge when we come to it." Amy signaled one of the busboys to clear their plates. When he finished, she thanked him before turning to Diane. "Back to your business plan. Are you and Caitlyn going to stay on at the inn?"

"For now. We'll need to find our own place, though, right after the reunion. Before that, if reservations pick up." One of the key goals of refurbishing the inn was to attract new customers. "I'd like to find someplace that has both office and living space."

Amy blinked. "Remember Mr. Wallaby's?"

"Gosh! That brings back memories." Diane cupped her chin in her hand. The money they'd earned from making beds and cleaning rooms at the inn burning holes in their pockets, she and Amy would ride their bikes to the little convenience store on the edge of town at least once a week. There, they usually went halves on the latest *People* magazine, which they'd read while drinking sodas they'd pulled from an old-fashioned icebox. Dr. Pepper for her and Orange Crush for Amy. Sometimes, the owner of the little store would give them a pack of Red Vines. "How is Mr. Wallaby?"

"He finally retired five years ago. His son, Ford, tried to keep the store open for a while, but he owns a furniture store in Fort Pierce. He couldn't manage both and finally closed the place last year. I'm sure he'd be willing to rent it to you."

Diane tugged on her lower lip. The convenience store was small—really not much larger than a postage stamp. If all she needed was office space, it'd be perfect. But she needed more than that. "I was thinking more along the lines of a small house for Caitlyn and me but with a mother-in-law suite that I could use for my office."

Amy grinned like the proverbial cat that had swallowed the canary. "That's the best part. Mr. and Mrs. Wallaby had separate living quarters in the back. You ought to check it out." She wiped a few crumbs from the table while she gave the rest of the bakery a cursory glance. "We have about a half-hour before I'll need to help out at the counter."

"We'd better work on the reunion stuff, then." Diane made a mental promise to check into the Wallaby property as she retrieved her notebook from the end of the table.

Twenty minutes later, she gathered up her things. "So that's it? That's everything we need?" she asked a final time.

"I think that's it. I'll put the staff to work making extra pies, cakes and cookies now. Anything that will freeze well. The breads, we'll just double our normal bake the week before so we have plenty." Amy jotted notes on a slip of paper she'd torn from Diane's notebook.

"I'll make a run to the big box store in Vero for everything else—paper plates, towels, napkins, plasticware, cups. I'll get a list from Kim, too." Their cousin had offered to serve as head cook during the reunion. "I know she already has her menus planned for the week."

"Sounds good."

Though it seemed early for planning meals and laying in supplies, the next three months would pass in the blink of an eye. Soccer season—or as Diane liked to call it, carpool season—was just around the corner. In addition to practices, they'd all attend Caitlyn's games and cheer for her and the team. The painters would erect scaffolding and begin painting the exterior of the inn later this month. Next came the Spring Fling and Easter. Sprinkle in a few birthdays and a couple of family dinners, and before they knew it, the reunion would be upon them. And after that, they'd start looking for a buyer for the inn.

Eleven

Belle

"Yum. Something smells good." The minute the words left her mouth, Belle realized how redundant they sounded. Ever since Kim had taken over the kitchen, nothing but good smells had wafted throughout the inn.

"You think?" Kim asked. She crossed to the oven. Another whiff of something wonderful filled the air when she cracked the door open to check on whatever she was baking. "I had planned to make broccoli salad for tonight's potluck, but it's so cold out, I thought something hot would be a better choice." Just as Jen had predicted, Saturday's rainstorms had put a temporary end to the warm front and ushered in another cold spell.

Belle rubbed her empty stomach. She could use something besides salad herself. It felt like she'd been living on nothing but greens and soup for weeks, even though it had only been three days.

Taking another glance at the oven, though, sent her thoughts in a different direction. Could a simple casserole actually be the sign she'd been looking for? She prayed silently. *Lord, if Kim takes something scrumptious and low-cal from the oven, I'll see it as a sign that I should follow my heart instead of my head.* Hope bloomed in her belly.

"What did you end up making?" she asked.

"Broccoli casserole. Wedges of homemade biscuit dough, chunks of crisp bacon, broccoli and ranch dressing. Oh, and cheese." Satisfied with what she saw inside, Kim let the door close. "It's not fancy, but it is filling."

Cheese, bacon and biscuits were definitely not low-cal. In fact, they were its exact opposite. Which meant Kim's dish was not the sign she'd wanted.

Belle sighed. She shouldn't be surprised. After all, that's the way things went at a potluck, wasn't it? From the basket of fried chicken provided by the Pirate's Gold Diner to that awful mashed potato salad Olivia Carruthers made to Clara Johnson's funeral potatoes, every dish on the table would contain at least a week's worth of calories in a single serving. She'd have to look for her sign elsewhere. And, unless she wanted to undo all her efforts to lose weight, she needed to fill up on lettuce and cucumbers before they left for the church.

Except she absolutely couldn't face another green leaf. Plus, cucumbers gave her gas.

At the counter, Kim snapped the lid on a plastic container, which she slipped into an insulated bag. "I steamed the broccoli that was left over from the casserole and tossed in some roasted chicken. There's plenty if you and Diane want some."

Belle's mouth watered as she stared at her cousin in disbelief. "I could kiss you on the lips right now. You know that?"

"Thanks, but I'll pass," Kim said with a laugh. "I consider it cruel and unusual punishment to be forced to go to a church dinner when you're on a diet. Remind me again why you're going tonight?"

"Because it means so much to Mama," Belle admitted, though, in all likelihood, she would have gone on her own if she'd had to. She couldn't put her finger on the reason, but something told her she needed to attend this particular gathering.

"She's been looking forward to this for so long." The December dinner had been canceled due to all the Christmas activities. Before that, her mom had missed a couple of potlucks because of her broken arm. "It's practically all she's talked about since they announced it during the service last Sunday."

The timer on the oven dinged. Kim shut everything off before she grabbed a pair of pot holders. A fragrant cloud of steam rose from the oven when she opened it. Carefully, she removed the casserole and carried it to the counter, where she rested it on a trivet.

"I wish we'd been able to take her last month, but things were topsy-turvy while we were having the floors redone. I'm glad she's getting to go this time." Belle quickly glanced away from the casserole, where crispy pieces of biscuit and broccoli poked out of a lightly browned cheese sauce. "And I think everyone is going to be glad you're bringing this dish," she finished.

"I hope so. It's risky to try out an unfamiliar recipe on a crowd, but I think this one's a hit." Kim tore a sheet of aluminum foil from a dispenser and loosely wrapped it around the dish.

Just then, the door to the family quarters sprang open. Margaret walked into the kitchen in a wine-colored knit dress with a ruched waistline. The full skirt flowed to mid-calf. A pair of black boots with sensible heels lent the outfit a timeless appeal.

"Mama, you sure look nice tonight." Belle fussed over her mom, who'd taken obvious pains to look her best. "Is that a new dress?"

"This old thing?" Margaret struck a saucy pose. "I've had it for ages, honey." She folded her hands atop her cane. "Are we ready to go?"

"Yes, ma'am. We're all set," Belle called. She brushed imaginary lint from the gray pants she'd paired with a loose-fitting black sweater.

"Where's everyone else?" Margaret's cane made thumping noises on the hardwood floor.

"Amy will meet us there, of course. Diane and Caitlyn left a few minutes ago. Jen went to bring the car around. Nat is going to stay here in case one of our guests needs something." As she spoke, Kim settled the casserole into a sturdy wicker basket and draped a towel over it.

Margaret straightened the straps on the handbag that hung from her arm. "I guess we'd better go then."

Jen slowly drove through the rapidly filling parking lot toward a boxy, two-story building next to the main sanctuary. Slightly newer than the rest of the church, the concrete block structure housed the reception hall and nursery, plus classrooms that were used for Bible studies and Sunday school. She braked to a stop beneath a wide awning that protected arrivals from the elements. Not that they needed it tonight. Not when stars sparkled against the velvet backdrop of a clear sky.

"I'll save you a seat," Kim told her sister as she stepped from the car carrying the wicker basket she'd held on her lap.

"I'll get your door, Mama." Belle unbuckled her own seatbelt and hurried around the trunk before her mother could struggle out of the car on her own.

Once Jen sped off to look for a parking space, Belle stuck close to her mother's side while members of the congregation and more than one guest filed in through the doors. Inside the rather austere hall, she paused just long enough to exchange the usual hugs and handshakes with the two deacons who'd been assigned to greet arrivals.

Aware that others were eager to get out of the cold, they didn't linger. But after they'd cleared the crush of people at the entry, her mother signaled their little group to a halt.

"That's our table over there." Margaret pointed to one of dozens of folding tables arranged in straight lines that ran the length of the large hall. "Kim, those are the food tables." She waved to several tables that formed a T at the front of the room as if her niece hadn't grown up attending the monthly Wednesday night potluck suppers with the rest of the family. "You girls help arrange the food and then come join me." With that, she hurried across the worn linoleum floor tiles as fast as a woman who relied on a cane could go.

Belle didn't dare glance at her cousin while her mom rushed off. If she did, she just knew she'd laugh out loud.

"I guess we'd better do as we were told," Kim whispered once the older woman was out of earshot.

"If we know what's good for us." Her mother's marching orders made her feel like a child again.

And she wasn't the only one. She and Kim no sooner neared the area where men and women were dropping off their contributions for the meal than Pam Hatch, an imposing matron with the demeanor of a drill sergeant, put them to work.

"Belle, you can start getting the knives and forks out of those boxes." Mrs. Hatch pointed to stacks of plasticware. She turned to Kim. "Arrange the dishes in their proper order," she said. "Appetizers and salads go here." She smoothed the paper tablecloth. "Casseroles and vegetables in the middle. Desserts all the way over there." She pointed to the far end of the line.

While Kim scurried off to do the woman's bidding, Belle began ripping open packages of napkins and cutlery and lining them up beside the plates.

"Don't clump the napkins together, Belle," Mrs. Hatch corrected. "People will take a handful, and we'll run out." Arms folded, she watched like a hawk while Belle began dealing out the napkins like cards. "Humph. Maybe you should just help Kim," she said, apparently not satisfied with her helper.

"Yes, ma'am." Belle felt her cheeks burn.

On their way to join Margaret a few minutes later, Kim leaned in close. "What happened back there?" she asked. "I felt like I was caught in some kind of time warp. What did she think—that we were fifteen again?"

"I haven't been spoken to like that in..." Belle clamped one hand over her mouth in an effort to stifle her laughter. She hadn't been scolded or summarily dismissed like Ms. Hatch had done in forever.

Diane and Caitlyn had already taken seats on either side of her mom by the time Belle and Kim found Jen in the growing crowd and the three of them joined the others at the table.

"Don't look now, but Tom Collier's on his way over here," Diane warned before Belle got settled across from her mom.

"Oh, yeah? Where?" Belle's head swung as she searched for the minister. She spotted him glad-handing his way through the crowd in their general direction. Her chest tightened when his searching gaze landed on their table. She gulped when, two seconds later, he abruptly changed direction. Tom clearly wanted something, but what? And from whom?

"I told you not to look," Diane hissed. "Now he's headed straight for us." The man's purposeful strides took him through the crowd like a hot knife through butter. "I hope he didn't find a problem with the church accounts," she fretted.

"Welcome! Welcome!" Tom Collier grinned widely and began working his way around the table, shaking hands and greeting each woman by name. "And Ms. Margaret," he said when he reached the senior member of their group. "It's a rare and wonderful day when you and your whole family joins us for Wednesday supper. Would you mind too terribly if I borrowed Belle for a moment?"

Belle canted her head. Had she done such a bad job with the napkins that Mrs. Hatch had sent the pastor over to chastise her? She shoved the ridiculous idea out of her head and sought the minister's warm brown eyes. "You need to speak with me?"

"Yes, if you don't mind." Tom bobbed his head over hands he held in a prayerful entreaty. "I apologize for intruding." Once again, he directed his comment to Margaret. "But this will only take a minute."

When Belle hesitated, her mom prompted, "Go on, dear."

Realizing she didn't have much choice in the matter, Belle pushed back her chair and followed the minister to a quiet corner of the room.

"Belle, I hate to ask, but..."

Knowing that Tom was about to ask for a favor, Belle resisted rolling her eyes when the man hesitated. Was this how the rest of her life was going to be? When she'd been at the top of her game, when she'd been a star, the people around her had shielded her from special requests. Now that she no longer traveled with an entourage, would she be expected to sing for her supper wherever she went?

"...But our music minister normally opens the potluck with a song and a prayer," Tom continued. "Unfortunately, Darius has come down with a rather nasty cold and can't be here tonight. I'm a man of many talents, but I think we'll all agree that the ability to carry a tune is not one of them."

Despite herself, Belle smiled. Every member of the church agreed that Tom must have been in another part of heaven on the day when the good Lord passed out musical abilities.

"So I was wondering if—well, you gave such a moving performance on Christmas Eve, I was hoping we could prevail upon you to sing another song for us tonight?"

Belle's shoulders stiffened. Of course, she'd done a good job that night. The candlelight service had been planned weeks in advance. She'd had all the time in the world to practice the music. But what Tom was asking her to do— to walk up to the mic and launch into some unfamiliar song in front of hundreds of people— no good could come of it. How could he possibly think she'd agree?

She clasped her hands together. She was being unfair. She'd been wrestling with the Lord these past few weeks, praying for him to give her a sign before she embarked in the direction either her heart or her head wanted her to go. So far, she'd gotten nothing in response. Maybe this was her chance to show the man upstairs exactly what he was asking of her.

"Of course." She tamped down her misgivings. "Did you have something in mind?"

"Really?" Happiness rippled across Tom's face. "How about "The Lord's Prayer"? That way you can kill two birds with one stone, so to speak. A song and a prayer."

Belle had spotted an old upright in the corner of the reception hall when they arrived this evening. She cast about for someone to accompany her on the piano. "Who's going to play for me?" Working with an unfamiliar pianist was a little dicey—after her experience in Nashville, she knew that better than most—but some accompaniment was better than none.

Tom gave his head a sorrowful shake. "That piano is so out of tune, it's pitiful. You'd be better off on your own."

The Lord's Prayer, a cappella. Belle swallowed. The song required a fiercesome vocal range. Glad she'd been running scales earlier in the afternoon, she looked around for a mic. She didn't see one. "I don't suppose you have any audio equipment?"

"We keep it all in the main sanctuary," Tom explained. "You don't really need it, do you?"

This. This was exactly why she should follow her head instead of her heart. Her head said restarting her stalled career in pop was the smart thing to do. That or branch out into R&B. Or, heaven forbid, give country another go. No matter what she chose, that's where the money was. And with money came the resources to do it right. The equipment. The backup band. The carefully orchestrated agenda.

But her heart, oh, her heart was leading her somewhere else entirely. If she followed it, was this what the rest of her life would be like? Singing for a handful of people in an unheated reception hall in the middle of the week, with no one to accompany her and nothing to amplify her voice? She shook her head.

Lord, you're going to have to give me a sign.

Aware that Tom waited for an answer, she gave the only one she had. "I'll do the best I can."

"Good." Tom clapped his hands together. "Let's get started then."

"Oh, you mean right now?" She couldn't help feeling shocked.

"Everyone's waiting." Tom gestured to the mostly seated crowd. "And the food's getting cold."

Dear Lord, what are you doing to me?

She'd been hoping for at least a few minutes to run through the melody. But it wasn't going to happen. Tom had already headed for the front of the room with all the confidence of a man who expected her to fall in line behind him.

Reaching the tables that nearly groaned beneath the weight of dozens of casseroles and platters, Tom turned to face the congregation. He clapped his hands, and immediately a few stragglers hurried to empty chairs. An expectant hush fell over the room.

When everyone quieted, Tom greeted the group heartily. "Welcome, everyone, to our monthly potluck. I want to thank you all for braving the cold and coming out tonight. And I'd especially like to thank all the men and women who contributed to what looks like a mighty fine feast." He hooked a thumb over one shoulder at the food. "Now we don't want the cold stuff to get too warm or the hot stuff to cool off, so here to lead us in a special prayer is our very own Belle Dane."

A polite smattering of applause greeted her. Lacing her fingers in front of her belly, she had no choice but to trust her voice to handle the high notes when she got to them. Instead, she focused all her attention on the meaningful words in the prayer of praise and supplication.

"Our Father," she sang.

The moment she opened her mouth, a bolt of lightning struck just beyond the walls of the building. Thunder clapped. Belle's entire body trembled when a white heat shot through her. Her vision blurred, and the room faded away until she and the music and the words were all that was left, all that mattered.

"Amen," she sang, not sure how she'd reached the end of the song or why she was still standing.

"Amen!" someone shouted from the back of the room.

"Amen! Amen!" quieter voices echoed.

They barely registered. Belle sucked in air like a drowning person. Feeling as though she might collapse at any second, she walked straight out of the room and through the double doors that opened onto a long hall. She hurried past restrooms, the church nursery and classrooms filled with tiny chairs and tables. At the end of the hall, a staircase led to the second floor, where adults and teens met for Sunday school and Bible studies. She ducked into the open space beneath the steps and pressed her back against the wall of the darkened recess. Aware that her cheeks were drenched, she wiped her eyes.

"That was quite the sign, Lord," she whispered when she'd caught her breath. She bowed her head in prayer. The fight was over. Her uncertainty had been stripped away by a bolt of lightning, a clap of thunder. What more was there to say?

"Have your way with me, Lord," she prayed. "Have your way."

"You didn't see the lightning? None of you heard the thunder?" Belle shivered despite the heat that came from the two tall patio heaters. Clutching the corners of the afghan she'd draped over her shoulders, she sought eye contact with each of her cousins and her two nieces.

"It was a perfectly clear night." Jen pointed to the cloudless sky. "It still is."

Unable to stop trembling after her experience at the church potluck, Belle wrapped her fingers around the cup of hot chocolate Kim had given her. She searched the heavens for anything that might resemble a rogue cloud. Not even a wisp of fog dimmed the brightness of the Pleiades, a constellation also known as the seven sisters, according to all those long-ago nights she'd spent stargazing with her dad. She blew out a breath. Was this another sign? Or was it just a happy coincidence that, including Nat and Caitlyn, seven women had gathered around the table on the deck after the potluck?

"Are you having auditory and visual hallucinations?" Diane leaned forward. "'Cause if you are, we need to get you to a doctor. Pronto."

"I don't have a brain tumor." Belle chuckled. There was nothing wrong with her head. But if there were, at least she'd know how to deal with it. Unlike the strange new territory she was about to step foot in.

"I heard thunder, Aunt Belle. Just a rumble. Now that you mention it, it did seem odd." Nat swirled her hot cocoa.

"Thanks, Nat." Belle reached for the girl's hand and gave it a quick squeeze. Nat's confirmation was exactly what she needed to dispel any doubt that what she'd seen was real. She glanced at the others. "I haven't lost my mind. It really happened."

"So if you're not seeing things, what's going on?" Diane asked.

Belle let out a long, slow breath. The time had come to share her problems—and the solution—with those closest to her, the people she relied on most in the whole world, her family. "I've been struggling lately, trying to figure out my next steps. My heart has been pulling me in one direction. My head wanted something vastly different. I couldn't choose, and it was driving me nuts."

Which was the understatement of the year. She'd been so confused lately, she hadn't known which end was up.

"There's no rush," Kim soothed. "You're still young. You have plenty of time."

Belle sipped her chocolate. The heat warmed her from the inside out. "I know, but I look at all of you making your dreams come true, and I feel this sense of urgency, you know?"

"We're just muddling through like everyone else," Amy protested from her spot beside Caitlyn.

Belle begged to differ. She swung, addressing each person at the table one by one. "Amy, you've taken on a partner for Sweet Cakes and plan on expanding the bakery soon. Kim, you've launched a new career with Royal Meals. Diane, you're on the cusp of starting your very own accounting firm—something you've wanted to do since college. Jen and Nat, you've taken the first step by coming here. You'll find your way. I'm sure of it."

She tapped the glass-topped table, her gaze

softening as she focused on Caitlyn. "And you, my dear, have changed the most of all. You're not the troubled young girl who stomped into that kitchen four months ago." Belle aimed a thumb over her shoulder. "Now you're excelling in school, making new friends, and if the coach has any idea what she's doing, you'll be the starting goalie on the Emerald Bay High soccer team."

"We're all so proud of you, honey," her mom said.

When the others echoed the sentiment, the girl hid her face behind her hands. "I like it here," she admitted with a shy deference. "I feel like this is where I'm supposed to be."

"Which brings us back to my dilemma," Belle said, sensing Caitlyn's discomfort at being the center of attention. "Usually when something's weighing on me, I'll distract myself and the answer will come to me. But I've prayed until I wore calluses on my knees. I washed windows until the tips of my fingers shriveled. I thought Jason's visit would do the trick—nothing like a good-looking man to take your mind off your troubles." She shrugged. "Things didn't turn out like I'd hoped."

"Poor guy," Kim murmured. "We all felt so bad for him."

"Me, too. I was afraid we'd have to take him to the emergency clinic." Belle took another sip of cocoa.

"Have you spoken to him since he left?"

"Oh, yeah." Belle gave a nonchalant nod. They texted back and forth several times a day and talked on the phone most nights. "He's recovered completely."

"I'm surprised you didn't ask him for advice. With his connections, he's in the best position to talk about your career," Diane said.

Belle shook her head. She and Jason grew closer with each passing day, but this was a decision she had to make for herself.

"He's a good guy. Correction. He's a great guy—but I already know what he'd tell me. He'd say take the smart path, the one that has the best chance of success. My head was in total agreement." Belle touched her temple with one finger before letting her hand drop to her chest, where she pressed her flattened palm. "My heart, though, was telling me something different, and it was ripping me up inside." She took a breath. "So I did the only thing I could do. I asked for a sign."

"And God sent a thunderbolt?" asked a wide-eyed Caitlyn.

"There might have been a few, less dramatic

signs before that one. I just didn't recognize them." *No, that wasn't quite right.* Forcing herself to be honest, Belle admitted, "Or I didn't want to."

"You sound an awful lot like the preacher who fell off a cliff," Amy said.

Belle puzzled over the remark. "What preacher? Tom Collier?"

"No, not him." Amy grinned. "Not one in particular. It's a joke about someone who doesn't quite understand how faith works."

Intrigued, Belle urged her cousin to go on.

"Okay." Amy glanced around the table as if she needed a little encouragement. When no one objected, she settled back in her chair. "So a minister and a monk are walking along a cliff when the preacher trips and falls over the edge. On his way down, he's lucky enough to grab a tree root. So there he is, clinging to this root for dear life, and he calls out, 'Lord, save me.'"

"Maybe I have heard this one," Belle murmured. She couldn't recall the punchline, but the setup sounded familiar.

"I haven't," Caitlyn complained.

"Go ahead and tell it," Diane urged.

"Okay, but I'll make it short," Amy agreed. "So the monk says, 'Hang on. I have a rope. I'll pull you up,' and he starts to remove his belt.

'Don't bother,' the preacher calls up to him. 'I prayed. The Lord will save me.' The monk thinks that kind of faith is all well and good, but he's a little more practical. He hurries into town to get help. While he's gone, a hot air balloon floats by, and the pilot says to the preacher, 'Climb in my basket. I'll fly you to safety.' But the preacher says, 'No, thanks. The Lord's gonna save me.' And the balloon floats on out of sight. By then, the monk has made it to town, where the people send out a rescue helicopter, which lowers a ladder to the preacher, who by this time is barely hanging on. But again, he says, 'No need. My Lord will save me.'" Her eyes sparkling, Amy paused for effect. "Well, you know what happens next."

Belle had a pretty good idea how the story ended, but she motioned for her cousin to finish.

"The preacher loses his grip and down he goes. He lands—splat—at the base of the cliff and dies. When he gets to Heaven, he walks straight up to the pearly gates." Amy stuck out both arms like someone who demanded answers. "'Why didn't you save me, Lord?' the preacher asks. And the Lord says, 'I sent you a rope, basket and ladder. What more did you want?'"

Shaking her head, Belle laughed out loud while giggles rippled around her. When the laughter died down and she'd sobered, she said, "In my case, the Lord sent multiple signs. Broccoli was one of them." She shot Kim a knowing look. "I found a reason to ignore them all."

"Until the thunder and the lightning?" Caitlyn asked, clearly impressed.

"I have to admit—I couldn't ignore that one," Belle agreed.

Amy cleared her throat. "Now that you know what you're supposed to do, are you going to fill us in?"

Belle stared at her cousin. Leave it to Amy to get right to the heart of the matter. She nodded. "I'm going to launch a new music ministry. Whether that means Gospel or Christian Rock, or a combination of the two, I'm not sure. But I have a gift, and I know that's how I'm supposed to use it."

A soft squeak broke the silence when Diane rubbed a finger on the glass-topped table. "How exactly...?"

"I don't know," Belle admitted. "Frankly, the whole idea scares me to death. I caught a glimpse of what it'll be like tonight when Tom asked me to sing at the potluck. No time to practice. No one to accompany me. No equipment. And I did it for free. What if I can't support myself?"

"That's a valid concern." Kim brushed her hair away from her face. "If you take this path, you probably won't ever be rich and famous again."

"Ouch." Belle pressed a hand to her heart. "You couldn't sugarcoat it just a little bit?"

"No." Kim's hair swung back and forth. "But I truly believe money isn't everything."

"My dad has money. He's loaded most of the time. That doesn't make him a good person," Nat said, showing an uncharacteristic disloyalty toward her father. When Kim gasped and the others looked equally shocked, the young woman shrugged her shoulders. "What? I've known the kind of man my dad is for a long time." She peered up at Kim. "Since way before the divorce, Mom."

As if she couldn't quite believe what she was hearing, Kim asked, "Why didn't you say something? I always thought you were on his side."

Nat showed her mom a rueful smile. "I'm ashamed of it now, but I was a selfish brat. I knew if I stayed on Dad's good side, he'd give me a big allowance and there'd be parties and trips and pretty much anything I wanted. All I had to do was pretend I didn't know what a jerk he was. In a way, I did the same thing Belle did when she overlooked the answers to all her prayers. But I didn't need a lightning bolt to show me the error of my ways. I've always known which of my parents honestly wanted the best for me."

Tears flowed onto Kim's cheeks as she slung one arm around her daughter and pulled the younger woman close. In a choked voice, she said, "You don't know how long I've waited to hear you say that."

Around the table, everyone fell silent, giving the pair the space they needed when Nat buried her head in her mother's shoulder. The two clung to each other for a long moment. At last, the younger woman's muffled voice rose. "Does this mean you'll buy me a car now?"

"Oh, you!" Chuckling and wiping her eyes, Kim relinquished her hold on Nat. She poked her daughter lightly on the upper arm. "It's going to be a long time before I can afford a new car. Much as I need one." Cupping her hand on Nat's shoulder, she turned to Belle. "Like I said, money isn't everything."

"And success isn't always what it's cracked up to be," Diane added. "It took me a while to realize it, but I finally saw how much I was giving up in the name of success." Alternating her hands, she tapped her fingers on her mug of hot chocolate. "I was on my way to the top at Ybor City. If I'd stayed there, I would have made partner within the year. But at what cost?" She glanced at Caitlyn. "Whatever it was, I wasn't willing to pay it."

Jen, who'd remained silent for most of the evening, broke into the conversation. "Who's the biggest record producer in the Christian music field?"

The name of a company in Tennessee rolled straight off Belle's tongue.

"What if, in order to be successful in this new field, you have to move there?" Jen asked. "Will you do it?"

"Leave Emerald Bay?" Belle felt her forehead wrinkle. "Why would I—"

Jen held up a hand. "I'm just saying, you moved to New York because that's where Noble Records was headquartered. Am I right?"

"You're not wrong," Belle said slowly.

"You'd leave here?" A heady mix of accusation and shock filled Amy's voice. "I get that you might move away from us." The baker twirled one finger in a circle that indicated everyone at the table. "But what about your mom? No one knows how much time they have left, but it's fair to say that she has less than the rest of us."

Belle pressed her fingers to her aching temples. "I have a lot of questions and not nearly enough answers. I'll have to figure them out as I go along. There is one thing I am sure of, though. Emerald Bay will always be my home. No matter what."

Her words struck a note that reverberated through her entire body. Nothing, certainly not something as fleeting as fame or fortune, could convince her to leave her mother or her cousins behind again. She'd made that mistake once, choosing a career over family. And though that career had spanned more than three decades, what had she been left with when it ended? Some trophies and useless records packed away in a box somewhere? A closet full of designer dresses she'd probably never wear again? No, she repeated, knowing she was making the right choice. Not even Jason could convince her to leave.

But at the mere thought of the man who'd come to mean so much to her, she froze. "What about Jason?" she asked, not particularly wanting to know the answer. "What if he doesn't support me in this?"

"Then he's not the right man for you, after all," Kim said flatly. "Look. As much as I like Craig, I couldn't be involved with him if he didn't encourage me to pursue what I want most out of life."

"The same goes for Max," Amy chirped. "Other than the people gathered at this table—and your mom," she added with a nod to Belle, "Max is my most ardent supporter."

"That's the kind of man you need, the kind of man we all need," Jen said, adding her own take on things. "You want a man who doesn't look out for his own interests at the expense of yours."

Was Jason that man? Belle hoped so, but like so many things these days, she didn't have the answer. "I guess I'll find out soon enough. He's planning another trip to Emerald Bay next month."

"Really?" Jen's eyebrows arched. "After his last visit, I'm surprised he's willing to show his face here again."

"I guess he thinks I'm worth it," Belle said with a smile.

"Enough about Jason," Diane said decisively. "You're the only one who can judge whether he's your Mr. Right or not. What I want to know—what we all want to know—is what's your next step?"

"Yeah, Aunt Belle," Nat said. "How can we help?"

Belle counted off a few items on her fingers.

"The first thing I need is someone to accompany me. I'm going to approach a couple of the members of my old band to see if any of them are interested." It was a long shot, but maybe one of them had felt the same pull she'd had.

"That would certainly be easier than breaking in someone new." Diane nodded her approval.

"Next, I need an equipment manager." The experience at tonight's potluck had taught her that much. Though the acoustics in the reception hall had given her voice enough lift to reach the back of the room, she couldn't count on that being the case anywhere else.

Jen, who'd rested her hands on the table, raised her fingers. "I know a thing or two about soundboards and systems."

Kim's head swung. "You do?" she asked doubtfully.

"Don't give me that look." Jen shook her finger. "I told you, I've worn a lot of different hats through the years. Some of the bars I've worked in didn't have their own sound engineers. Learning how to run the system made me a more valuable employee. What can I say?"

"You can say you'll put those skills to work for me," Belle said without a moment's hesitation.

"Sweet!" Jen gave a thumbs-up sign. "What equipment do you have?"

"A couple of mics. Not much else," Belle admitted. She hadn't needed to lug speakers and mic stands in and out of performance venues in a couple of decades.

"Not a problem." Jen's voice held enough conviction to put Belle's fears to rest. "We'll need a mixer, a couple of speakers and mic stands to start, plus all the wiring, of course. All that can be pricey, but we'll hit the pawn shops in Vero next week. I bet we can put together a decent system at a good price by buying used."

"I'm meeting with Tom Collier tomorrow morning to go over the church's finances," Diane began. "Between him and Darius, they know everything that happens in this part of the state. I'm sure they'll be more than happy to spread the word that you're available. You might as well start getting your name out there."

"Thanks, Diane." Belle nodded. "And please tell Tom I'll stop by to speak with him soon." She wanted to personally thank the minister for asking her to sing at the potluck. He'd been an instrument of change tonight, and she thought he needed to know it.

"I'm pretty good with websites, Aunt Belle. I'd be happy to build one for you."

The girl's offer touched Belle so deeply that tears welled in her eyes. "I'd love that, Nat," she said. She'd seen the work the young woman had done on the inn's website and knew she had the skills to do the job right.

"We should also start shifting your social media presence away from Belle Dane, Pop Star to Belle Dane, Gospel Singer, if that's the direction you're leaning. I can help with that, too."

"Honey, I can use all the help I can get. I am beyond grateful for all this." Feeling both humbled and amazed by their support, she waved a hand at the women who'd gathered at the table. As she did, a thrill passed through her. Yes, there were many details yet to work out, but this was really happening. Bowing her head, she breathed a silent prayer of thanks.

"If you ever need a place to practice, you're welcome to use the kitchen," Kim suggested.

"The kitchen?" Belle frowned. The open, airy room probably had the worst acoustics of the entire inn. Nor was it quiet. Either Kim was whipping up something scrumptious on the stove or Caitlyn was rushing in to refill her water bottle and grab a snack or one of their guests was wandering through on their way to the backyard. None of which created the best environment for trying out new material.

"Sure. I could always use an extra set of hands with the dishes," Kim deadpanned.

Warmth flooded Belle at the simple reminder. She'd discovered her voice while washing dishes in the kitchen. She'd realized she had talent while drying the pots and pans. She'd learned harmony singing with her cousins while she wiped down counters and put things in the exact spot her Aunt Liz had wanted them. There was no doubt about it—the kitchen—and her family—were her roots. She'd left them for far too long, and in her absence, she'd achieved what many would consider success. Now she'd come full circle. Back where she'd started from and where, God willing, she'd stay.

Twelve

Belle

"The layout, the colors, the images you've used are all perfect." Belle peered over Nat's shoulder at the screen, which displayed a final version of her website. "I can't believe you pulled this all together so quickly. How long have you been working on it?"

"It's been three weeks since the potluck. I started roughing it out the next day. I could have finished it sooner, but I wanted to make sure every detail was exactly right."

"Well, I think you nailed it. Can you scroll back to the main page?"

"Sure." Nat slid the cursor across the top of the page.

An instant later, the screen filled with a photo

Belle hadn't even known existed until she'd seen it in Nat's rough drafts. The picture had been taken at the Christmas Eve service, and the photographer had caught her with her head tilted back, her arms raised. With the darkened choir loft in the background, the light of a hundred candles cast her face in a luminescent glow.

Belle tsked. She'd posed in hundreds of photo shoots, some with the best names in the business behind the lens. None of them had come close to capturing her inner soul the way this one had. But it wasn't the picture that had demanded her attention. It was the banner at the top of the screen. The banner that hadn't been there the last time Nat had shown her the work-in-progress.

"Belle Dane, Full Circle," read the caption.

"Where did you get those words?" she asked, her heart in her mouth.

Nat shifted nervously in her chair. "I, um. They just came to me, but we can change them if you want. I haven't launched the website yet."

"No, no." Belle placed a calming hand on the girl's shoulder. "I don't want you to change a thing. It's perfect just the way it is."

The banner was another sign that she was on the right track. She should be getting used to them by now, she told herself. In the three weeks since the potluck, things had come together at a pace that far surpassed anything she'd ever thought possible. Along the way, she'd received a slew of little signs letting her know she hadn't strayed off the path.

Like when she and Jen had driven to a pawn shop in Vero Beach. Just inside the door, they'd nearly tripped over a stack of practically brand-new audio equipment someone had dropped off earlier that morning. Happy that he didn't have to find space for it on his already crowded shelves, the owner had sold Belle and Jen exactly what they needed at bargain-basement prices.

Or when Diane had arrived for her appointment with Tom Collier only to walk in on the pastor and the music minister discussing whether or not the youth choir should attend a Christian music festival in Orlando this summer. Diane had snagged a flier, and by early afternoon, she'd secured a spot in the lineup for Belle. And then there was Kim. Belle could nearly guarantee her cousin hadn't considered the outcome when she'd mentioned Belle's new venture to Craig. Without even being asked, the mayor had added Belle to the roster of performers at the Emerald Bay Spring Fling.

Not that she hadn't encountered a few glitches. Both Hank and Vic had been enthusiastic about the prospect of working with her again, but neither of them had been willing to uproot themselves or their families and move to a tiny town on Florida's east coast. Which left her the thorny task of finding someone to join her on stage. A problem which Caitlyn, of all people, had resolved.

Belle smiled to herself, thinking of how excited the girl had been when she burst into the house after youth group last week, tugging on the arm of a boy who was all arms and legs.

"Wait till you hear him play," she'd practically shouted. "He's incredible."

Belle had had her doubts, but she'd handed the kid her guitar. She hadn't been expecting much, but sixteen-year-old Daclan turned out to be the best-kept secret in Emerald Bay. A self-taught child prodigy who literally jumped at the chance to work with her. A flurry of phone calls, meetings with parents and ten grueling practice sessions later, and she had herself a guitarist. One she knew better than to think she could hold on to—Daclan was too young and far too talented to stick around forever—but for now, he was the answer to her prayers.

"So you think it's okay? Really?"

Belle flinched when Nat's question pulled her out of her thoughts. "I, um…"

"I can change it, Aunt Belle. If you don't like the colors or the images, I can—"

"Nope. I love it just the way it is," Belle assured the young woman.

"You want to go live with it then?" Nat's finger hovered over the keyboard. "Everything's ready. A couple of keystrokes, and in a matter of hours, you'll have a whole new presence on the Internet."

Belle took a deep, steadying breath. Once Nat launched the website, once it was out there for all the world to see, there was no turning back. Was she ready?

"Yes," she said. "Definitely."

"Okay." Nat's fingers flew over the keys. "I'll let you know when it's up."

"I'll be in Rosario if anyone needs me." Her mom had given her the cottage to use for practice sessions until the family reunion. She gave the image on the screen a final glance before she headed out of the room. Tamping down a last-minute shiver of doubt, she turned away. What's done was done. It was too late to change things.

"I'm on my way," she whispered.

On an electric keyboard she'd borrowed from the church, Belle picked out the melody of the song she was working on. Humming the final bars, she scribbled a few corrections on the sheet music before she started over from the top and played it all the way through. As she struck the last chord, she smiled. It would do.

Her phone trilled with an incoming text that let her know Daclan was on his way. Ever punctual, the boy would be right on time for their practice session. She nodded to herself and messaged Jen to join them at the cottage. When her cousin replied that she'd be there "in 5," Belle's attention returned to her song.

This particular piece of music wasn't one they'd play at the Sunshine Villa open house this weekend. For that, they were mostly sticking to tried-and-true hymns, though Daclan had lobbied hard to cover a few of the more popular Christian Rock songs. Belle felt her smile widen into a full-fledged grin and did nothing to stop it.

Their first gig.

It wasn't like they were performing in front of thousands at Madison Square Garden. In all likelihood, the audience would consist of a dozen or so visitors plus the residents of the retirement home, but she couldn't be happier. And, truth be told, Daclan might be one of the most gifted musicians she'd ever known, but the youngster had never performed in public before. This weekend would give them a chance to work out all the bugs in their routine before they stood in front of a bigger crowd.

She ran through the song again, this time paying close attention to the lyrics. She'd nearly reached the chorus when she heard a knock at the door of the cottage. Belle let her hands fall away from the keys. As the last note faded, she called, "Come on in, Daclan. The door's open. Jen's on her way."

Instead of the usual scrape of the teenager's sneakers on the floor, though, she heard whoever was on the other side of the door knock again. Louder this time.

"Who is it?" It wasn't Daclan or Jen. Both of them knew to come straight on in and start setting up for their practice session. For that matter, neither of them would bother knocking.

She stood and hurried across the room. Swinging the door wide, Belle blinked. Jason was the last person she expected to find standing on her doorstep on a chilly late-February day. Her hands flew to her face. She rubbed her eyes, certain she was mistaken.

But there was no mistaking the spicy, manly scent that tickled her nose. Or the intense focus of the gray eyes that stared down at her. When the man in front of her didn't disappear, she stared at him.

"Jason? What are you doing here? I thought you were in London." She was certain he'd flown to England on business and wasn't due back for another week. "Did I get the dates wrong?"

"Something's wrong, but it's not the dates." Jason thumped a rolled-up magazine against an open palm.

The movement drew Belle's attention. She stared down at the latest edition of *Variety*. Only one corner of the cover protruded from Jason's grasp, but it was enough. She read the headline.

Belle Dane—Where Is She Now?

Her stomach sank. "How?" But she knew how. The Belle Dane, Full Circle website had been live for over a week. It had only been a matter of time before one of the magazine's reporters had stumbled across it. She'd thought—she'd hoped— it would take them a little bit longer to go to print with the news. Or—here's a thought—contact her for a quote.

Apparently not.

"So it's true?" Jason demanded. "You've launched a whole new career without letting me know? We talk practically every day, and you didn't even consider such a monumental move worth mentioning?"

Belle bristled. "I didn't think I needed your permission." She struggled to keep her voice soft and even despite her emotions. "But I was going to tell you. Next week, when you came to Emerald Bay. I'd planned to tell you all about it then."

Jason fell silent, his face an impassive, unreadable mask.

Was this the end of them?

Belle held her breath. Was Jason the kind of man who would support her dreams, her ambitions? Or not? There was only one way to find out, and she stared up at him, searching his face for a sign.

Was that anger she saw in the depths of his gray eyes? Or something else?

TREASURE COAST REVIVAL

Thank you for reading
Treasure Coast Revival!

Want to know what happens next in
Emerald Bay?

Sign up for Leigh's newsletter to get
the latest news about upcoming releases,
excerpts, and more!
https://leighduncan.com/newsletter/

Books by Leigh Duncan

EMERALD BAY SERIES

Treasure Coast Homecoming
Treasure Coast Promise
Treasure Coast Christmas
Treasure Coast Revival
Treasure Coast Discovery
Treasure Coast Legacy

SUGAR SAND BEACH SERIES

The Gift at Sugar Sand Inn
The Secret at Sugar Sand Inn
The Cafe at Sugar Sand Inn
The Reunion at Sugar Sand Inn
Christmas at Sugar Sand Inn

HEART'S LANDING SERIES

Cut The Cake
Save The Dance
Kiss The Bride

ORANGE BLOSSOM SERIES

Butterfly Kisses
Sweet Dreams

TREASURE COAST REVIVAL

HOMETOWN HEROES SERIES

Luke

Brett

Dan

Travis

Colt

Garrett

The Hometown Heroes Collection, A Boxed Set

SINGLE TITLE BOOKS

A Country Wedding

Journey Back to Christmas

The Growing Season

Pattern of Deceit

Rodeo Daughter

His Favorite Cowgirl

NOVELLAS

The Billionaire's Convenient Secret

A Reason to Remember

Find all Leigh's books at:
leighduncan.com/books

Acknowledgements

Every book takes a team effort. I want to give special thanks to those who made *Treasure Coast Revival* possible.

Cover design
Chris Kridler at
Sky Diary Productions

Editing Services
Chris Kridler at
Sky Diary Productions

Proofs
Raina Toomey

Interior formatting
Amy Atwell and Team
Author E.M.S.

About the Author

Leigh Duncan is the award-winning author of more than three dozen novels, novellas and short stories. She sold her very first novel to Harlequin American Romance and was selected as the company's lead author when Hallmark Publishing introduced its new line of romances and cozy mysteries. A National Readers' Choice Award winner and *Publisher's Weekly* National Best-Selling author, Leigh lives on Florida's East Coast where she writes heartwarming women's fiction with a dash of Southern sass. When she isn't busy writing, Leigh enjoys cooking, crocheting and spending time with family and friends.

Want to get in touch with Leigh? She loves to hear from readers and fans. Visit leighduncan.com to send her a note. Join Leigh on Facebook, and don't forget to sign up for her newsletter so you get the latest news about fun giveaways, special offers or her next book!

Made in the USA
Monee, IL
28 June 2024